An Artist's Impression

By

Beatrice James

The moral rights of Beatrice James & Obilium
have been asserted.
First published in Great Britain in 2013
Revised edition - 2018 by:
OBILIUM
Straight Road
Colchester – CO3 9DN

ISBN 978-1-909868-03-8

For
Patricia & Irene
And all mothers
who love their children
unconditionally.

'It's harder to heal than it is to kill.'

- Tamora Pierce

Prologue

My name is Kate. I am a serial killer and remain the greatest mystery of the nineteen-sixties. You may find some of my aliases on the internet, but not my real name.

My picture never appeared in any newspaper or journal. An artist's impression was compiled from witness reports. The face of a murderer. An iconic image of evil.

The Damsel of Death, as the press described me, killed, then disappeared. For years they wasted their time trying to find me. Eventually they connected the crimes, but they were never sure of all of them. To this day I'm an enigma, my motives were unfathomable.

What could possess a woman, to kill all those innocent victims? What connection could there be? Were they the random acts of a psychopath? There are so many questions. Be patient and I'll answer them all for you.

Don't judge me yet, hear my story first.

1

Monday 20th May 1963

Kate left Green Park station behind her, crossed Berkeley Street and turned the corner into Dover Street. The neon number one above the door, meant she'd found England's first legal betting shop. Hours of research were paying off, she thought, as she checked her handbag for the notebook.

A middle-aged gentleman in a trilby hat opened the street door in front of her. He side-stepped, held the heavy wooden door ajar with his left hand and tipped his hat with his right. The well-executed gesture caught her off guard. She was unfamiliar with acts of chivalry and an awkward pause preceded her grateful 'thank you sir.'

She recovered her confidence at his smile.

Holding the wrought iron hand rail, Kate climbed the carpeted marble staircase, to the first floor. Still nervous of her new environment, she entered Jack Swift's gambling emporium. Furtively, she avoided the gazes of the punters gathered in the dingy den. Spotting a Sporting Life pinned to the wall, she went to check details she already knew.

There it was. The list of runners and riders for the 3.15 race, at Worcester. She pretended to pick a horse randomly with the hat pin she pulled from her handbag. Squinting through eyes she appeared to close, she deftly landed the point on Faraway Lad. With the curious Boardman staring over her shoulder, she noted the horse with a Waterman pen and paper from her bag.

'You won't win anything like that Lady.' Harry said, trying to be helpful, though sounding condescending.

Kate didn't speak and forced a smile toward the ruddy face. Don't engage, she told herself and she had no need to. The 'Blower' broke the silence announcing the on-course odds for the coming race. The cashier was free, so Kate crossed to his window and told him the story she'd used three times already.

'Are you sure you're in the right place Madam,' the cashier gestured round the male-only, smoke and gin-scented room.

'I think so,' she replied. 'I want to place a bet on a horse.'

'That's what we're here for and lady customers are a rare treat.'

'My dying mother has given me some money, with the wish that I gamble it. She hopes that fate grants me fortune and happiness, away from a miserable marriage. But can I count on your discretion, my husband must never find out? He's a spiteful man and he'll hurt me, if he suspects what I'm doing.'

'Of course Madam, my lips are sealed on pain of death. Now, how much were you thinking of wagering?'

Kate pushed a pile of notes across the counter.

'Seventy-five pounds,' said the man as he counted it.

'Yes. I'd like to put all of it on,' pausing to refer to the note. 'Faraway Lad. He's running at Worcester in the 3.15, this afternoon.'

'I know lady, it's my job to. What odds do you want, SP or the current on-course price?'

'SP?' Kate repeated.

'Starting price.'

Appearing ignorant she said. 'What's the difference?'

'In the old days there wasn't a choice, your odds

4

were fixed moments before the start of the race. Nowadays you can take the price at the time of placing the bet.'

'And…' Kate tilted her head.

'Well, our Boardman Harry over there has just chalked up 12-1 for your horse, so that's the price you can take now. Or I write SP on it and you get the odds when the OFF is called.'

Seeming unaware, Kate said. 'Will the price go up or down?'

'Ah, I can't help you there Madam, it's more than my job's worth. It's the gamble you take. And, I don't want to put you off all-together, but there's another choice to make. Do you want an each-way bet, or do you want it, to win?'

Kate knew the answer, but a charade's a charade and she'd come a long way to be part of it.

'Each-way?' she repeated, with a question in her voice.

The cashier drew on his reserves of patience and resorted to a diagram. With a sigh he wrote, winner; second; and third on the page.

'If you bet to 'Win', you only win if your horse crosses the line first. If you bet each way and your horse finishes in the top three, you will win a quarter of the amount, plus…'

Kate cut him off mid-sentence, time was getting short and she didn't want to miss the opportunity.

'I definitely want to bet to win!' and knowing the horse was going to start at 15-1… 'And I would like the starting price. I'm feeling lucky!'

'You'll have to be Lady. That horse is one race away from the glue-factory!'

'Please don't explain. I've just had lunch,' said Kate

5

pulling a face.

'Suits me, I've said too much already. Here's the slip. Are you staying to listen?'

The 'Blower' interrupted with the latest betting from the course. Among the changes, the commentary reported Faraway Lad was on the drift to 15-1.

Kate couldn't resist. 'I told you I was feeling lucky.' She beamed.

Even though the shop clock was just past three, she didn't feel able to keep the act going throughout the race.

'No, I'm going. If I'm late my husband will demand to know where I've been. I'll read the result in tomorrow's paper, when my husband won't sense my joy or sadness. If I'm fortunate, I trust you'll prepare my winnings, to collect?'

'Yes Ma'am, we keep enough cash in the safe, to cover the unlikeliest of results. Jack Swift is a very honourable man and so is his Company!'

Kate, turned and steered through the eight or nine speculative male punters, straining to hear the on-course atmosphere. It was now close to quarter past three and she had to open both doors to the street, herself.

Once outside in the spring sunshine, Kate turned right past the market and continued towards Bond Street at the top.

'That went as well as could be expected,' she thought to herself. 'I'll be back tomorrow for my winnings!'

As she walked through Burlington Gardens, she stopped outside the Royal Academy. She never tired of that building. One of London's finest, with statues of great Englishmen, like Milton and Newton sharing a place with Plato, Archimedes and others, it was always an inspiration.

Kate crossed several more streets, including Regent Street and arrived back in Carnaby Street. She took a deep breath and pushed open the anonymous door, as earlier that day. Not being a smoker, the air in the small shop meant she had to stifle her cough reflex.

'I've been expecting you.' He pushed a manila envelope through the window. 'First-time lucky, not many can say that!'

'Ooh goody.' Kate acting again. 'How much did Bob's your Uncle make?'

'Well, you shrewdly took the course odds of 11-2 when you came in. So you won a hundred and ninety-two pounds, ten shillings and you get your thirty-five pounds stake back too. There's two hundred and twenty-seven pounds, ten, in the envelope. Enough for you and your husband to celebrate tonight.'

'No! I told you,' looking over her shoulder, 'he must never know!'

'Ok, ok,' tapping the side of his bespectacled nose. 'Your secret's safe with me!'

'Thank you, you're a gentleman.'

Kate clasped the bag tight shut with her prize safely inside and left the shop.

Without stopping to window-shop the boutiques, she turned right into Great Marlborough Street, towards Tottenham Court Road. She was pleased the sun was now obscured by cloud. The charity shop coat and hat seemed appropriate for the trip, but wasn't ideal for serious striding busy West End pavements, at the end of May. The Big Freeze winter was well and truly over and the weather in London was unusually warm. No time for discomfort now, she thought, restocking the wardrobe can wait until after Charlotte Street.

Another patronising bookmaker, with an unkempt

beard, to match his wit.

'Don't spend it all at once dearie.'

She stifled an urge to say. 'Don't dearie me, you sexist little man.' Instead, she gave a sickly smile.

'I'll try not to!' Putting her right index finger to her lips and snatching her winnings with her left, said, 'our little secret.'

'Don't you want to know how much is in there?'

She didn't tell him she already knew and without turning back, 'no, I love surprises.' The door swung shut behind her.

'Taxi!' Kate waved at a passing cabbie. 'Harrods, any entrance.'

2

Frances

We all have secrets. That's how I felt growing up in the Scottish town of Bathgate, after the second world-war. There was still austerity and rationing, but the spirits of the locals were high after a difficult few years. The future was bright and optimism was in the air.

Like most small towns, on the surface, there was harmony of sorts. The people going about their everyday business. Shopkeepers, office workers and housewives with their broods of children. It was respectable. Everyone was polite and there were words of acknowledgement as you walked along the high street. 'Hello Frances, how's your mother?' 'Good morning Frances, what a lovely day.' Manners were important and was drummed into me from early age.

You learn to put a face on. Whatever is going on in your thoughts, you smile and politely reply. It's a kind of Scottish stiff upper lip, I suppose. We're tough cookies. Whatever adversity awaits us, we deal with it and move on. Everything is not always as it seems though, look closer and you see cracks appearing.

If I'm honest I hated childhood and told myself I was adopted. My background of choice was to be the love child of a Prince, visiting one of the large castles near Edinburgh. Prince Whoever fell for a local girl and I was the result of their affair, then my royal father left the area, unaware of me. My poor mother couldn't keep me and I was adopted by a local family. The new guardians had recently married and wanted a large family. That would explain why I felt like a fish out of water. This of course is utter nonsense and they'd be horrified to know my notions of grandeur.

I loved my real parents, but I hated the close-knit area where we lived. Nothing was private and everything eventually became common knowledge. That's normal in working class areas, where the back door's always open and neighbours double as friends and confidants. It made me uncomfortable and I couldn't really explain why. My mother's working day began at five, when she prepared the fire and heat water for my father's wash. Then she made his breakfast and continued her routine. At seven he'd go downstairs to open the small post office & general store that had been in our family for years.

I can't remember much about my very early childhood, but my first memories are downstairs in the shop. I remember large jars of colourful and attractive looking sweets which were taken down and weighed on ancient scales, in ritual ceremony. I wasn't allowed to touch anything, of course. I would sit on the step dressed in an outfit, handmade by my mother and watch it all.

As the day wore on, customers would file in and I'd recognise their faces and the conversations with my parents. Even at a young age, it all seemed very provincial and banal. Vegetables were often a topic of conversation, including the size of the marrows and leeks, at the weekend show in the church hall. The weather was another talking point, despite the fact it was always grey, or so it seemed to me. For some it would have been an idyllic upbringing and I'm starting to sound like an unpleasant little girl. But my parents were kind, there was always enough to eat and I had some lovely outfits. God was it dull though, dreadfully dull and I planned my escape from around the age of eight.

I attended the local Catholic school and religion became very important to me. I loved our local church and the ceremonies. I liked seeing the congregation in their Sunday best and the graveness of the occasion. It brought hope to me and I loved the glamour and colourfulness of the service in what was a beige life.

My parents were traditionalists, my father read the paper in the evenings, my mother washed the dishes after dinner. I was required to help her clean up. She worked harder than my father, in the shop, keeping house and cared for my baby brother and me as well. Twice a week she read to two local blind women and did other community-spirit activities like the church flowers. My father had an easy life from what I could see. He'd gossip in the shop, take deliveries, orders and paperwork was about it.

Mother occasionally took me to Edinburgh and we would look round the shops. I loved those outings, it was like escaping to another world. The sights and smells of the big city attracted me I looked forward to the time when I could spread my wings.

I was very capable academically, but there was no point staying at school if my parents couldn't afford to send me to University. At that time in the fifties, it didn't happen very often anyway. Women were second-class citizens in every sense. Despite holding the country together during the second world-war, it was back to the kitchen sink once it ended.

I still remember mother's delight at getting her first vacuum cleaner. I was horrified she got such pleasure at the gift from my father. I hated household chores with a vengeance and vowed I'd never fall into domestic servitude. I witnessed enough growing up.

As was quite normal I left school at fifteen. Most of my friends took employment in Bathgate, working in hotels, shops or hairdressers. I set my sights a bit higher and applied to Jenners department store in Edinburgh, as a trainee buyer. I was sent a brochure that I still have, describing the store as the Harrods of the North. I knew this was the world I wanted to be part of. I had a sense of style in my dress sense. My mother made my clothes from a young age and I designed outfits like ones in magazines and she dutifully copied them for me.

So when I travelled to Jenners for my interview, it was a self-assured fifteen year old that entered the revolving doors. The confidence of youth and more importantly the ambition that my family lacked. This girl's going somewhere, I told myself as I applied a third coat of lipstick and blotted. I smiled coquettishly at Mr Brown, the chief buyer, while I told him what I could bring to the job. I was from the provinces, but in my mind I was already part of the Edinburgh set. I convinced him and got the job. Goodbye Bathgate, hello world.

My parents worried about me, alone in Edinburgh, without any family support or guidance. My mother and I found suitable lodgings just outside the city. I was so excited to start work, I didn't give a thought to how she felt. She had my brother to look after, but I knew she would miss me. I never returned home to live, but mother and father were proud. I was part of a new generation, entering the swinging sixties.

Three years later I was ready to go to London, which was a radical move at that time. Most girls were dreaming of marriage and babies by the age of eighteen. I wanted to better myself and dreamed of moving to England's capital. That was where it was all happening and I needed to prove I could achieve success in a man's world. I still had some small-town girl qualities though. My faith was important to me and I couldn't see myself as a swinger, I abhorred the idea of drugs and free love. I wanted people to take me seriously and I must have seemed older than my years. I moved to Harrods, although not for a promotion. I still had to prove myself and my ability, before I could move on in my career. You'd probably describe me as a bit of a social climber. I hate that expression, it sounds negative rather than ambitious. Men never seem to be described in that way.

I lost my Bathgate accent, well apart from when I spoke to my parents on the phone or in person. Sometimes my accent a bizarre mix of the two voices, as I sought to fit into the London lifestyle. Most of the women I worked with came from good families and only there until they found a husband. I was supporting myself and trying to give the impression of someone at home in the swanky Department Store.

Another aspect of my re-invention was changing my name. I didn't tell my parents of course, but when I came to London, Frances seemed as dull as the town I had escaped from. I became Francesca. Only two more letters, but somehow it suggested the glamour and sophistication of the life I aspired to. It was part of the transformation I had to make, but looking back, I was a bit shallow in some ways. I had to create an image and an impression I was someone, to behave in the way I did. Men always had more confidence and in the sixties women had to struggle to get anywhere. Some elected to sleep their way to the top, but not me. I was still a good

Catholic girl, even if I'd acquired a taste for the finer things in life.

I never embraced the women's movement that developed at that time and had a more independent approach. I couldn't see the point in action groups and politics, that's how naïve I was. I believed in myself and my own abilities and worked hard for the next few years to move up the ladder. I moved into a better flat in a nicer area and felt I was going somewhere. Men however, didn't necessarily see it that way. I encountered some who wanted women to be grateful for the attention. Some older men I met wanted to keep me, but that was never going to happen. I wanted a self-made, successful man with the same ambition as me, to look up to and respect.

I set out to find him with the same determination I'd shown in everything I wanted to achieve. Call me calculating if you like, but I attended conferences, dinners and social events, scanning every room for Mr Right. There were a few Mr Right-Nows, but it started to feel a bit hollow. Val, one of the women I worked with, told me to let my hair down. I was a bit hurt. I felt my image as a professional woman didn't need any tweaking. She reminded me I was twenty-four, not forty-four.

I agreed to attend a house party with her that night in West London. It wasn't really my scene, but I had a sense of loneliness I couldn't describe. I wasn't estranged from my family, but I didn't feel part of it anymore. I attended Church, but there wasn't such a sense of community in London. What was wrong with me? Was I too proud, or too uptight?

I borrowed something from Val's wardrobe. A printed Pucci shift dress in shades of purple and pink. A bit loud for me, but when I slipped it on, it hugged in all the right places. I found a stole I hadn't had much opportunity to wear and the look was complete.

I met James that night, the light and love of my life. The answer to a prayer I hadn't even made. I am laughing as I write this, he was everything I didn't want in a man. However long I live, I'll never forget having the rug literally pulled from under me. I mellowed in his presence and he stepped up his game, to become the man I needed.

We married and set up our first home together. We called it the Love Shack and it was full of passion and laughter. James despaired at my lack of domesticity and I burnt beans and fused lights. I didn't have a practical bone in my body and I still don't. Luckily, he does and proved himself pretty quickly. He wasn't the man I thought I wanted, but ended up being everything I did.

We had some spectacular arguments, but that was part of the fun. He was quite a free thinker and had strange views about certain subjects. I was still the moral Catholic who did things by the book. He smoked cannabis and I hated it. I liked red wine though, so we had to tolerate each other's habits. The sixties turned into the seventies and I was desperate for a baby. James, who I knew would make a great father, was of the opinion you couldn't force things.

It became an obsession. I was spoilt in many ways and used to getting what I wanted. I'd progressed in my career the way I planned to. I had staff that respected and admired the way I climbed the ladder, without the privileges of some. Apart from a child, I had it all. There was a gaping hole within me only a child could fill, even though when I was younger I never saw myself as maternal. My work had defined me, but I had more to give. I was a woman in a man's world, but it wasn't enough.

I had two miscarriages in the difficult years ahead. Two baby boys that didn't live long enough to take their first breath. It was heartbreaking and I felt a failure. I grieved for my sons and wondered what sort of God would take them so cruelly. I didn't lose my faith, but clung to the hope God would give the gift of a child. We didn't try to understand the reasons why. We just loved each other and tried to focus on positives. When I became pregnant for the third time we almost held our breath with hope. I was frightened to dream too much. We both prayed for a healthy child, though James didn't voice his faith in the same way as I did. He professed to be an atheist, but I knew better.

When Kate arrived, safe and well, we were ecstatic. It wasn't an easy labour, but it was the best day's work I've ever done. She was beautiful. All new mothers feel that way I suppose. My feelings for her transcended love. It was something else.

Nothing could take the edge off our happiness. A perfect baby girl, she would always be the star in our universe. Whatever the future brought, she would shine. I was sure our daughter had been sent to us for a reason. Our miracle, she could do anything. She could change the world.

3

Kate

I met my parents on the eighth day of March in 1975, at quarter past nine in the evening. I was much anticipated and a very wanted baby. I suppose I was a miracle, they'd tried for so many years to have a child. Mother told me she prayed to God every night for me. After losing two babies, in as many years, she believed she was never to experience the joy of motherhood.

Her faith made her stoical. Perhaps God had other plans for her. She was blessed with a sharp wit and an intellect that enabled her to succeed in a world, dominated by men. She lived during an era, when a woman's expectations were limited to keeping home and pleasing a happy husband. She needed all of the self-belief and determination that she possessed in quantity.

By the mid-sixties, Frances had carved out a career for herself as a fashion buyer, for a large department store, in the heart of Knightsbridge. All that was missing in her life was love. Fiercely independent, she scared away all the men she encountered, in both her business and private lives. So, as she once confessed to me, she was totally unprepared for the intensity of her feelings, when she met my father. For once in her life, she wasn't in control and she didn't know where it would take her.

They met at a party. Jimi Hendrix was blasting out of the speakers and the air was thick with the smell of weed. Whilst my mother never described herself as a free spirit, she thought she'd create an air of mystery.

Like a chameleon, she shed her proletariat roots and adopted a more cultured, bohemian persona alien to her own parents. She created a new life in London, away from the prying eyes of the Scottish provincial town where she grew up.

So, it was a new Francesca that made her entrance in a tatty house, in an unremarkable street in Chiswick. Dressed in a Pucci print shirt, killer heels and a fake-fur cape, Frances had changed and she was never going to be the same again. For the first time in her life, she looked and felt fabulous. She danced and drank more than she was used to. Somehow, she sensed something magical was happening, but didn't predict it was the young man, a few feet away. He was mesmerised by the vision in purple and wondered how to become part of her world.

James McLean wasn't ambitious. Talented, artistic and creative, but he lacked drive. That particular evening, a desire to succeed enveloped him. He watched the girl in the printed dress, dancing languidly in ultra violet light. The beer and the joint he'd smoked earlier took the edge off his nerves, just enough to make a move. As he approached her, with a confidence he wasn't really feeling, she smiled and they started to talk. Within an hour they told each other more about themselves than was usual. Hopes and dreams exchanged, a lasting bond was formed.

The rest, as they say, is history, my history anyway. It's strange, thinking about your parents as young, crazy, in love and living life to the full. But they were and I'm the result of their passion for each other and life. I'm a lucky girl.

Who thought my beautiful, social climbing, deeply religious mother would fall for a man who didn't care for money, material things or God. Self-effacing, kind and spiritual, he worried not what the world thought of him. He hated pretentiousness and organised religion, with equal passion. Despite himself, he loved my mother with an enduring faithfulness he drew on, in the years to come.

I like to think, that in the most unfashionable fashion, they completed each other. Francesca's sharp edges became blurred and her sense of the world being a place of black and white, merged into more realistic shades of grey. James realised he might need to give up his dreams of living in a farmhouse, growing vegetables and cannabis plants. It was the sixties, but even free-love comes at a cost. For Francesca and James, it meant compromise. They would manage, their love was enough.

They married in a small Catholic Church, in Bathgate, on the outskirts of Edinburgh. If the decision had solely been my mother's, it would probably have been Edinburgh Cathedral. James by agreeing to the church wedding and the promise to christen children Catholic, demonstrated enough commitment. They didn't need any further pomp and ceremony, to prove anything to the friends and family, who attended their modest ceremony.

My father was and still is a man of principles. Although he grew to accept Francesca's beliefs and the doctrines of her faith, he never made the life changing journey, she had hoped he would.

As a small child, I loved looking at my parent's wedding album. I would sneak into their bedroom and open the ornate gilt trunk, purchased on one of their adventures to India. Rummaging through the pictures and love-letters, with their time-curled edges, until I reached the ivory silk covered book. The photographs, slipped between crisp vellum and tissue paper, gave me a warm feeling of security and a childish sense of romance that would shape my adult life. Would I ever find a love like theirs? I hoped so with all my heart.

Amongst the treasures in their chest, was another thick volume of precious memories. It was my own baby box. James had resisted the cheap looking versions given as presents from well-meaning friends and relatives. Instead, he spent hours of his precious spare time locked in his favourite place, the wooden log cabin that was his retreat from the world. The intricate carved lid read 'Katherine Patricia McLean - Born 8th March 1975 - 7lbs 2ozs.' A glass covered frame was enclosed within the lid, with a tiny photo taken at the hospital.

The box was a jumbled trove of nostalgia that could keep me occupied for hours. Francesca regularly threatened to buy some albums and re-arrange the photos in chronological order, mainly to satisfy her need to organise, but it never happened. Maybe James's strong sense of disorganisation eventually rubbed off on her. To me, it always signified my childhood memories, engulfed in the strong framework, of my father's protective love. A wooden metaphor. It was his precious gift to me.

4

Monday 20th May 1963

Once inside the taxi, she had a change of mind. 'Driver, I still need to go to Harrods, but can we go via Marylebone High Street?'

Muttering under his breath, something about indecisive women, he said. 'Which end?'

'I don't know really. I want to go to Robert Dyas.'

'I know where that is…'

'Oh and I need a sweet shop,' Kate added.

Whilst the driver was trying to make small talk about how the weather had finally cheered, Kate was counting the proceeds of her last collection. She smiled. Ten twenties and four tens, spot on she thought. Gala Night hadn't let her down. But then again, it couldn't.

She didn't pay much attention to the journey, she was almost getting used to her new surroundings. After all, the streets and buildings were all in the same place.

'Here's Robert Dyas, and there's a sweet shop three doors further up. Shall I wait here for you?'

Kate agreed and left him and the black Hackney Cab. Ten minutes later they were on their way to Knightsbridge, once more.

'We're here' The driver interrupted Kate putting four hundred pounds into a zipped compartment of her bag and the rest in her purse. 'Seven and six please love.'

Kate gave him a ten shilling note, curious to see what shillings and pennies looked like, she waited for change.

'If I give you half a crown, does that leave you

21

enough change for a tip' That's cabbie speak for, you will be giving me a tip won't you.

Kate very nearly said, what's half a crown, before realising there were gaps in her research of the period. Instead, she managed… 'No, you better give me one and six back, I've no other change.'

Passing the two coins the cockney driver remarked, 'very generous and no mistake.'

The driver had made a U-turn, so she was only a pace or two from the main doors. Harrods was always a familiar place. She had been taken to the store dozens of times by her mother, who had an office at the rear of the first floor. She strode purposefully through the perfumery department and on up to luggage. When she got there, she had to ask where it was. China & Glass was in its place. Once she had been helpfully directed to the third floor, she found what she wanted.

A suitable travel case was needed for her travels. Choosing quickly to save time, Kate opted for medium sized, black, mock lizard skin. Or was it real lizard, in this age of un-protected species. A plain black, calf leather, medium size handbag was also chosen. She didn't want to look out of place. Three pounds seventeen and six seems a lot in the scheme of things, but time is shorter than cash this week, so the assistant on the till was given a five pound note. Pausing long enough to notice her first half a crown, she pursed the change and headed for lingerie. A girl can't live without clean knickers. The irony of her thoughts didn't escape her. She was deliberately focussing on the task in hand, rather than the tasks in front of her. It was a coping mechanism.

Shopping for underwear shouldn't take as long as it did, but these unusual fabrics with the lack of stretch,

Lycra not existing yet, took Kate time to get used to. Besides, she would need some special items, if things went to plan. She was being tempted by the Christian Dior & Balmain ranges, very much. After choosing, she handed an assistant her choices, including seven pairs of 'sensible' under-garments; twenty pairs of stockings, in four colours and a selection of suspender belts, garters and other means to hold them up. Two more departments, including shoes and nearly thirteen guineas later, she had all her essential wardrobe items.

Leaving the side door, she made her way up Knightsbridge to where she believed a chemist had been trading, since the war.

'We're closing shortly!' said the twenty-ish assistant in the black pencil skirt. Kate looked at her watch, just past five twenty. I'd forgotten London hasn't always had the seven-eleven mentality. Grabbing a toothbrush and paste, face cream and some hastily chosen make-up, including a Nail Varnish called 'Woltz' that was advertised as; 'lasts longer than a holiday romance!' Smiling, she paid and hit the street. Pausing at a bench, she packed all her purchases into the suitcase.

Turning into Beaufort Gardens, she walked halfway down and found the Knightsbridge Hotel's entrance, on the left. A liveried door-man held it open and offered assistance with her case. Kate absorbed the opulent surroundings and her thoughts were wandering when she was asked, 'Can I help you Madam?'

'Oh, yes, of course. Sorry I was just admiring the beauty of this building. I would like a room for tonight please. I'm sorry I didn't have the opportunity to book in advance.'

'No problem Madam. Would that be a single, double or a suite?'

'Well,' said Kate, 'I'm travelling alone, but I do like space, so I think I'll spoil myself and take a double. Then again, a suite sounds good. How much would that be?' She convinced herself that this was a rare opportunity to sample such luxury and after all, her budget was limitless.

'It's £55 per night for the Beaufort Suite, Madam.'

'I'll take it,' she said reaching for the cash. She filled out the registration form with the first of many aliases she would use. Margaret Downing. She would need to get used to this, she couldn't afford to make any mistakes.

After checking in, Kate stowed her suitcase in the second-floor suite and returned to the Lobby and out into the spring evening. Back on the main road, she found a newspaper stand with the day's Evening Standard, piled high. The '3d' printed in the top corner threw her for a moment, before fishing around in her purse to find a twelve-sided coin, with three pence embossed round the edge.

With the paper under her arm, Kate returned to the hotel. Safely back in her room, she scanned the paper while running a bath. Ignoring the politics, editorial and even the racing pages, Kate made straight for the classified ads section, cars in particular. Making a list of the Dealers' details, she turned off the water and even though it was nearly six thirty she optimistically returned to the Hotel reception.

'Can I use the hotel phone', she asked the uniformed man behind the desk.

'If you give me the number, I will connect you to it,' came, the efficient reply.

'It's more of a speculative list of car dealers that I was going to try to speak to, or leave a message for…'

Her voice trailed off as the thought occurred to her that the answerphone was probably not yet an everyday item, even in business.

'It's not likely that any staff will still be working at this time of night, to take messages, but if it pleases Madam, I am willing to try. If anyone answers your phone will ring and you will be connected.'

Kate thanked him and offered her list to him. Taking the codes and numbers and a note of the room-number from the key she was holding, he gestured to a booth at the rear of the reception area. She sat inside for what seemed like quarter of an hour and was getting out of the red plush chair, when the bell sounded. She picked up the receiver. The male voice was almost triumphant.

'I've managed to get an answer on the twentieth ring to Finchley 5842, I'm putting you through.'

There was a click and the voice changed to an impatient older man saying…

'Come on, I've got a Kaluki game I'm late for. What do you want at this time?'

Kate resisted an apology and said, 'I am in urgent need of a second-hand, reasonably inexpensive, but reliable car.'

The voice paused… 'Then you are a very lucky Lady. On three counts.'

Before Kate could ask…. 'Firstly that I had to return to the office before going out this evening and heard the incessant ringing of the phone… Secondly, that I have today taken in to my showroom, the Late Mrs Kaufman's Morris Minor, a fine example of the marque, which owing to her ill health in recent times has more miles left than sadly, did its owner… And thirdly, if you are willing to pay the asking price, I'll make my excuses to Sydney and Sylvia and deliver it to your Hotel this evening. I believe the young man I spoke to said the Knightsbridge.'

'Wow, that's quick! How much are you selling it for? What colour is it?'

'Ain't that like a lady, tell you they're in a hurry and then that you're too forward! The men ask me about the engine, you the colour! The price is a hundred and eighty pounds and the colour's a very fetching shade of Forest Green… I'll accept cash, or cash and I'm robbing myself at that price, but you sound like you can spot a bargain enough to know that…'

There was finally a pause long enough for Kate to think. 'What's your name, mystery car salesman with the silver tongue?'

'I was going to say you should know you rang me, but then again, you didn't. Morris Lesner. Morris Motors, Finchley's finest Morris car dealer, where…'

Kate interrupted. 'Ok Morris I submit, I was taught by my Father to start any negotiation twenty per cent below the asking-price, however time is short and I get the impression you'll win anyhow.'

Without hint of victory, he said, 'I'll be there in an hour, what name shall I ask for at the desk, it's easier than getting you to carry a rose. All those thorns….'

'Margaret. Margaret Downing, I'm in room 312.'

'I'll phone Sydney then I'll make my way to you.'

'Thank you Morris, see you in an hour.' The line clicked twice and she replaced the handset.

Kate left the booth and waited at the main desk, while Mr Uniform finished explaining to an American couple, directions to the Albert Hall. 'Thank you for your perseverance, that was very fruitful.' Kate said to him when she had his attention. 'Do I pay now?'

'No Madam, a nominal amount will be added to your account, for settlement when you checkout. Will you be dining in the Restaurant, there is still time, the chef's on until eight thirty.'

'Yes. Table for one, I'm alone,' she said looking at the lobby clock, but I'm meeting someone in an hour, so it'll have to be something light.'

'Very good Madam, I shall call the Maître D',' he said in an impeccable French accent.

Whilst making a mental to do list for the day ahead, she dined in the art deco restaurant. The crab and asparagus risotto she ordered was avant-garde in early sixties England.

The sommelier had tried to tempt Kate with a 1959 Chablis Grand Cru, from the Blanchot vineyard. Under normal circumstances she would have loved to sample a wine of such quality, but she wanted to keep a clear head for this week's assignment. She couldn't tell him that.

He was thanked for his excellent recommendation, but told that alcohol was dangerous to mix with her medication. He discretely suggested a Schweppes Indian Tonic Water with ice and lemon. Kate made him put a bottle of Britvic Grapefruit juice in it, just to take the edge off the Quinine.

She had then met Morris, looking fine in his camel cashmere Crombie. He had parked in Hans Place, a beautiful garden-square behind Beaufort Street. The car had been as described and the engine sounded healthy. So after he had walked her back to the hotel Kate happily settled her debt, before the dapper gent disappeared into the Knightsbridge night.

Back in her room, she wrote up the plan in her notebook, bathed in complimentary Fenjal bubbles in the

Edwardian style décor and tried to ignore the fact that the bed didn't have a duvet.

After her bath, using the Robert Dyas drill bit set, she carefully enlarged the holes in the ends of half of the specially chosen sweets. Then using a page from a complimentary copy of Vogue, rolled into a cone, she 'injected' a small quantity of Paraquat Dichloride powder into each of the holes. She then filled the holes with a paste made from sugar and water and left them on more pages of the magazine to dry. She flushed away the remaining chemical and washed her hands three times, Lady Macbeth style, before enjoying the opulence of her very expensive London apartment.

5

Kate

Some people describe certain events in their lives as 'light bulb' moments. It's that moment when everything makes sense. It could be a great idea, or a realisation that someone isn't who you think they are. Or even a life-changing decision that will influence future events in your life. Those 'light bulb' moments don't always happen when we expect them to, or for that matter, when we want them to.

My life is made up of those moments. Share them with me and you will begin to understand, how I became the person that they still talk about. That evil, conniving, calculating woman who steals people's most precious moments. Who leaves their lives without hope, shatters their dreams for the future and leaves them bereft. I wasn't always that person, so stay with me for the journey, please.

I was a strange child. At least, I believe that now, although at the time I had nothing to gauge it by. I spent too many hours thinking, dreaming and pondering some of life's many questions. Whilst other children of my age were engrossed in watching Button Moon and Bananaman, I was pondering the reason why we are all here in this life and what did it all mean. It seemed to me that we had all been invited to one big party, but no-one's been told what we're all celebrating.

I would have strange feelings, reaching down to the pit of my stomach, wondering if it was all real. Was I really here? How big was the Universe, was I really a tiny atom in a huge ball of fire and energy?

I learned to take my mind to higher levels and eventually I could do a strange thing. I could separate my mind from my body. Is that levitation? I could lie in my bed for hours at night and eventually it would happen. I could look down on myself and it was a very peculiar feeling. It gave me a sense of who I was, even at such a young age.

One of my earliest memories involved watching a very long film at school, about poverty in India. It made me cry. It could have been tears of joy, I realised that that child, encrusted in grime and engulfed in poverty, could have easily been me. Despite knowing nothing different, I couldn't take my comfortable life for granted. I had a sense of the wider world even at a very young age.

My mother described my feelings in her own inimitable fashion. 'There but for the grace of God, go I.' That phrase has stayed with me, throughout my life. Who decides? Does God decide? And if he does, then what does he base his decisions on? My Catholic guilt would kick in and I would give all my pocket money to Oxfam, for a few weeks. Perhaps I will be a communist, I thought, it seems fairer somehow. Then I read 'Animal Farm' and it changed my mind. Human beings are too selfish. There will always be someone who takes control. Would I ever be that person? You know the answer to that, don't you? Even though you don't understand why yet, you will.

As a child your mind is a blank sheet, uncluttered with knowledge, doctrines and beliefs. In time, you learn to hate, or look down on people you don't understand. Prejudice raises its ugly head, or maybe, you meet the wrong person and they lead you down a path you wouldn't otherwise take. Childhood should be innocence and joy. I know that now but the reality is different for many. I have taken childhood from many, who will never realise their hopes and dreams. Can that ever be forgiven?

My parents were eager to channel some of my expanding thought processes into something more productive, my education. I was too introspective, too deep. They looked forward to the time when I would start my formal education and start to mix with other children. That subject however, caused some disquiet in our home. James and Francesca were unable to agree, on the form it would take. As an only child, there was a danger I could become too solitary.

James was at home with me during my younger years. His hand-crafted furniture was in demand in the leafy suburb of London, where we lived, so he had the luxury of working from home. Wealthy clients commissioned him to make beautiful kitchen cabinets and furniture that would stand the test of time. This suited James very well. He could not have envisaged a nine to five existence and had never in his life wanted to join the dead-eyed convoy of faceless commuters, shuffling for position on the packed trains and buses.

No he was still a free spirit at heart, having the skills and patience to do the work he loved. Spending hours teaching me to read and write, even before I would enter the school gates. He taught me the name of birds that visited our garden. Flowers and trees, I could name easily and I would be encouraged to paint and draw nature's inspirations.

He would have made a brilliant teacher. I realise that now. He had the patience and tenacity to deal with an inquisitive four year old, who wanted answers. He

31

believed in peace and he believed in people. He was a good combination of role model and human being.

He started researching schools that would stimulate me and encourage my 'free-thinking.' Summerhill School became his first choice. Their ethos was that the school should be made to fit the pupil, not the other way round. Run as a democratic community, pupils could decide whether or not to attend lessons. I loved the idea of the school, my only reservation was, that it was a Boarding school. I prepared myself for the possibility though, by reading Enid Blyton's 'Mallory Towers' collection. As it turned out, I needn't have bothered.

My mother's face turned a strange shade of purple. As a child of four, I couldn't identify the colour as anything I had ever painted in my growing collection of work. The faces in my pictures were always pale pink or light brown. This colour seemed to be the one I got when I mixed red and blue!

She was clearly very angry. It followed a discussion with my father about my education. I remember being told, in an unusually harsh tone, to go to my room, which I duly did. I tried to use my levitation techniques, to mentally remove myself from the situation. It didn't really work well enough. I could still catch some snippets of the argument. 'You can't be serious' and 'leftie commune,' made me realise that my mother was not in agreement with Summerhill School.

6

Tuesday 21st May 1963

At ten to seven, Kate's dream was disturbed by a loud knock on the room's door. A baritone voice said, 'Good morning Madam,' this is the wake-up call you requested. Kate mumbled a thank-you and turned over, pulling the blankets up to her ears. She was drifting off to sleep again, when her sub-conscious jabbed her into focus. Time! Not enough of it to waste! She ran another bath, a quick one, not the soak she'd had the night before.

She laid out the new garments from the case, hoping they'd be comfortable enough for the long drive ahead. Dressed and downstairs, Kate sat in the same seat in the restaurant, as the previous evening. A cooked breakfast would take longer than toast to prepare and consume, but it meant she wouldn't need to stop for lunch, en-route. It also gave her time to thumb through the Daily Express, found outside number 312's door. The back pages first, she couldn't resist the results from the previous day's eventing. Faraway Lad - 1st. SP 15-1; was the first line under the Worcester 3.15 sub-heading. Kate smiled and looked for another. Worcester 3.45: Silly Billy 9-2.

Kate put the paper down and concentrated on the fried fare, toast and marmalade. The Wedgewood bone china crockery made the experience all the more enjoyable. The waiter had asked her to choose from Earl Grey; Darjeeling; Assam; Orange Pekoe; or Lapsang Souchong teas. Orange Pekoe was Kate's absolute favourite since discovering it on a holiday in Italy, some years ago. She now bought it from Twinings by mail order, because it's so hard to find. When it came to the table in the matching, cobalt blue, Florentine tea pot, the waiter skilfully poured the golden brew through a solid silver tea strainer, onto the half inch of waiting milk, in the equally beautiful cup. Kate thought if she wasn't in heaven, she must be close.

Fifty minutes later, at ten past nine, she asked at the desk to use the phone once more. The response was standard.

'I'll dial it for you Madam.'

'I'm afraid I don't know the number, but if you put me through to the Operator, I'll ask for her help.'

'Very good Madam.'

Back in the phone booth Kate was connected to a girl's shrill voice.

'Operator. Which service do you require?'

Kate cleared her throat and said. 'I need to make a trunk call to a School in Bishop's Cleeve. Unfortunately I don't know the number, but I think it's a Cheltenham exchange number.'

'Don't worry caller I'm used to it. What is the name of the school?'

Apologetically, she answered, 'I don't know that either,' then added, 'but I do know the address is School Road, in Bishop's Cleeve.' She could hear the conversation between the cockney and west country voices. She heard the phone being answered and Kate's inner actress was summoned to perform. When the call was over Kate gathered all her new 'retro' belongings and checked out of the hotel.

She walked in the spring sunshine to where the car was parked. She put the case in the boot and climbed in the front. Morris had shown her round the car when he delivered it the night before, but in the light of day it looked even more basic and un-impressive than the first time she had seen it. The seat was even more uncomfortable than it looked and the steering wheel felt too big in diameter and yet too thin in construction. Then she remembered that Morris had shown her the starting handle and suggested she get help with it. Turning an engine over is not for Ladies of substance, he had said. 'If only you knew Mr Lesner, if only...' she'd thought as he said it.

A cabbie parked two vehicles away from her was duly recruited to help. She was amazed that men willingly help 'damsels in distress' in this era. In the twenty-teens she had seen them step over girls lying in the gutter. When he cranked the handle the engine coughed into life. Unlike the evening before, it sounded noisy and lumpy at tick over, she wasn't convinced that it would get her as far as Berkshire, let alone Gloucester.

She thanked her less-than-glamorous assistant and without signalling, she put the gear lever in first and moved off. The clutch was harder to depress than she was used to and she nearly hit a parked car when she should have turned the first corner. No power steering she grumbled and had visions of the bulging biceps she would have by the time this mission was over. Another irritation was the noise the gearbox made as she crashed through the gears. It was deafening. She was planning a phone call to Morris to complain about the state of her purchase, when a voice through the window said.

'Who taught you to drive Lady, didn't they tell about double-declutching?' It was her new friend the Taxi driver and his cheeky grin. He was trying to be helpful but Kate wasn't in the mood for humour. She scowled at him and said. 'What are you talking about?'

'If you don't let the clutch up in neutral between gear changes, the cogs inside are going at different speeds and it won't go in to the next gear without a fight. It then makes that terrible noise and you'll need a new box inside a week!'

Even though Kate had no intention of keeping the car very long, she couldn't stand the noise any longer. She thought she'd out-cheek, Mr Cheeky.

'That double clutch thing wasn't necessary on my last car. Can you show me how to do it?'

'It'll have to be a quick lesson. I'm in the middle of a wait and return. Move over.'

He threw away half a cigarette and climbed in. 'Must be some fancy car your other one, foreign was it?'

'Italian I think. I thought you were in a hurry.'

'Watch carefully, as I move from first to second, I dip the clutch move the lever into the neutral area and let the clutch up and wait for the engine to slow down before dipping the clutch again and putting the lever in second. If the engine and gearbox are going at similar speeds, you'll get a smooth change. That's the easy bit. When you change down, like this…

… You have to blip the accelerator while the lever's in neutral to increase the speed of the engine, to the same as the gear you're moving in to.'

He drove round the square a couple more times, performing the demonstration, while Kate tried to wear a suitably admiring grateful look. He suddenly pulled up and jumped out. He'd spotted his customer returning to his cab and he was gone, running as if his coat was alight.

Kate needed to collect her winnings from Jack Swift's shop in Dover Street. As soon as she had circled the square enough times to get used to the new driving technique, she headed off in the direction of Park lane. It's not the shortest route to Dover Street, but certainly the easiest in an unfamiliar car. Already she realised that there were gaps in her careful research. Why hadn't she bought a vintage car and tried to drive it? Mentally chastising herself for the oversight, she wondered what else had she missed.

She couldn't help noticing that although the car was more difficult to drive, the streets weren't. At that time of day the journey would take twice as long, at least. She was in Dover Street in no time, but parked round the corner in Stafford Street. The car didn't really fit in with the 'impoverished wife' story.

The cashier handed Kate an envelope. 'Beginner's luck?' he quipped.

'Beginner's luck', she repeated. 'How much is here?'

'£75 at 15-1 plus your stake, makes £1200 Lady. Jack's distraught, he was coming in this morning but when I told him last night that a Lady chose her winner with a hatpin and took us for over a grand, he drowned his sorrows in pink gin last night. His wife has phoned me to say he was staying in bed this morning.'

'Tell Jack I hope he can afford it!' Kate put the money in her bag and headed for the door.

'He can, don't you worry about that…'

Back in the car, Kate was thankful for the flat shoes she'd bought the day before. Driving a 1950's car is hard enough, but in heels, impossible! She turned West at Knightsbridge towards the 'A4' and almost crashed into a bus because the place looked so different. She drove through Chiswick and its surrounds, noting the changes, on the route she had researched and memorised.

Heading on to the new bit of the 'M4' by Heathrow, she was making reasonable time, in fact better than predicted. However, even though Morris hadn't delivered it empty, it wasn't going to reach its destination on a quarter of a tank of fuel.

Somewhere between Colnbrook and Slough, Kate spotted a rare 'filling-station' and pulled in. Unconsciously she parked next to a pump, got out and with her right hand, grabbed the nozzle from its holder. She was still trying to unscrew the filler-cap with her left hand when a rotund little man with a grumpy face spoilt her mood.

'What are you doing?' He clearly wasn't happy.

'Getting some petrol,' Kate retorted.

It was just as 'Napoleon' was about to verbally roast her when she had a 'splash' moment. ('Splash' unlike 'light bulb' is slow-delivery realisation.) Self-service Petrol Stations were about fifteen years away. Kate's sharper brain cells took over…

'I'm so sorry,' she schmoozed, 'I don't know what came over me, I was miles away.'

Napoleon's face changed, thankfully for the better. 'Oh. Oh, that's OK. I only wanted to prevent you from getting your lovely clothes dirty and protect the skin of your lovely hands.'

Kate stifled the frown, if not the thought. 'Too many lovelies little man,' and let Mr Self-important take over. At only four and six a gallon, she told him to fill it. She didn't want to repeat this exercise any more than she needed to. She didn't let him keep the change though. There was still something unpleasant about him.

The overall journey time was supposed to be three and a quarter hours, but not in an old Morris Minor, so it was a pleasant surprise to reach Witney not long after midday. Thirty-seven miles to the target, she was able to relax slightly, but not too much. After all, getting to Bishop's Cleeve was the easy bit.

7

Kate

L et's cut to the chase. My mother won the battle and the war. I would start at the Maria Fidelis Convent School in September. I felt sorry for James and worried that it might cause a rift between my parents. I had by that time resigned myself to going and was already aware that there was no point in arguing with Francesca. There was never the remotest chance that her only child wouldn't attend a Catholic school. James relented, remembering the promise he had made at the wedding and lamented again that religion was the catalyst for disharmony.

Was she right? Probably yes, but the logical part of my brain would suggest that I would have needed to attend both schools to give an accurate answer. You can't be in two places at once though. Well you couldn't in 1979 anyway. So the decision was made.

My first day at school came around too quickly. The long days of summer became shorter and every day spent in the garden with my father became more precious. I went shopping with my mother to John Lewis to purchase my uniform. I have never quite inherited the sense of style I associate with my mother, although over the years I have tried. I recalled the Summerhill brochure whereby the pupils could choose their own clothes to reflect their identity. So I definitely wasn't prepared for the tartan kilt and red jumper that was presented to me by the sales assistant. Inwardly telling myself to shape up, I entered the changing rooms, demonstrating a level of stoicism that made my mother proud. ('Light bulb' moment, you don't always get what you want in life, but make the most of it and move on.)

The day dawned and I awoke early with a sense of trepidation. My parents however, were up even earlier and as Francesca was at a business meeting, James was the designated driver. The building itself looked large and daunting, though looking back I was very small, so I guess it was all about perspective. I would remember that first day, many years later, as I approached another young child moving towards the school gates, holding the hand of his mother, smiling at the prospect of seeing all his friends. I stole that moment from him, as you will shortly find out.

The convent was so cold. Large rooms and high ceilings didn't help. I needed that red jumper more than I realised. Those thick tights were for a reason, I know that now too. Never a high fashion item, but I was glad of their warmth. I was welcomed into the class by Sister Bernadette and things brightened up considerably as she emanated warmth and humour, in a quiet Irish lilt.

I adapted quickly to my new environment. Mealtimes took some getting used to and I became aware of the expression often used by my mother, 'waste not want not.' It obviously related strongly to the convent kitchen. We were not allowed to leave the refectory table until our plates were clean. That is a habit that remains with me to this day. It also means I will eat almost anything.

During lessons I still found I could 'switch off' and my mind would easily wander. This followed on from my early experiences as a young child and could be useful. It did however get me into trouble on occasion, particularly if Sister Ursula was teaching. I had a few problems with the concept of 'original sin,' perhaps because I thought about it too much, rather than learning it parrot fashion as many of my fellow pupils did. If the lesson went on too long, or I didn't like the subject matter, my mind would be somewhere else contemplating more important matters. Maybe I had too short an attention span.

My habit of thinking too much seriously affected my ability to accept some of the teachings. At home, my mother talked to me at length about it and I would argue with her, even as a young child and at times she would despair.

My best friend at school was a ginger haired girl named Bridget. We met on our first day and I was immediately smitten. She was a scholarship student from Hackney in the east end of London and her background was a contrast to mine. Her father was a fishmonger and unfortunately the smell permeated her clothes, due to the cramped living conditions in the flat above the shop, where she lived. I didn't realise this at the time, I just overheard two older girls holding their noses and calling her fish-cake.

She was already in tears when I approached the group. I intervened by pulling her way and doing the best impression of my mother I could muster. After reprimanding the culprits in a way that they would not easily forget, we marched off together arm in arm. Looking back the motivation to intervene was probably inherited from my father, who generally favoured the under-dog.

Bridget's background was very different to mine and her accent made me laugh. We would mimic each other relentlessly. She would do an impression of me, sounding more like the Queen and I would respond with an impression of a cockney that would put Dick Van Dyke to shame.

Bridget and I grew up together. I had no siblings, no one to share silly secrets, hopes and dreams. She filled that gap admirably. We struck up a friendship that would stand the test of time and would include some life-changing events. I defended her cause on many more occasions during our years at the convent, but she repaid me in full as a loyal friend and confidant.

I loved the chaos of her home, her crazy family and the kindness with which I was treated. Her parents were earthy and didn't hold back in terms of expressing themselves, especially her father Joe. He was a union man through and through and could swear like a 'trooper.'

His socialist views made my father look positively right wing and I loved our discussions about politics. He opened my eyes to many inequalities and gave me grounding in subjects that would influence me throughout my life. Strangely Bridget wasn't that interested. She wanted desperately to better herself and there was no better time to do that than during the eighties. Her father embarrassed her, but I found him fascinating.

We would discuss issues such as 'Crime and Punishment' and argue vehemently. He still believed that there should be a death penalty and he would quote 'an eye for an eye' and other snippets from the bible, that suited him at the time. I couldn't even contemplate the idea that the state had the right to take someone's life, whatever they had done. Surely that was God's job to judge. What sort of person could press the button, or administer the injection? Surely that would make them murderers as well. These beliefs served me well for many years. I was a true liberal in every sense of the word. What changed I hear you ask? Don't worry you will find out. I won't leave you hanging, if you will excuse the pun.

Bridget was and is a true friend. At school, she regularly proved this on Thursdays, when she made the ultimate sacrifice, eating my faggots. The grey lumpy, gristly mix was enough to turn any meat eater into a vegetarian. I could not stomach them and Bridget agreed to take one for the team. The alternative was to sit there all afternoon and miss netball, my favourite sport. She was a star.

We squashed up together on her single bed and shared our dreams for the future. I would become a Barrister and she would run her own company and make loads of money. I would be famous for representing notorious criminals and fighting injustice and she would become very rich and buy her parents a bungalow in Clacton, where they had enjoyed some memorable family holidays. We had it all planned. It helped spur us on during some of the more boring lessons and gave us a focus for the future. We were both searching for our destiny and neither of us would have any idea what was going to happen in the next few years. Suffice to say that life has a way of surprising you and changing the path you are following. Maybe it's destiny, or fate. You decide.

8

Tuesday 21st May 1963

Kate arrived in Bishop's Cleeve just after one-thirty on that Tuesday afternoon. The Morris Minor needed to remain unseen, so she parked in Pecked Lane, at the end of School Road. She was earlier than the estimated time she had given the Headmistress, but if the afternoon's classes had already started, she guessed that wouldn't matter.

She gathered her thoughts and her handbag. She opened it to check the most important contents. To ensure that the noxious content didn't pollute any other items, the paper bag containing the sweets was placed inside a second paper bag. She locked the car and walked up School road towards the familiar buildings. St Michael's church and graveyard was on the right and the newer stone and slate school on the left. The symmetrical building had no visible front entrance, so Kate went down the left hand side of it until she found a way in.

Once inside she quickly found the door marked 'OFFICE.' She knocked firmly, but politely on it. A lady's muffled voice said, 'come in.'

Kate took a deep breath. 'Could she do this?'

Inside the room, a diminutive woman in her fifties looked up from behind a typewriter on a dark wood desk.

'Good afternoon,' said Kate, 'my name is Patricia Friel. I spoke to Mrs Bowen this morning about my visit.'

'Ah yes, you're here to see Rosemary. I'll tell Mrs Bowen you are here,' as she swept out of the room, leaving the door ajar and 'Patricia' still in the room. No more than a minute later, she returned and beckoned for her to follow, saying, 'Mrs Bowen is ready for you.' They entered another larger room with a brass plate on the Buckingham-green door, with 'HEADMISTRESS' embossed on it. Kate was greeted by a dark haired lady, of a similar age to her secretary, in a Harris Tweed skirt-suit and white cotton blouse. Her hand outstretched she said 'welcome' and gestured for her guest to sit on a comfortable looking chair with arms, in front of her desk.

'Thank you,' said Kate.

Returning to her chair, Mrs Bowen sat down and said, 'how can we help?'

'As I explained on the phone Mrs Bowen, my name is Patricia Friel and I am a child welfare officer attached to Devon and Cornwall Police constabularies. I am here to investigate an incident which happened some months ago in Plymouth, involving the Letts family. I need to ascertain, if possible, whether there is a case to answer.'

'I see,' said Mrs Bowen, attentively.

'I have been specially trained in techniques that allow me to gain the information we need from children, without actually interviewing them formally.'

'Go on,' said the Head.

'If, as I'm sure you are aware, you directly question a child, they tend to clam up.'

'Indeed they do.'

'My methods allow a child to chat and I direct the conversation in subtle directions, until I have heard all I need to.'

'Why here at school? Surely she would be more

talkative at home?'

'Not in this case. I can't say too much about this particular child's home life, but it is not as normal as it would appear. That's why I need to see her away from that environment. School is a perfect place.'

'Very well and I would like to watch and learn from you. How should I introduce you?' Mrs Bowen was now well and truly on-board.

'I realise you must be fascinated to see how it's done, but unfortunately this exercise only works on a one to one basis.'

'Oh,' said Mrs Bowen, looking disappointed.

'I have to gain the child's trust and that is quickest achieved if there are no distractions. I have to be extremely patient and sometimes it takes more than one visit.'

'Of course, I understand. Should I take you to her now?'

'Yes. Please.'

Mrs Bowen stood and left the room. Kate followed her out. As they walked to the classroom Kate said.

'Please introduce me as the welfare officer, here to talk to Rosemary about her new school and the move from Devon.'

The Head stopped at a classroom door, knocked and entered. Kate waited in the corridor. She could hear the child being asked to come with her. Moments later a dark haired ten year-old was being introduced. She had shining brown hair, an olive skin and big brown eyes. In her head, Kate couldn't reconcile this attractive child with the pictures of the adult, she would become.

'Rosemary, this is Mrs Friel. She is a welfare officer from the council. She wants you to show her round your new school. Will that be all right?'

The child looked at Kate, smiled, looked back at the Head and replied, 'yes Mrs Bowen.'

'In that case I'll leave you two to get acquainted.' With that, she turned away and returned to her office.

'Hello Rosemary. What shall we look at first?'

'I could show you the playground if you like?'

'Ok, after you.'

The youngster had a slight and probably nervous skip in her step as they walked the length of the corridor. On Rosemary's instruction, Kate opened the door at the end and they went outside.

'Do you like your new school?'

'Am I allowed to say?' Said the child in a quiet voice.

'Of course. Say what?'

'Well, the school's ok. It's smaller than my last one, but nicer. My teacher is lovely and she's tried to help me to find some new friends.' The child chatted away as they walked.

Kate could tell that she was a simple, unsophisticated and not unpleasant young girl. She sensed a 'but' coming, so she said, 'but…'

'But the girls and boys here don't like me, because I'm new and I speak funny. They tease me and won't let me join in their games at play-time.' The smile had gone. It was now a saddened Rosemary that stood before her.

It was difficult to make the connection between the girl she was talking to on this day and the adult that she would grow up to become. Kate had to remain strong. She didn't want to waiver, but her Catholic guilt was questioning her behaviour. Could she be the wrong one? Was it really necessary? Her mind was so far away that she almost fell over a low bench that Rosie had side stepped. The blow to her shin brought her back to the matter in hand.

'I've got something to cheer you up. Would you like a sweet?' Kate opened her handbag to get the paper bag out. Holding the offering she opened the two layers of paper and showed Rosie the contents.

'Oh thank you, but no thank you.'

Kate looked startled. 'Why ever not? I thought everyone liked sherbet lemons?'

'Oh no, it's not that. It's my father. He says I'm not allowed sweeties between meals.'

'Well in that case you are a very good girl for obeying your Daddy.'

Rosie smiled.

Kate went on, 'I don't see why you couldn't have some to take home. To have after your tea, this evening.'

The child's smile grew even wider.

'It can be our secret. Don't tell anyone, especially your brothers or sisters. They are all for you, as a reward for giving me such a good guided tour of your lovely school.'

'Oh thank you Miss, but my dress doesn't have any pockets.'

'Have you got a satchel?'

'Yes I have, it's not very big though.'

'Where is it? Can you show me?'

'Come with me then Miss.' She almost danced back down the corridor. She pushed open a door, opposite the one of her classroom and waved for her to follow.

As she entered the cloakroom, Kate felt like Gulliver in Lilliput. Everything in the room was so small. The benches were the height of a footstool. The clothes pegs were just above her waist height and the open door of a cubicle revealed a miniature china toilet pan. She was thinking back to her convent days, when a voice called her. It wasn't a Lilliputian, it was a triumphant sounding Rose.

'Here it is!' Amongst some coats on the low down pegs, Rosie held open a schoolbag.

Kate put the double paper bag inside. 'Remember to hide them as soon as you get home and don't share them. They are all for you!'

'Oh I definitely won't,' said Rosie promising to follow her instructions and because of her sneaky expression, Kate knew that is exactly what would happen. The child still had an obedient streak. Her work was done.

'Thank you for showing me round.'

'Thank you for my sweets Miss.'

'Now you had better get back to your lessons.'

Kate turned and walked back round to the offices. She heard Rosie go back into her class. She didn't look back. She couldn't. The feeling of nausea meant she needed more fresh air. She paused at the half open door.

'Thank Mrs Bowen for me please,' she said to her secretary. I have all the information I need. You will hear from my superiors in due course. Now I must go, it's a long way back to Yeovil.'

Goodbyes were exchanged and Kate marched firmly away. Deep breaths of Cotswold air and she started to feel better. At least she hadn't had to witness the consequences.

A sudden visualisation of the child doubled up in pain in front of her family, was the work of a religious conscience. She repelled the vision as best she could. This was the easiest one. The others would prove to be more hands on. She needed courage, determination and stamina. She went back to her little green car. The mission had begun.

9

Kate

We decided that most of our school friends were shallow. Bridget worried about her freckles and her titian locks that weren't yet fashionable. She tolerated her braces and pretended that they didn't matter. She had no time for boyfriends anyway. I secretly worried about my pimples and inheriting my mother's unruly curls. But we were grounded in so many ways and knew our own minds.

My parents loved Bridget. Initially my mother thought she was 'common,' reflecting an ironic level of snobbery, given her own modest background. This soon changed as she got to know her better. She recognised a clever girl who was striving for a better life when she saw one and would often return home from work with samples of items that were miraculously the perfect fit for skinny Bridget. In turn Bridget was thrilled and could differentiate between love and charity. Our convent education could justify not looking a 'gift horse in the mouth,' even if it didn't have any origins in Catholicism.

I would return from Bridget's home with a bag of Dover Sole, from Joe. One of my mother's favourite dishes evolved from this, eventually becoming her signature dish, 'Soul fish risotto' a strange combination of tomatoes, peppers and cheese. Quite adventurous for the eighties. My father usually cooked, but would allow Francesca in the kitchen on occasion, to try out one of her recipes. It was such a happy time, with our blended families and we counted ourselves lucky as many of our fellow pupils parents were splitting up and divorcing.

I loved my time at the convent. It could be harsh and tedious at times. The nuns believed that education was more than the sum of the subjects we covered in order to pass our 'GCE's. There was a moral backbone to our education that made us aware of our weaknesses. Nevertheless, it also encouraged us to be confident young women, who could make a difference. I can cry inwardly if think too much about it now. I actually can't think about what I have done and absolve myself.

Sister Bernadette told us that we are all here for a purpose. She could never have condoned my actions under any circumstances whatsoever. Her ultimate faith in God was enough for her. He would deal with it all, in this life or the next. I couldn't quite share her optimism or devotion. I tried and God knows that I struggled with the decision I made. Am I evil? Perhaps only 'He' can answer that. How important is the greater good? It's a tough question. Maybe you will find the answers yourself. We are ultimately all responsible for our actions aren't we?

10

Sister Bernadette

Mine's a dull old tale I expect, compared to most. I haven't had the life experiences of Beverley, or suffered like my good friend Kate. I am not sure what I can add to the mixture really, but I am always happy to talk about Kate. I have known her since she was a little girl. Obviously I don't have children, but if I did have, she would have been the daughter I would have wanted.

At the convent school you can't always take to the girls can you? God helps you to teach them and watch over them, but he can't make you like them. A lot of the girls come from privileged backgrounds and quite frankly, they are ruined before we get them. They're not interested in education, just getting the newest fancy gadgets and showing off in front of their friends. Some are so used to getting their own way that they become bullies. Now you have to be a good judge of character in this job. You try to lead them on the right path, but it can still be a rocky road, sure enough.

I am generally a happy upbeat kind of person. I joined the convent when I was seventeen years old. You probably have some of your own opinions about nuns, especially Irish ones, but let me tell you I am not a stereotype. I can put the fear of God into you if I choose to, but mostly I don't.

Kate was a great student. She made my day, often. I love the girls that have a brain, but also have a mind and some imagination and question things, including the doctrines. It's good to be challenged and it keeps you on your toes. Kate questioned everything and I mean everything. As she got older the subjects changed. Her opinions changed, but she still couldn't help questioning and probing. Kate didn't accept the principle that the world isn't fair.

'Why should we accept poverty?' That was one of her favourites. She wasn't afraid to discuss women's rights, including abortion. We didn't agree on some of the issues, but it made for an interesting discussion.

A lovely thing about Kate is her interest in you. She cares and she wants to know about how you are feeling. When she was about ten, she sat me down one day on our usual bench and asked me a question.

'What's your story Sister Bernadette?'

I asked her what she meant by the question and she replied

'Well, an intelligent and kind woman like you could have had a husband and a family. Why would you choose the church? It doesn't treat women well, does it?'

'Too many questions child,' but I did tell her about growing up in Kilkenny, the only daughter in a family of five children. I told her about my mother and how she slaved all day in a tiny house, cooking and cleaning and looking after us all, without a complaint. I told her about my father and his hard drinking and gambling. I watered it down a little, but she was a clever child who couldn't be patronised.

'Did he hit you Sister Bernie?' she asked nervously, not really wanting to hear the answer.

'Yes Kate,' I replied. 'He hurt me both body and soul, but he hurt my mother far worse. She loved him you see. Love can be destructive if in the wrong hands. I remembered my mother sobbing into her pillow when she thought no one could hear her. Meanwhile the great Niall Malone would be supping Guinness with his pals, boasting that he could outdrink them all and then seek to prove it.'

'What happened?' said Kate. My story had taken some weeks to unfold as we sat and had our little chats during break. I told her how my mother had become ill with cancer and passed away just before my fifteenth birthday.

'I made her a promise Kate. I know she had more faith than any woman I have ever known and she would have taken strength from my decision to become a nun. She had always wanted one of the boys to become a priest, but they were a feckless lot. I knew that I would take to the life of a 'Bride of Christ.' He couldn't let you down in the way that most men can,' I laughed.

She knew that I was happy with my life. As she got older she still challenged me, but her maturity helped to accept the choices people make. She became more tolerant. Kate had her whole life ahead of her and she had the brains and personality to be a success.

I tried to teach her more than the curriculum. We enjoyed our talks about everything and everybody. She educated me in some of the ways of the world that I wasn't aware of and opened my eyes to important issues. I was ignorant in many ways and had the protection of the church and my environment as a safety net. Kate's social conscience rubbed off on me and I began to see the importance of going out into the community and getting involved. I started helping in a women's refuge and began to understand some of the issues that had affected my mammy. I realised you can't live in a bubble and I thank Kate for that gift.

11

Tuesday 21st May 1963

The drive from Gloucester to Norfolk had for the most part been uneventful. Apart from the extremely strong winds, which had made piloting a car without power-steering feel as if she had been in a five hour wrestling match. Add to that an incident near Thetford involving seven escaped cows, Friesians by the look of them, thought Kate. It took 'Farmer Giles' twenty minutes to persuade them to return to their field. She thought about turning round and going another way, but in a land without satellite-navigation it seemed not to be her best idea.

The delay gave her some unexpected thinking time. Trying not to let the whistle of the weather and the gentle rocking motion distract her thoughts, she made bullet points and some disturbing doodles. Dark satanic scribbling she thought and little wonder really. The reminders included the phone call to Fraserburgh and booking the Hotel in Bradford. She made a short list of some random names to use for the rest of the journey. She didn't want it to make it too easy for them to track her movements.

The way ahead was finally cleared and she resumed her way up the A11. It was getting dark early because of the heavy clouds being blown about, but she knew the way round Norwich well enough. That's the payback for all the expensive and painstaking hours of research over the last few weeks. Although the landscape and especially the City looked different today.

Thankfully there were still enough buildings of a certain age to navigate by.

At a little after quarter past eight she was in Tombland and facing the Maid's Head Hotel. She turned right at the entrance and parked in Palace Street. Gathering her bag and case she walked back the way she came and entered the Hotel lobby. It hadn't changed much. Dark wood panelling that pre-Victorian carpenters had installed doesn't age, she thought. The man on the desk spoke first.

'Can I help you Madam?'

'Yes you can. I'm travelling alone and I need a room for the night.' Kate was assertive enough without growling.

'A single room for just the one night or are you intending to stay longer in Norwich, Miss?'

'Actually it's Mrs. and just the one night, but I'd like the oak-beamed attic room if it's not taken.'

'Oh, you've been here before Madam.' Said the broad vowel Norfolk accent.

'Not exactly.' Kate, side stepping continued, 'I've been told how lovely it is and the views of the city and cathedral are apparently not to be missed.' She lied. She had stayed in that very room two weeks ago.

'You're in luck Madam, Tuesday evenings are one of the quieter nights in the Hotel and we have several large rooms available, including the one you enquired about. What name shall I put in the register?'

'Mrs Jarvis. Brenda Jarvis. 22 Acaia Avenue, Surbiton.' Kate's lies were a tapestry.

The friendly night manager offered her the book to sign. 'I'm afraid you are too late to dine in the restaurant, but I could have a light supper sent up to you if you need it.'

'I'm not overly hungry, but it's been a long day and I should have something. What do you suggest?'

'How about poached eggs and anchovy toast?'

'Agatha Christie style?' Kate couldn't resist. It was the author's favourite dish.

'Why yes,' said the manager, 'she stayed here some months ago and had us making it all the time for her. Now we've added it to the menu.'

Kate smiled. 'Sounds perfect and I'll be in good company.'

He pressed the counter bell and a younger man appeared, straightening his jacket and then led the way, with the bags.

Once inside the almost familiar space, Kate noted the changes. No TV. No WI-FI. No walk-in shower and natural stone bathroom. Heavier curtains, a proper bedspread, valance and sheets. And no telephone.

She ran a bath, but delayed getting in until the young man had returned with her snack. The old-style tub was so deep that both took about the same amount of time. She gave a pound note and his eyes nearly left their sockets. She remembered to ask him for a wake-up call at seven. Once he was on his way back down the stairs, Kate disrobed and got in the bath and took her plate and a fork in with her. There's something deliciously decadent about eating whilst enjoying a soak, she mused. And the best bit was, there were no distractions, at all.

So exhausted was she from her arduous cross-country trek that she fell asleep whilst still immersed. When the water had cooled enough the brain woke her up, to find somewhere more comfortable. She got out and dried herself with the Egyptian cotton towels, rubbing hard to restore the circulation. Before letting the water go she retrieved the plate from under the water. The last two anchovies were still floating on the surface. It doesn't matter how wet they get, they'll never swim again, she thought.

Putting on the flannelette nightdress she had bought in case it wasn't warm enough was located in the bottom of the case. She put it on in a hurry. The weather was blowing hard outside the single paned windows and it was barely fourteen degrees in the room, she sensed. It was now after ten-thirty and with little source of entertainment to distract her, she got into bed. Light out. She lay there, shivering on contact with the cold sheets.

Eventually the shaking to warm up stopped and she felt reasonably temperate, but not that tired. Her mind was working overtime on the events of the past couple of days. It was time to meditate. She had been taught the 'art,' twenty or more years ago, whilst at Cambridge by a fellow student. For the last few years she had an app on her phone that guided her through it and sent timed reminders. She could do with her smart phone right now, in so many ways. She was out of practise doing it manually and it wouldn't happen. She couldn't shut down the mental process.

The sight of Rosie drifted in and out of her consciousness. Sometimes smiling; sometimes vomiting; occasionally lying in a vale of death. The death mask images would wake her frontal lobes and the sleeplessness would continue. Kate tried looking out of windows, pacing the floor, counting sheep and an assortment of mental exercises. It didn't improve. Her restlessness would have needed an anaesthetic to curb it and so the long night continued.

Something woke her again. Not a child's image this

time. It was her sub-conscious urging her to act. Urgent thoughts, but why? It was light outside, but then it was nearly June, it gets light from five o'clock. She found her watch on the dresser. She looked twice. She thought her eyes had too much sleep in them at first. Twenty to ten. What? What's going on? Kate had planned to be back on the road soon after eight.

Young Master Bell-hop must have forgotten to write up her request for a seven o' clock knock. A cat's lick wash and day-clothes later she tackled the Duty Manager.

'Why was I not woken at seven as I requested with the Porter last night?' Kate demanded.

The manager lifted his head from his journal with a surprised look and said. 'I don't know Madam, but I'll find out.' He called out 'Peter' into the room behind him. Another young face appeared.

'Yes Sir?'

'I gave you the 'wake-up' list this morning. Mrs Jarvis in the attic suite was on it, why didn't you knock for her?'

'I did Sir.' He shot a look at Kate. 'Mrs Jarvis replied to me. I heard her say thank you, so I came away.' They both looked at Kate.

Something was dawning in her mind and she mumbled 'Oh my God. I'm sorry. I can vaguely remember it, but I must have been dreaming. I was awake most of the night so at seven when I was finally asleep I was obviously deeply unconscious. Please accept my apologies, it's all my fault.'

'That's quite all right Madam, we're used to it, aren't we Peter?' Peter nodded. 'Can I set the table for breakfast? I think Cook is still in the kitchen.

'No thank you. I'm very late for an appointment, I

must check out and go.'

'My bags are packed.' She turned to the young assistant. 'Would you bring them down while I sort out my bill?'

He barely spoke, but was up the stairs in an instant and back in no time. Kate let them keep the change from the twenty pounds she handed over. Guilt, for causing a fuss? Perhaps, but they'd remember her anyway when the detectives will come with their questions, so in the great scheme of things it wouldn't matter much.

12

Kate

Love is more than a four letter word. I am also my mother's daughter in more ways than I realised. I wasn't ready to fall in love and like Bridget believed that we didn't need a man to make us happy.

The Sixth form of the Covent didn't give too many opportunities to meet boys apart from the occasional party, where a group of boys from the local Grammar School would turn up and the more shallow girls from our year group would plaster on make-up and stake their claim on the nearest spotty prize. Not for myself or Bridget. We were not interested. This was the nineties. Things were changing and we didn't need to cheapen ourselves in order to lose our virginity. I had high expectations. Watching James and Francesca cuddled up on the sofa at home during the evening was a constant reminder that love did exist and that it could last. As someone once said to me, disappointment is linked to expectation. Mine, had a life force of its own. Looking back we were probably hated by some of our class mates.

It's a shame we don't have the American School Year Book in England. You know the kind I mean. Tiny 'photo-booth' pictures of the whole class with various comments, like; 'Prom Queen' and 'Most likely to be married by eighteen.' British humour and cynicism would make for far more interesting reading. I imagine that my classmates would have written comments such as; 'Thinks she is a cut above us' and 'Doesn't mix socially so we don't really know her.' 'Clever, but stuck up.' 'Ideas above her station.' Am I being harsh on myself? Probably.

Sister Bernadette got me. She understood. Despite joining the convent at seventeen, she had a worldly knowledge that was quite amazing. She encouraged me to study harder, stop day-dreaming and eventually to apply for Oxbridge, despite my protestations that this was out of my league. When I was awarded a place at Cambridge to study Law, she acted like a proud parent.

I already had two very proud parents, so a third was a bonus. James and Francesca were both pleased and slightly surprised. My father particularly thought I would choose a less traditional University, given my frequent vocal outbursts that education is not just for the elite. I still inwardly cringe when I think about how opinionated and objectionable I was at seventeen. My soap-box was the favoured platform of choice whilst lecturing James and Francesca on their privileged Bourgeois lifestyle.

I realised my principles could be adjusted to suit my changing views. I truly didn't think I had a chance of getting to Cambridge so hadn't really thought about the wider issue. When the envelope arrived I instantly saw my future in a different light. I am clever enough to go to Cambridge. The world really is my oyster. I can still help the poor, the deserving or undeserving, I can still be a Lawyer, but other doors would open for me. How did I equate this to not having privilege, I don't know? I wrestled with my social conscience and my notions of equality, but there was never really a question of whether or not I would go.

I braced myself and went to Bridget's. Joe was ready for me. I was expecting the worst, bearing in mind his beliefs and some of the arguments we'd had in the past, but he was kinder than that. His jokes about me being too good for the local Polytechnic were expected, but I had a sense that he was genuinely happy for me in a strange way. He was always good at stepping into other peoples shoes and although he didn't hold with 'the establishment,' he could see why I had applied to Cambridge.

Bridget was going to York University. She believed their Business Studies BA was her best option. She wanted to work in the City eventually, although Joe was trying to persuade her otherwise. We were going our separate ways. It was scary. Many tears were shed during the following weeks leading up to our respective departures. Francesca sensing our pain treated us to a week's holiday in Crete. It was the first one on our own.

We let our hair down. We had studied hard, sacrificed nights out and parties, as our A-Level exams approached. We stayed in a white-walled villa with a small pool and an attractive pool attendant. We sunbathed during the day until even Bridget's milky white skin turned a light shade of caramel. I looked at her, seeing her for the first time in a different light. When did she become so beautiful? I hadn't noticed, seeing her every day at school. Braces gone, long titian curls and her piercing green eyes. The locals noticed too and she was regularly pursued around the island by Greek gods on their scooters.

I wasn't invisible either and had my fair share of attention. It was fun to flirt and drink cheap red wine as the sun came down. We ate beef Stifado and lamb roasted in herb filled parcels. We sipped Retsina and talked about the next part of our lives. It was carefree and just what we needed. Rested, we returned to a damp and gloomy British summer day and promised we would holiday together next year. Little did I know that my life would change so radically that the week in Crete would become a distant memory. Life was never going to be the same again.

I packed another box to take to the college where I would be living. Francesca had made a special 'Soul Fish risotto' to mark my departure from the family home. We sat around the large wooden table that had been such a big part of my childhood. I had painted on that table, written my homework, made my first attempt at spaghetti Bolognese with Quorn. (I was going through a vegetarian phase at the time.) I was already feeling nostalgic and I hadn't actually left home. Everything Francesca said seemed poignant and James was his usual funny, kind self. They were both pretending that they wouldn't miss me and to some extent I almost believed them.

We piled up my belongings in Francesca's Volvo and we all set off early in the day. By the time I was settled in my room with some familiar belongings around me at seven that evening, I was starting to panic. My parents had left half an hour earlier, after presenting me with a shiny new mobile phone, so there would be no reason not to keep in contact. James was practical, Francesca was emotional. He took her to the car before he started to get upset. 'It's a milestone' he said. 'We will cope,' she said.

13

Bridget

W hat can I tell you about Kate? That's she is loyal, funny, spirited and kind. That's a start I suppose. When I first met Kate it was as if I had always known her. You know that feeling you get, not exactly déjà vu, but a sense that the person is already familiar to you. You somehow just realise that although some friends will come and go through your life, some are there for keeps and Kate was a keeper.

As Miss McLean marched up to the bullies who had already made my life a misery for the best part of a week and verbally reduced them to tears, I knew that she was a force to be reckoned with and I was more than happy to be on 'team Kate.' To this day I don't know exactly what she said, but I do know that they never called me 'fishcake' again.

In fact looking back they didn't really speak to either of us again. Colleen MacIntyre spent the next few years actively ignoring both of us, with a haughty air of indifference. She was the worst of the three by far, her pudgy face and small lips which were permanently pursed and she fancied herself to be a cut above the rest of us, because her father owned a transport business. It didn't matter how much money she may have had though, it couldn't improve her appearance or her personality.

She immediately spotted her prey on our first day and my ginger hair was the flame that drew the moth. The freckles didn't help either and the fact that my dad was a lowly fishmonger was music to her ears. Did I smell of fish? I would like to think not, but looking back our flat was over the shop and it is hard to avoid the smell when it's part of your childhood. Kate didn't care though. She wasn't interested in why they were bullying me, she just wasn't having any of it. She hates injustice and although I am the one with the ginger hair, she was the one with the fiery temper when roused.

She was my protector at first. I was a bit overwhelmed by her interest in me. My father Joe had pushed me to apply for a scholarship to Maria Fidelis School. Although I passed the exams I was worried I would be out of my depth with the fee-paying girls. Even at a young age you can feel out of place. You become aware of your own social status, I suppose.

Don't get me wrong, I wasn't ashamed of my working class background, but I was certainly aware of it. I was a proper 'cockney' then and was a strong contrast to Kate's cultured West London tones. Opposites can attract though, can't they? Our sense of sisterhood went beyond class and money and we formed a true bond of friendship.

What did we have in common? Well very little on the surface. My background had made me ambitious from an early age. I wanted to succeed in business and make money. I wanted to be out of the Fish shop and the flat in Hackney and my education would help me rise above my humble background. Kate on the other hand was more for the underdog. Perhaps her background and privilege was taken for granted by her, to some extent. She wanted to right the world's wrongs and make everyone equal. We were both passionate about life in general and tended to set ourselves apart from the other convent girls.

I loved going to Kate's home. We would pitch up at about four-thirty and if James hadn't picked us up, we would have experienced the joys of London Transport and would be giggling as we entered the house. We shared a sense of humour and loved to observe others, people watching I suppose. We would often sit next to a 'down and out' on the tube. Kate would inevitably start a conversation and it would end with her getting out her purse. I couldn't help but laugh at how easily she was often taken in. I was a bit shrewder and also had a lot less pocket money to spare so I suppose I could be the more cynical one at that time.

We entered the house and most of the time James would come out of his 'shed' in the garden when he heard us slam the door. The kettle would go on and we would recount our latest adventure. He was a quiet man and a great listener, unlike my dad Joe who is a great talker! I felt at home there and it was a haven of peace and tranquillity compared to Hackney.

Francesca would arrive home about six-thirty, a haze of Chanel No 5 and always full of drama. She worked at Harrods, so to me she seemed unbelievably glamorous and important. She would sit down with a gin & tonic and tell us all about her day. Funny, witty and wise, she was the person that Kate and I looked up to in our own different ways.

I was gangly and skinny until about the age of seventeen. With ginger hair and braces, you can get the picture. Kate on the other hand was tall without being a beanpole, slim without being skinny and her hair was long and hung in curls that she despised. As teenagers we could always see the potential in each other without necessarily seeing it in ourselves.

Francesca had the knack of throwing together an

outfit and looking a million dollars. She had a sense of style that couldn't be taught. I had very little money to buy any clothes during those years and she would push a thick green plastic bag towards me, with the gold emblem of Harrods embossed on the front. 'Just some samples Bridget darling,' she would say and my heart would thump with excitement. Over the years I started to collect a wardrobe of classic clothes that shaped my own style and personality, thanks to Kate's mother.

Kate was an only child and although I know Francesca would have liked a large family, it didn't happen for her. They all made me feel as if I was an honorary McLean though. James was a great cook and I looked forward to dinner, wondering what delights he had dreamt up or found in his stash of cook books. My dad didn't cook. Despite being a master Fishmonger or whatever it's called and having the knife skills of a surgeon, it was as much as he could do to make toast. My mum was a traditional type of cook, taught by her own mother. So unless Dad had brought up some fish, our meals tended to lean towards hotpots, stews and pies.

It felt bohemian at Kate's house. You never quite knew what was going to happen, or what sort of discussion would take place at the dinner table. Unpredictable is good. At home I knew the routines all too well. I had three younger siblings, so there was a regimental air about the day and mum worked hard to keep it all going. Dad was out in the evenings quite a lot, due to his duties as a councillor and my mother wouldn't sit down until her work was done. Don't get me wrong, I have loving, caring parents and I am very lucky to have such a family. But we didn't do spontaneous and sometimes the daily stuff felt black and white, rather than the technicolour of Kate's home.

We all want the things we haven't got, I guess. Kate loved the organised chaos of my flat and liked spending time with my brother and sisters, who she thought were 'cute.' I tried to tell her that they were not so cute when you wanted to study, watch TV or just have a bit of quiet time . She would have loved some brothers or sisters, looking back. We tended to study at Kate's home rather than mine and I would often sleep over at weekends. For many years we were inseparable and although we would argue frequently about politics, world events and the like, we didn't argue about our friendship or loyalty to each other. I know that we may have appeared aloof to some of our classmates, but we grew up at our own pace and didn't feel the need to follow the gang. Some of our classmates were drinking, smoking and meeting local boys. Not us, we had our places in the world mapped out and we wanted to get out there and do it.

I remember our first and last holiday together when we were eighteen. We broke free from the confines of our studies and went a bit wild. We didn't have a gap year, but we let our hair down and partied for the first time. Do I make us sound dull? I hope not. We just had our own rules and wanted to set ourselves apart from the others. Fortunately, we were both natural students and we were able to achieve the results we wanted. Boys could wait, or so we thought.

14

Wednesday 22nd May 1963

With Norwich behind her, Kate was on the Cromer Road and had already passed Aylsham, but she was almost three hours later than intended. She had planned to get to the school before the parents and children arrived to start the day at nine. It was now nearer twelve o'clock. In 2017 she would have needed to wait until the end of the school-day at three-fifteen, to get another opportunity. However, this is 1963 and school meals haven't become the norm yet. If Kate's research was accurate the children would be going home soon for their lunch.

So she pulled the car into verge and reached in her bag for a scarf and dark glasses. More a cliché than a disguise, especially on a cloudy day, she tied the scarf over her head, covering her hair and as much of her forehead as possible. She was finally ready for her first experience of 'hit and run'. She switched off the emotional side of her brain almost without realising. She was in a way on automatic pilot. Anything more and she would have turned back.

Turning from High Noon Road into School Lane, she could hear her heart now racing faster than the Minor's engine, but nerves were not going to spoil months of work. Round the long bend and there was the School on the right, just where the road has a slight double kink in it. The building looked even smaller than in pictures, she thought and wondered how any serious teaching could be done in cramped conditions. She pulled her thoughts back to logistics.

She drove round the long way and had a second look. This time she parked just before the long bend straightened, out of sight of the school entrance. The parents of the village would approach from the other direction. Kate let the engine idle and sat quietly, breathing slowly and deeply to slow her heart. It was clear that adrenaline wasn't going to allow that to happen. She got out of the car for a stretch of the tension-filled limbs.

She looked at her watch, it was just before twelve. She climbed the bank to a height that would bring the school into view and scanned the scene. Some parents were gathering by the gate, but not that many she thought, but then again this was a time when children walked home by themselves. A lady in a blue coat with a pram caught her eye. Could she be? There were no others with younger children or babies, so it seemed likely. Kate would know for sure when the children emerge, if she met two boys, she would be sure.

The following minutes seemed like an eternity, until her focus was restored by the bell. They would be coming out from class any moment. Returning quickly to the driver's seat, Kate slipped the clutch and inched forward, until she could just see Pram Lady. Sure enough she was greeted by two boys, one small excitable young lad and an older brother. The smaller one looked as if he hadn't got used to the routine of school days and ran round and round like a headless chicken. 'Let's go' she thought to herself.

Kate seized the moment and with as much acceleration as the old car could muster, she aimed the car at the group. She was in third gear and close to twenty-five miles an hour, when she tweaked the massive steering wheel, to cause the car to swerve. Kate was almost physically sick when she felt the impact. Even though she had rehearsed for it, the reality was unbearable, she had killed a child. The screams drowned out the sound of the tyres as the car skidded to a stop.

The mother was still screaming 'Steven' as Kate looked back. Shocked school staff were running from the gate and the child's brother was bent over his sibling trying to shake life back into a pale and bleeding shell. All their immediate attention was on the child and not on the car and Kate's original plan, to run back to the group and offer her profound sorrow at losing control of the car, no longer looked like a good one. The new plan formed in an instant. Get the hell out of Erpingham!!

The school would call for the Ambulance and Police and because Cromer is only five miles away, they would likely be dispatched from there. That meant if she went south, back to Norwich, she should be able to avoid being caught. Driving faster than was sensible, Kate drove back to the city on the road she had used an hour before. She abandoned the dented Morris next to the Adam and Eve Public House, built in the thirteenth century to refresh the Cathedral's stone-mason builders. Leaving the scarf and glasses on the passenger seat, she made her way on foot to the station, as briskly as she thought wouldn't attract attention.

'Single to Peterborough, please and when's the next one due?'

'First or second, Madam?'

'The first of course. Why would I want the second train?'

'I meant first or second class Madam,' said the ticket-clerk with a quizzical look.

Thinking it might be the place to be less visible, she

replied 'second.'

'That'll be twelve shillings and sixpence and then next one is at half past one, from Platform 2. It gets there at twenty to three, Madam. Do you a need a porter to help with your bags?'

Kate was still un-nerved by this chivalry thing. 'No, thank you I'll manage.'

Kate made her way to the platform, but it wasn't quite quarter past and she felt as conspicuous as a murderess should. She went and hid in the corner of the waiting room until the train was nearly ready to depart.

Steam trains if you're not used to them are impressive beasts, assuming you ignore the noise and the smells, though the 2nd class carriages are less comfortable by modern standards. The red leather benches were firm to the point of hard and the very upright position meant the next seventy minutes were going to drag. The next time she was asked the question, she would have to say 'first,' after all, 'I can afford it.'

At Peterborough, she alighted the train, gave her ticket to the collector and crossed the station concourse to the ticket office. She enquired the best way to Bradford and bought a first class single ticket.

She needed to hurry to platform one because a fast service to Newcastle was almost due, stopping only at Grantham before Leeds and Darlington. Then a change of train at Leeds, with almost an hour to wait meant she wouldn't get to her destination until after seven o'clock.

This is more like it. Kate congratulated herself on choosing a first-class carriage, this time. From the added touches like crisp white cotton antimacassars and the tables with gilded light-fittings, to the seats like armchairs that she sunk into and didn't want to get out of. She asked the attendant to wake her up before Leeds if she got too comfortable. He said he would and then offered her a pot of Assam tea. She felt she needed something stronger, but the tea would have to do.

Suitably refreshed, her mind returned the task. Her planned phone call to reserve a room at the Midland hadn't found an opportunity because of the unplanned start to the day and the lack of time in Peterborough. It should be ok, she thought, but would ring from Leeds station, in case she needed to switch to the Great Victoria Hotel instead.

On arrival at Leeds, Kate found the phone-boxes and made the call. The Midland Hotel, which forms part of Bradford station is very used to late arriving and weary travellers, took the booking quickly and efficiently. So much so that she was able to press the phone-box's button 'B' and get most of her pennies back.

It was now ten past five and with more than forty minutes until her train's departure, she had asked a passer-by for the nearest department store. She was pleased to find that Schofield's was less than a five minute walk. 'But don't dawdle,' was the added advice, 'it shuts at half past.'

After the over-sleeping debacle that morning Kate was desperate for an alarm clock. An assistant in perfumery told her where to go and she wasted no time, running up the wooden escalators. Clocks and watches, on the second floor, was a wonderful department and she rued not having the time to browse the 'vintage watch' display.

The travel alarms by Westclox were practical and familiar to her. She chose the tan leatherette case with the gold metal and ivory square face, but with a slight curve to the edges. The very same one that she'd admired as a young girl, at her Grandmother's house in

Scotland. Sometimes nostalgia gives a warm feeling.

15

Kate

C onvent girls are the worst ones,' said Harry with a leer. I had drunk two pints of scrumpy cider, so I took the comment slightly less badly than normally I would. We were sitting around the student's union bar having formed a small group within the first few days of 'Fresher's week'. I was getting used to Harry by now. He was very rich, very clever, but had the social skills of a five year old. He spoke his mind constantly and although initially quite funny, after he'd had a few drinks he could be extremely irritating.

I had made a few friends already and was feeling that University life may suit me. I didn't have to work as hard as when I was studying for A-levels and although I found some of the lectures quite dull, it wasn't too difficult to keep up. I hadn't realised Law was so dry. A free thinker like me needed a bit more stimulation and I began to think I might have made the wrong choice. Did I really want to be a lawyer that much, I was unsure for the first time in my life. It had seemed such a clear path and choice that I started to wonder if I had really given it enough thought.

As I was pondering this, with my group of new classmates, a man walked across the room to our table and asked if he could join us. He had an American accent and I hadn't seen him around before. He introduced himself as Jackson Maze. An unusual man with an unusual name, I was intrigued and decided I wanted to get to know him. His hair was unfashionably long, his eyes were the brightest blue and he was looking at me with an intensity I wasn't used to. The 'light bulb' moment happened very quickly and seemed more like a lightning bolt. As he started to talk in his slow southern drawl, I didn't hear a word he was actually saying, I realised later. He was clever, he was funny and I wanted him.

Luckily he wanted me too. Badly. We left the student bar in a hurry, we had an urgent need to touch each other as our arms entwined. My heart was racing and I could feel a smile forming on my face as we walked through the streets of Cambridge. It started to rain, but it didn't matter. Nothing mattered apart from this man. This was a totally new experience for me. Kate was cautious, Kate was sensible, Kate didn't run off into the night with a stranger. This strange new Kate broke all the rules and didn't care.

Lust or Love, I didn't know at that stage, but I did know I needed to get to his flat and find out. He lived alone and had been in Cambridge for a year doing a Masters in some sort of Physics. He was sponsored by an American company he had been working for in their research department, so he wasn't your typical student.

We spent the weekend in Jackson's large brass bed. I hadn't thought about when and how I would lose my virginity, but as experiences go, it was up there. He was tender and clearly knew what he was doing, which was just as well. I didn't. A rush of warmth ran through my veins that was not just linked to the amazing sexual experience with Mr Maze. It was like a drug. He was like a drug.

I always said to myself I wouldn't sleep with someone until I really knew them, Kate McLean didn't do one night stands, What had happened to me. I felt like the cat that had got the cream. I watched him sleeping, his dark hair curling on to the pillow and I knew I was home. He was home, how the hell had that happened?

I didn't really leave. I moved some clothes from my room in the college and gradually other items followed. It was so easy. Too easy? We quickly became known as a couple and our life together started. I would sit in lectures, remembering what we had done that morning in bed and a flush would actually come over me. It felt like a languid sexual haze. I couldn't stop thinking about him, when we were apart. We couldn't wait to fall together on our brass bed when he came home and I would be waiting.

He was the brightest man I have ever known. We could and did talk about anything. He wasn't troubled by my weirdness and understood all my thoughts about life the universe and everything. He could visualise a world where we could all levitate and travel into other worlds or through time. It didn't seem crazy when he said it. We drank red wine and argued about existentialism. How did we know we were actually alive? I knew I was alive. He made me feel more alive than I had ever felt. I didn't 'drift off' when I was with Jackson. I savoured every moment.

16

Thursday 23rd May 1963

Kate awoke at seven, when her new alarm clock's little bell rattled out its hollow chimes. She'd had no idea how primitive the alarms were in 1963. The one she had purchased couldn't have woken a butterfly, but the new sound was unfamiliar enough for brain to alert her. With her nerves already rattled, bleary-eyed she made her way to the bathroom. After splashing her face with water, she opened the door to collect the morning paper. What confronted her stopped her heart for a moment.

She saw the red Daily Mirror banner, but to the right, in very bold black letters was the headline she had been dreading.

'CHILD POISONED BY MYSTERY WOMAN.'

Underneath was an artist's impression. A picture of Kate, as described by Mrs Angela Bowen, Rosie's Headmistress. She read on with dismay.

The Police are looking to interview a woman who they believe gave poison-filled sweets to a nine year old schoolgirl. The girl died on Tuesday evening. That same day a mystery woman had come to her school, to ask her some questions. The visitor purported to be a Child Welfare Officer attached to the Devon and Cornwall police forces.

The identity she used was found to be false when the two police forces and both county councils denied any such person's existence. The woman managed to talk her way into the school and spend some time with the child on her own. No one, as yet, can offer any explanation for the sweets, other than the time spent alone with the mysterious 'Patricia Friel.' The headmistress, Mrs Bowen is said to be distraught and has provided the police with a full description of Mrs Friel.

'DO YOU KNOW THIS WOMAN?'

Kate looked at the artist's impression. It was grotesque. The eyes were not hers and too far apart, her hair looked thin and greasy. She felt offended. Then she took a hold of herself. Kate, she thought, for God's sake. You are upset at how you have been portrayed in a Police wanted poster. She cringed at her own vanity. Would anyone recognise her from this?

Now the public would be looking out for a dark haired woman in her late thirties to early forties, travelling on her own. This was one part of the plan, she hadn't really considered and she was angry at herself for not having a contingency. This wasn't a game. She chastised herself. It could be life or death.

She dressed quickly and started to consider her options. She thought of going out at nine to find a chemist and purchase some peroxide, or some other kind of hair dye. She realised she should have done some research. She guessed she wouldn't find any kind of product she could just shampoo in. To lift the colour from her hair would take some kind of bleach and be a laborious process. Kate knew her technical abilities were limited. She could end up with a head of yellow fluff or at worst it could all drop out. She couldn't risk a hairdresser. The Police could be asking too many questions.

She jumped into the taxi, waiting outside the station, just before eight-thirty. The headscarf trick she had used in Norfolk wasn't enough of a disguise for her to feel inconspicuous. They arrived in Leeds just on nine and she virtually ran into Lewis department store as it opened. The taxi driver grinned as he kept the meter running. This would be a good fare.

Approaching the wig department, she saw an eager shop assistant coming to meet her. 'Can I help you madam?' She enquired.

'Yes please,' said Kate in the best Yorkshire accent she could manage. 'I need a few wigs love, for me Aunty. She's having an operation and her hair's going t' drop owt.' It wasn't going to open up a new career as an 'Impressionist,' but the assistant didn't notice, or care?

Fifteen minutes later, she had a blonde bombshell backcombed beauty, a red bob, that Lulu would not have been ashamed to wear and a short black sleek wig. That should cover the next few days and she breathed a sigh of relief. As an afterthought, she stopped to pick up a sharp pair of scissors on the way back to the taxi. If she didn't reduce the amount of her real hair, the new hairpieces would look like the wigs they were. Not great when it's a disguise not a fashion statement.

As the taxi headed back towards Bradford and her hotel, she started to worry that she might have overlooked something else. She hadn't seriously thought about getting caught until this point. It was a possibility, but she consoled herself by thinking that the Police would always be one step behind. After all, because the crimes had no obvious pattern, they couldn't predict where or when she would turn up next. She'd change her appearance and her accent regularly too. At college and university had met friends from all over Britain. She could do this. She had to do this.

Back in her room she cut her long tresses as close to her scalp as she could manage without injury. Then she decided on the red wig for the day's task ahead and played around with it until it looked as natural as it could. The eyebrows were giving the game away though, but she'd have to deal with them later. Because each wig had come in its own discrete cloth bag, with a drawstring and didn't weigh much, she elected to take the Raven black style with her in her bag.

She checked her watch and was disturbed to see it was half past ten. Time was slipping away. Furtively she sneaked down the stairs and past reception as best she could.

Originally she had planned to get the bus to Bingley, but now she would have to play catch up. In a 'scouse' accent she instructed another station taxi to take her to the Hairdresser's in the main street in the town. She didn't want to go there at all, but she had to be dropped off somewhere and every town's main road has got a Lady's Hair Salon. The story she spun out as they passed through Manningham, Heaton and Cottingley, was that she didn't know the name of the shop because her cousin had recently acquired it and had invited her down to see it. She'd said 'you can't miss it!'

When the cab reached Main Street and stopped outside a random Hairdresser, she moved quickly from her seat, saying that's it. Putting two pound notes in his hand before he even told her the fare might have been foolhardy, or genius. He'd care more about the overpayment than her face.

She walked past the shop, up Wellington Street and entered Bingley Railway station. On the wall opposite the ticket office she found the Timetable for the service back to Bradford. It would be quicker than the bus and less chance of being spotted than another taxi. The trains were half-hourly, at a quarter to and quarter past the hour. She checked her watch with the station clock. They both declared it to be five past eleven. She would time her return to coincide with the train's departure. It wouldn't be sensible to loiter.

Kate bought a single ticket to Bradford, left the station and walking with purpose she made her way toward Bailley Hills Road. Although she had made this journey a number of times on Google Earth, the town looked very different today. After initial confusion about Old Main Street not existing, she found the way to her destination. Apart from a lack of cars, it looked familiar.

The main entrance to the Cemetery beckoned on the left, but just past it round the corner was a smaller gate and path that led through the trees. That was her chosen route and she made her way into the grounds. As quietly as she was able, she continued through the leaves, until the majority of the graveyard was in view. She remained, just camouflaged enough to be 'invisible'. She scanned the scene.

There was no sign of him. 'Surely he's at work by now. Even a habitual late-comer would be at work before (she checked her watch) twenty past eleven!' She thought, 'wait a minute, this is 1963 and Elevenses is still a national institution.' Even her father still liked his tea & biscuits at this magical hour. The minutes ticked by, as she waited patiently to see if she was right. She was tempted to carve her name in the bark of a Yew tree she was leaning on for support. She trawled her memory for the words of a Tennyson poem.

Old Yew, which graspest at the stones
That name the under-lying dead
Thy fibres net the dreamless head
Thy roots are wrapt about the bones…

She was transported back to a childhood love of poetry, when a noise disturbed her concentration.

Kate peered through the foliage in the direction of the sound. 'He's here!' Her heart raced again, as it had the day before. The maker of the sounds, a male youth, wiry with dark hair, had returned from his break and had jumped into a hole in the ground. It must have been quite deep, because the ground level was almost at his shoulders. In her head, Kate paced the distance. Thirty to thirty-five yards at a guess and the hole was angled obliquely away from her.

'What now?' No matter what you rehearse in life, there are still some details that have to remain ad hoc. Kate had hoped for some 'local' inspiration for the next act in this unfolding tragedy. She smiled at the thought that the other member of the 'cast' hadn't even been blessed with a script! This one was different, she felt herself becoming the part she had created. A monster, she thought. Images of young women in their prime flashed in front of her eyes and gave her the courage to continue.

She waited, barely breathing in case he heard her. After half an hour, the mounds of earth flanking the hole had grown. The sinewy digger had disappeared completely, ten minutes ago! Kate was beginning to doubt her own sanity for thinking she could get any kind of result here. She had come unarmed and less prepared for the task than was her usual way, remonstrating with herself in her head about the lack of prep. 'Fail to plan – plan to fail', was one of her old lecturer's favourite mantras. Maybe she would have to de-camp to Bradford, for a rethink.

Then, without warning, a shovel flew out of the hole. A head followed and then chest, torso, knee and the young Peter was back on the grassy surround. He turned back to face the hole and sat on the edge of the short side nearest to Kate. He reached into the pocket of his soil-dusted waistcoat and pulled out two shiny objects. He's stopped for a smoke, Kate anticipated. The tobacco tin and lighter were out of sight, but she was sure enough that the boy was rolling a cigarette.

The next mental process in Kate's head involved dragging forth the memory of an old flame, from Amsterdam, who wouldn't smoke anything he hadn't made himself and how long it took to roll and then enjoy it. Seconds later, she worked out that he would be busy for... long enough! It's now or never! The handbag was already on the ground and the coat was off in an instant and cast down with it.

Kate crept towards the hole. She took her last deep breath, ten yards from the discarded shovel, stealthily reaching for its handle. A split second of Catholic guilt made her decide against using the sharp edge of the tool, or was it because she hadn't brought a change of clothes? Another oversight. Being a murderess wasn't an easy occupation.

Peter must have sensed the movement behind him. As Kate swung the makeshift weapon, the lad turned to see what was moving behind him. Unfortunately for the young man, he didn't turn himself far enough to avoid the inevitable. In fact he had matters worse. What would have struck him on the back of his head now impacted his right temple. Kate, the daughter of an 8-handicap golfer, had swung enough clubs in her life not to miss with this one.

The noise and the vision were different to those of the small child and the Morris Minor incident. The feeling of nausea was the same and if she'd had time to be sick, she would have done, but she still had work to do.

The blow had knocked the boy into the six feet deep cavity, he had just created. He was so far down that even though he was motionless Kate couldn't tell if he was dead or not. Not taking any chances, the idea came easily to her. She tossed the lighter and tin after the body and back-filled the hole with fresh soil. In a hurry to go, she opted not to fill it completely. The mounds were on an apron so close to the edge that pushing half of the soft earth was a quick and easy task.

Satisfied that Peter wasn't going to return from his premature burial, she stopped work. The spade was stuck into the remaining earth to make it look as though the young employee had deserted his duties and she made her way quickly back to the trees.

A last look round the cemetery and then up Bailley Hills Road to check her escape route. An elderly woman, with her shopping and small mongrel terrier, took what seemed like an eternity to reach her house and go inside. When the pavement was clear, she left the site using the same gap in the wall she had entered through, just over an hour and a half before.

Back in Main Street, she slowed her pace enough to window-shop, partly to delay her arrival, partly out of curiosity for the merchandise on display. She had missed the 12.45 train and kept an eye on her watch to make sure she caught the 1.15. It was hard for her to drag herself away from the sights and smells of a 60's northern town, but time wasn't going to wait for her to be nostalgic.

17

Kate

J ackson was due to finish his work in July. It was now December and we had been together for three months and three days. His parents were in San Diego and he hadn't planned on travelling back there for Thanksgiving or Christmas. It was just too far and too expensive.

It was very unlike me, but I made a radical decision. I phoned my parents and told them I would be staying in Cambridge for Christmas, instead of coming home for the family celebrations around our huge dining table in London. I told them the truth. I had met someone and had fallen in love. I didn't want to share him and I couldn't imagine us at home with my mother and father, it felt too awkward. We were still in the honeymoon stage and it was addictive. Was this very selfish of me? Probably, but it would also prove to be a bad decision. Had they met Jackson, they may have understood. Had they seen us together, they would have known our feelings for each other were real and not a passing whim.

Hindsight is a wonderful thing isn't it. They were upset at my decision, but they understood, they still remembered the heady feeling and the first months of their relationship. I don't deserve them really.

Jackson Matthew Maze was born and raised in Southern California. His family owned some land and an Avocado farm, which I thought was wonderful. He had his first chemistry set when he was three and was hooked. A true academic, he excelled at local schools and at 17 won a scholarship to Harvard. He had a limitless brain and a heart to match. He talked of his parents fondly, but he had outgrown their world long ago. He made regular trips home, though he spoke of feeling smothered in the small town atmosphere and the rigidity of the folks there. His southern drawl remained and turned me on without fail, especially in the large brass bed where he would whisper, 'come on baby' and I would already be removing my clothes. First love, nothing can touch it? I knew then, no one would ever match up to him, whatever happened in my life. I waited for things to change, would he make a stupid comment, or show a side to him I didn't expect or like. It didn't happen. He remained perfect. Well to me anyway.

I became a different Kate. He softened my edges and I began to see how different my life could be. I no longer yearned for the Courtroom and couldn't envisage being in that world. Wigs and pomp and men, who thought they were God's gift to women. I began to yearn for a simpler life. Jackson was a combination of laid back southerner and yet when it came to his work, he would go through the night with an idea or a problem until he had solved it. He was always on the verge of a breakthrough and although I couldn't follow half of what he was doing, I was always interested in his ideas and theories.

He made me laugh. I have always had an ironic sense of humour, inherited from my father James. Jackson was drier than a bone in the Sahara. His observations about the British had me in tears of laughter and I began to see our country from his eyes. His star shone so brightly, I could not see anything else.

Everyone else in my life faded away and I didn't care. I didn't have time to answer Bridget's letters and emails. I am ashamed to say I managed a few texts, but although I felt guilty I just couldn't focus on anyone, or anything else.

On Christmas Eve we shopped and bought some supplies for the flat. A chicken, champagne and cheese. We stayed in bed, played scrabble and made love. He presented me with a silver necklace with a tiny snoopy on it. We both loved Peanuts and I was thrilled. I bought him a telescope. We lay by the open fire. I look back to that day and realise that life's pleasures are often simple. It was a perfect day.

We had a 'love in,' popping out only to buy food and drink. We were wrapped up in our love and each other. We gazed at the stars. He showed me Orion's Belt as his own arms were tightly wound around my waist. 'One day,' he said, 'we will travel through time baby. I will show you how.' I knew I believed in him. He had the power to change the world, I sensed it. He had my world in the palm of his hand.

My studies suffered, I lost interest. My tutors remarked on my apathy and change of attitude. They reminded me of what a great opportunity I had at Cambridge. I didn't care. I would have been happy packing avocados, as long as Jackson was by my side.

Winter turned to spring and soon it was time for him to return. I started to panic, I could feel the anxiety creeping through my veins, spoiling our last few weeks together. He was going to Seattle to start a research project. He was being paid a pittance, but he was so excited at the prospect of the work, he failed to see the dark cloud hovering over me.

He made me promises. I made him promises. We

would visit each other. I would go to Seattle during the long academic breaks. I was sure my parents would help me out financially. We would email, we would ring each other. It would be all right, wouldn't it?

As he boarded the plane at Heathrow, tears poured down my face. My heart was so tight in my chest I thought I had stopped breathing. He had hugged and kissed me at the gate for the last time. I felt that my world had ended. I was being ridiculous. I knew it, but I couldn't help myself.

My sense of self diminished. I began to see myself as a failure. Jackson hadn't loved me enough to stay. If you love him let him go, echoed through my mind. He had a future in the USA. He was brilliant. Why would he want me, a millstone around his neck?

My pain turned to anger. Just like a bereavement. How could he leave me? Why hadn't he asked me to go with him? Perhaps I was just filling in the time for him. Because he wasn't around to re-assure me, the negative thoughts took hold. His letters arrived daily, but I didn't answer. I changed my mobile phone and threw away the old one.

I was being stupid, stubborn and proud, but I was my mother's daughter. She spoke to me on the phone, asking about Jackson and when I told her, her response was predictable. 'Move on my lovely Kate,' she said. 'You will meet someone else, if it was meant to be he would have stayed.' I should have realised she was from another generation and followed my heart. Then things changed forever.

In my grief and despair I hadn't noticed that my period hadn't come or gone for two months. I was pregnant.

18

Thursday 23rd May 1963

She'd been a redhead when she dispatched the gravedigger. Back in Bradford, Kate needed a change of hairdo. She found a mirror in the town council's Public Toilets. When no one was looking, she swapped the red look for the sleek black bob wig she had been carrying around with her all day. Satisfied with the difference in her appearance, she felt ready to have a punt on an afternoon race.

'Honest Ron Wilkins' shop beckoned her in. 'Honest,' she thought to herself, 'I doubt it!' Anyone who has to announce their reputation can't have earned one. Kate was used to heads turning when she entered the male domains that are the country's turf-accountants. This afternoon in Bradford was very different. A small group of punters were jumping and shouting and ignored her completely. Slightly put-out at the lack of attention, Kate moved to where she could see better what was going on.

To her astonishment, on a makeshift table (the sort a decorator would use to paste wallpaper), to one side of the shop, were five small white mice with different markings, moving haphazardly along the table. Each rodent had a small woollen figure sitting just behind the rodents' shoulders. The men surrounding the table were barking orders to move faster at the creatures, but seemed to make little or no difference to their movement.

Kate approached the clerk, still looking over one

shoulder.

'Can I help you Madam?' said a smallish man, with thinning hair.

'Well, I came in to place a bet for my sick husband, but…. (looking back once more), what on earth is going on?' She had planned an Edinburgh accent for this charade, but the surprising sight inside the shop made her forget herself.

'Oh that, the mice racing was how we kept open during the winter's seven weeks without National Hunt racing!'

'I thought racing has been normal again since March?' Kate said in a questioning tone.

'Oh yes Madam, it has, but the boys love it and can't seem to give it up, so I let 'em.' He replied in a discernible Middlesbrough accent.

'If I had more time and a mouse of my own, I might be tempted…'

'A shilling each from Reg's pet shop…'

'No really, I've got other errands to run. Now why did I come in…? My husband is bed-ridden, but has asked me to put this (sliding two five pound notes under the bars), on Imperial Prince in the 3.30, at Haydock.'

'Five pounds each way on…'

Kate interrupted. 'No, to win!'

The clerk pulled a face. 'Is he on medication? That horse is 25-1 and he's risking ten pounds on it.'

'Yes he is actually if you must know. Very strong doses. He woke up earlier today and he had dreamt that someone was calling his name and… (By now Kate was letting her theatrical side make mischief)… told him God wanted him to know, his Prince was going to come. He thought it was a sign.'

The clerk was speechless, but gave Kate a receipted

slip, with a slight smile that said, loser. Kate took the slip, nodded her thanks and left the shop. She had another mission. The steam train age was romantic and the buses utilitarian, but neither gave her the flexibility she needed for the next phase of her journey. She had to find another car and soon, before she headed north. On the train back to Bradford, she had picked up a local paper left on the seat opposite. Among the 'missing dog' and 'found dog' stories, an advert promoting a local car dealer, Brian Turner Automobiles, had caught her eye.

19

Francesca

I believe that as you describe past events in your life you are able to put them into perspective. I have never been great at appreciating that fact at the time. My life looked on paper to be a series of goals, as I mentally crossed my achievements off the list.

I hope I don't make the birth of my daughter sound that way. From the minute she was born, she was her own person and it stayed that way. From an early age, she had her own ideas and views of the world around her and although James and I tried to shape those ideas, essentially they belonged to her.

She made me proud to be her mother, but I know I can be pushy and opinionated and this especially applied to her education. I felt really strongly that she should be given the best chances we could provide. As someone who left school at fifteen, I knew that all too well. I grew up in the workplace and I always felt inadequate about my schooling and lack of University credibility. I would like to think that I am an intelligent woman, but my lack of higher education had been a distinct disadvantage

I wanted more for Kate. I wanted her to have the opportunity to achieve her potential and not have to worry about earning money and proving herself too soon. She was a clever girl and she had the advantage of being a free thinker. She had an intellect that could dissect an argument and play devil's advocate, without any problem. I felt that she would make a brilliant

Barrister. She downplayed it, but she had a bit of the actress in her that I could see would make her a credible lawyer. There is a theatrical air in the British Courts that demands a certain personality to succeed.

I believed she might struggle though, with the lengthy course work and the dry nature of Law. She had a great memory, but if something didn't interest her, she didn't try to retain the information. We talked about this quite a lot before she went away to University. She knew she would have to knuckle down and probably work harder than she had so far. She was prepared for this and I think she was excited about the prospect of leaving home and starting her adult life.

When she got her place at Cambridge, I was overwhelmed with pride. I had deliberately not pushed too hard when she said she wanted to take the Oxbridge exams. It was reverse psychology. She would have sensed how desperate I was for her to get a place. This would have put pressure on her and she may have decided to follow Bridget to York instead.

So for the first time ever I took a step back and waited. It paid off. When the envelope dropped on to the mat, I think my stomach turned more somersaults than Kate's. As she nonchalantly picked it up and went into the kitchen, I was so excited I couldn't breathe properly. I mentally chastised myself for being so self-centred. This was Kate's moment not mine, I reminded myself. James and I stood next to each other in the doorway as she opened the letter.

My daughter has never been one to hide how she is feeling and this moment was no different. A smile curled around her mouth, getting wider by the second as she realised she had been successful. We shouted, we screamed and the joy was palpable. Even laid back

James was moved to tears by our daughter's achievement.

We dressed up that evening and went to the Ivy. It cost a fortune, but it was one of the best evenings of my life. I have a picture somewhere of the three of us outside the restaurant. James looking fabulous in a charcoal suit by Spencer Hart that he didn't get enough opportunity to wear. Kate wore a green, vintage Ballgown that I had bought for her on impulse, whilst shopping one lunch hour. She looked absolutely beautiful. Her chestnut curls framed her face and I couldn't believe that it had been eighteen years since her birth. Where had the years gone?

The next few months passed in a haze of preparations and anticipation. I took some well-deserved holiday from work and we shopped, packed and had some mother & daughter time that I will always treasure. We both knew it was a milestone and nothing would ever quite be the same again, though not in the way I thought, unfortunately. If disappointment is in fact linked to expectation then my hopes and dreams for Kate were about to come crashing down.

On her last night at home, I cooked my, by now famous, Soul fish risotto. James and Kate didn't let me cook very often, but her last night was special and warranted a meal that held some sentimental value. I couldn't eat much, as I watched James and Kate tucking in. In my mind, tomorrow had already arrived and she was gone. We drank too much champagne and toasted Kate's future.

The following day we moved her in to her lodgings in the college. The place seemed huge and unwelcoming and the buildings looked as if they had been around forever. This was a whole new world to me, the academic centre of excellence in the heart of Cambridgeshire. I watched the lecturers and students striding around the buildings with an air of confidence, even arrogance.

Would Kate change? I wondered if she would become one of the elite I could see all around me? Would she become a different person? I panicked that she might have made a mistake. She didn't belong here with the 'hooray-Henrys.'

Although I had always considered myself a bit of a snob, these people were in a different league. Perhaps I was feeling my own sense of inadequacy. Kate and James seemed fine and not phased at all. James had been to a good Public school so it was to be expected I suppose. We helped her unpack and took her for a late lunch. It was already time to go. This was harder than I expected. I gave myself a talking to. Francesca, for goodness sake, she is only two hour's drive away. She will be fine. James looked at me with a twinkle in his eye. He knew me too well.

We drove home, initially silently and then we couldn't stop talking. We had our own thoughts about Kate, but we were full of hope and happiness for our little girl. She had waved us off and whatever she was feeling she didn't show it. That was for our benefit, we decided.

As we entered the front door, the house seemed empty. Ridiculous isn't it? People talk of the empty nest syndrome and when your child leaves home, at first it's a reality. Kate's bubbly personality had filled the rooms and her absence took some getting used to. We snuggled up on the huge sofa and talked about Kate all night. In a strange way it reminded me of her birth.

On our first night out together, when we had left

her with a reliable babysitter, we sat and looked at each other. We had booked a table in a local restaurant so we could get home easily, if there were any problems. Then we sat for two hours and talked about our baby daughter. People sitting nearby must have been bored stiff. We hadn't lost our identity as a couple, but things would never be the same. A little whirlwind had entered our lives and she was here to stay.

So we talked and looked back over the years and toasted our daughter's future. The moment was even more poignant as she would return less than a year later and turn our lives around again.

Kate was quite good at keeping in touch. We had bought her a new mobile phone, on a contract, so there was no reason not to. The phone was more for our benefit than Kate's really. She would phone us most evenings and tell us how her day had been. She would sometimes text from lectures, usually witty comments about the subject matter or the lecturer.

She found all the pomp and ceremony amusing. Unlike me, she wasn't intimidated by it at all. She reported on the ridiculousness of some of the rituals and couldn't somehow relate what happened at Cambridge to real life.

Then something changed. She was very casual at first, about a man she had met, but it didn't fool me at all. Kate didn't do anything half-heartedly. She had been out with a few boys during the last two years, but no one had held her attention or interest. This man was different. I could hear it in her voice. He was a bit older than her and was an American scientist. She didn't know that much about his studies, but she was clearly infatuated with him, that much was obvious.

I raised my anxieties with James. He laughed them

off in his usual manner. I was being over protective, worrying too much. As it turned out, I wasn't worrying enough to stop the chain of events that was to follow.

Kate was happy. Kate was ecstatically happy. She became harder to contact. She would only answer her phone when it suited her. Love can make you selfish. I wasn't so old that I couldn't remember that feeling. That all-consuming feeling, when you fall in love and nothing else matters. I was lucky enough to have found that love with James. Would Kate be the same?

I envisaged her in years to come living with Jackson and having the same feelings of security and happiness that I had found.

But it was early days. She had just started her course. This wasn't a good time to fall in love. She became quite obsessive and I had never seen her like that before. Instead of coming home at weekends, as she had initially promised, she didn't leave the flat.

I knew she was sleeping with him because I asked her outright. That was my way. She was hardly in her own room at the College that was costing a fortune. She spent all her time at Jackson's flat. He was being sponsored by a company in America, so money wasn't an issue for him. He was hardly a typical Cambridge undergraduate. He certainly wasn't a spotty geek with glasses or any other kind of scientist stereotype.

She sent me some photos of Jackson including one of him half naked, well with his shirt off anyway. I could see why she had fallen for him. His face was tanned with that all-American glow and he had bright blue eyes that shone with intelligence. Hair slightly longer than fashionable, but nevertheless he was incredibly attractive. Was Kate just one of his conquests I wondered? Or was he the real thing?

That girl had no shame. I was her mother for goodness sake. Why was she throwing this relationship in my face?

Then I remembered our bond. Of course she would tell me, she always told me everything. What she was thinking, what she was feeling, that was Kate. This time wasn't different. She was having a new adventure and she had to share it with me. She fell in love with the same enthusiasm and passion she showed for everything else in her life. There is nothing half-hearted about Kate.

I felt as if I was losing her. She was slipping away from me. I lay awake at night worrying that she wouldn't finish her studies. Jackson was leaving next summer. Perhaps she would go back to America with him.

Anxiety became my friend. I was constantly worrying about her and her future. James had a much more relaxed attitude. He was happy she had met someone and believed whatever would be, would be. 'How quaint,' I thought angrily. I remonstrated with myself again and would try to let things run their course. That was the answer.

Christmas approached. I was desperate to see Kate and finally meet Jackson, maybe. She had only been away a matter of months, but everything had already changed. I shopped like a mad woman, spending more at Harrods and Fortnum & Mason than I normally would have done. I asked James to decorate the house. I was going to wait for Kate to do the tree on Christmas Eve. That was our tradition. She would unwrap the baubles and decorations we had collected over the years and spend a long time dressing the tree to her satisfaction. This year would be no exception I told myself, it just might mean an extra person around the table.

I ordered a goose and a ham, enough for twelve people. I always tend toward extravagance on certain occasions, but it seemed even more important this year. I bought some handmade crackers and started to feel the excitement building. I love Christmas, it's my favourite time of year. I love the crisp cold air and the snowy streets of London. I love that everyone's bustling towards the big event.

The store where I worked looked fabulous. People would come for miles to see the lights and the window displays. I loved watching the faces of the small children who gazed up in wonderment and anticipation, whatever class or creed they were. It is a celebration that brings everyone together. A family time.

She phoned the day before we were expecting her home. I knew from her voice that she wouldn't be coming home. She really didn't want to disappoint either myself or James, but she was adamant, in that selfish, youthful way that you might recognise.

I was speechless, initially with disappointment then with anger. I didn't show these emotions to Kate as I fought to keep my voice's normal tones. I put her on to James who was much better at this than I was. I could feel the tears emerging through the anger as my vision of Christmas evaporated. Spoilt and selfish, I thought to myself. Ungrateful, rude and inconsiderate girl.

James looked at me across the room. Suddenly I remembered something. It was in the early days when James and I first met. Probably about a month or two into the relationship, I rang my boss to say I had the flu. I recalled putting on a pathetic, croaky, rasping voice as I explained that I wouldn't be in for a couple of days, at least. We then closed the curtains and spent the next two days entwined in each other's bodies and laughing at the prospect of unplanned laziness. James would run out to the nearest local shop for some provisions, but we were oblivious to everything and everyone. I understood. We would get over it. Perhaps we would stay in bed over Christmas ourselves. After all, we had no one else to please.

Poor Bridget was also missing Kate. Expecting her home, but worried that she hadn't been in touch for a while, she turned up on our doorstep a couple of nights before Christmas. As we sat around the dinner table, we were all very aware of the missing diner. We all loved Kate and we all wanted the best for her, but I sensed Bridget was hurt that Kate hadn't confided in her in the way that she always had in the past. We all pretended that it was fine, in that way that only the British can. It's often what is not said that really counts. We would get over it. There would be other Christmases.

So I began to soften towards Kate. James and I got on with our busy lives. We even had a week away together in the Maldives, an unexpected treat arranged as a surprise for my birthday. We let our anxieties about Kate remain in the back of our minds. James and I became a couple again, for a few months anyway. We rediscovered ourselves and realised that we still found each other intriguing, both physically and mentally. We were a good team.

The bombshell happened when we were least expecting it. In our minds Kate was at University finishing her first year exams. Probably spending too much time with Jackson, but nevertheless coping. What we didn't expect was the front door opening and Kate appearing, looking as if she had spent the last week crying. She couldn't be pacified. I had never seen her like this. She was inconsolable. I would have done anything to take the pain away from her.

We worked out what had happened. It was a combination of miscommunication and Kate's pride. Jackson had returned to the States and was expecting Kate to join him, initially for a holiday and also to see how things went. Once he had left she began to get angry. He had expected her to follow him? What about her life, her career? She punished him by ignoring him. This unfortunately is a family trait, on the female side of the family. She began to form ideas in her head that he had just been using her to pass the time at Cambridge. I think she was being irrational by this stage.

Then she uttered the words I wasn't expecting to hear. Well not yet anyway. The golden girl, the Barrister, the successful student looked down at her feet, then at James and at me and changed the course of all our lives.

'I'm pregnant,' she said. 'I am going to have a baby. I'm sorry.'

Not as sorry as me, I thought to myself. Kate you stupid, stupid girl. Why are you throwing away the chances you have been given. It was the worst news she could have given me, but as a Catholic, I knew there were no other options for her. She would have this baby. Her life would change. Would she be a single mother? I wondered. What about Jackson? She didn't contact him of course. She dug her heels in and decided to go it alone. I despaired inwardly and only James knew how I really felt.

So it remained, until the actual day of the birth of course. That's when the world changed again. I spent the day holding Kate's hand as she went through the pains of labour. She remained strangely silent most of the time. Perhaps it was her penance. I knew what she was feeling, as the grip on my hand tightened. Some long hours later, she gave a final push and granddaughter Emma made her entrance into our lives.

Kate was exhausted, but proud and tearful. James and I looked at each other in amazement. We would look after our girls. Life doesn't always take the route you expect, but we could cope. We were strong enough and there was enough love to go around.

20

Kate

As I looked at the white stick in my hand, turning blue, my whole life changed irrevocably. The path I had envisaged for myself, vanished in the time it took to form two inky lines. Oh dear God, I don't know what you have in store for me, but this wasn't supposed to happen. What would I do? A strange calm came over me that I hadn't felt since Jackson told me he was leaving. This was right. Somehow this was right.

I went back to London to tell my parents. As expected my father took the news better than Francesca. She was furious. 'You stupid girl,' echoed in my head, as she ranted like a mad woman. 'You have thrown away your chances.' 'You are nineteen years old for God's sake.' 'You had your whole life ahead of you.' What's happened to the wonderful Jackson?' 'He didn't hang around long enough to find out'. Her words sliced through my heart like a blade. As a Roman Catholic, abortion was never an option to Francesca and she didn't consider whether or not I wanted a baby at the tender age of nineteen. It was now a reality.

The more they wanted me to tell Jackson, the more I resisted. He had spent a month trying to reach me, through the college, mutual friends, letters and phone calls. Over time, he apparently got the message. What was the message? I didn't know. Would my baby have a father? I started to think about the logistics. Travelling to America every few months, to see a father wrapped up in his work and his inventions. My heart hardened and I made a decision that would change the course of my life and his child's. I will go it alone.

Emma Jane McLean was born on February 22nd 1995. She was a healthy weight, eight pounds and three ounces. 'Mother and baby are doing well.' So said the cards sent out by my parents to various family and friends.

I, Kate McLean was in love for the second time in my life. I gazed down at the soft, flushed face of my baby daughter and felt at peace with the world. I vowed to let no-one hurt her or harm her and promised her the world. A promise, as it turned out, I would not be able to keep.

Luckily, Francesca also adored her granddaughter. Enough for her to allow me to move back home and for James to build on to the house, so we virtually had our own wing. Enough for her to allow James to babysit, whilst I went to work. Enough to forgive me for having a child out of wedlock and becoming a single parent. Emma was surrounded by love and she thrived. She was a beautiful, sweet natured child. Caramel curls framed her heart shaped face and the sight of her bright blue eyes brought a tear to my own. Jackson was here, in spirit at least. I was looking at our child and started to worry that I had somehow deprived her of a father. I brushed those thoughts aside. Life was challenging and the days were long. I didn't have time to dream. That part of Kate was diminishing. I had to live in the here and now.

After dropping out of Cambridge, I considered my future. I had a child to support and although my parents were comfortable, they weren't rich. Both still worked to keep it all going. The house cost a fortune and the extension had taken the last of their savings. I needed to look for something that would suit me and fit in with Emma's needs.

Fate intervened yet again. A friend of mine from University rang me. She knew I was looking for work and suggested I get in touch with her father. He was a Senior Probation Officer in Inner London and they were advertising for trainees. I was interested in criminology and the idea that I would be paid, whilst I did the training sounded very good. I had done some voluntary work at a homeless shelter when I left University, during the long months of my pregnancy, so I knew the sorts of issues their clients would be facing. I had loved the work at the shelter. Some of the men were drinkers or drug users, but they all had a story. How had they ended up there? They loved to talk and I loved to listen. A hot bath, clean clothes and food, made all the difference to their lives. I was a friendly face, someone to talk to, who wouldn't judge them or their chosen lifestyle. My eyes had been opened to the seedier side of London. Beyond St Paul's, Buckingham Palace and all the sights that tourists adore, was an underbelly of deprivation and poverty. I found myself softening again. 'There but for the grace of God,' reared its head again.

Some of the men were wonderful characters, with hearts of gold beneath their harsh, drunken personas. I think Oscar Wilde once said, 'we are all in the gutter, but some of us are looking at the stars.' It took my mind away from my own situation which was a good thing.

The job in Probation sounded intriguing, so I gave him a call. He asked me to come in and see him and we spent some hours discussing the work. He asked me how I would deal with child sex offenders, rapists and murderers. Would I be able to work with them, challenge them and make a difference or would I be repelled by their behaviour. I gave it some thought. I wasn't a judgemental woman and started to think about some of the people I may deal with. What kind of lives have they had in order to commit such heinous crimes? Yes I could work with people and make a change. People can change, I genuinely believed that. You can hate their crime, but you don't have to hate the person. Everyone has good in them. Yes, I truly believed that to be true. Don't mock me now. I made a mockery of my own words. I pretended I was God and made my own judgement.

I got the job. I went back to college to get my Diploma. Living in London and studying at home was much easier and the support I received from family and friends helped enormously. After I qualified I went to work in a local probation office, a few miles from home. There was a pattern to my day, a routine that I needed. Not too much time to think, it was a busy time.

I enjoyed my work immensely. I liked writing reports for the Courts, to assist the Judge with sentencing. It gave me a sense of purpose. I was glad I hadn't joined the legal brigade whose empty words in court, often gave little explanation for their client's behaviour. I pored over the psychiatrists and psychologists reports, learning about the human psyche and personality traits. I could have been quite obsessive about some of my cases, but the little girl waiting for me at home balanced out my life and gave it meaning.

I loved coming home to Emma and James. It reminded me of my own childhood so much. She grew and developed into an interesting mixture of charm and mischief. Her enquiring mind certainly came from her father and she loved looking out at the stars. I bought her, her own telescope and she began to watch the stars at night before bedtime. Her curiosity extended to her father. She didn't understand why she didn't have a daddy. My own father filled the gap admirably, but she liked to hear me talk about Jackson. I told her he had to go back to America, which was a long way away and couldn't come back.

She had a piggy bank at this time and started collecting pennies and coins in her pig. She told me that she was saving so she could go on a plane and see daddy when she was a big girl. My eyes welled up and I had to leave the room. Would she hate me when she was older? Was I wrong?

As time passed the decision became clearer. I couldn't contact him now, it was too late. He probably had his own family by now. I had 'googled' him one night, after a few too many glasses of wine with Bridget and he was a man of substance. A proper scientist. One of a hand-picked team, working on the Hadron Collider in Switzerland. This sounded a bit far-fetched. It didn't mention any family, but that didn't mean he didn't have any. He was a rising star in his field. He didn't need me or Emma in his life.

21

Thursday 23rd May 1963

In Lumb Lane, Kate found the entrance to the car showroom, through a narrow pair of double doors. She wondered how they could get the cars in and out?

Before she entered, she checked the plan with herself. The new wig, she thought, gave her an Italian look, so the idea was to pretend that she was born there. Sicily if she was asked.

Her first thoughts were that the room was too lovely to sell cars in. It had a wide, solid stone staircase rising up through an ornate ceiling, with coving and plaster roses. The opposite wall was different. Large floor to ceiling windows were flanked by stone columns with Doric detail at the top.

A sober-suited man with a burgundy tie, looked up from behind a large captain's desk, at the back of the room. He had lifeless dark hair, parted on the left and brylcreamed into a 'pulled-curtain' shape across his forehead. The man was about to speak, but Kate didn't wait, she was in a hurry. 'I need a car,' she said.

'Certainly Madam, you've come to the right place.' Looking over her shoulder, he continued, 'is your husband not with you?'

With big eyes and a pout, Kate spoke in a purr. 'Oh no, I don't have a husband anymore. I'm a single woman again.' Inwardly she was fed up with the sixties-males' sexist ideas that a woman has no value, unless she is on the arm of a man. Thank God we've moved on.

'I have to go on a journey and my Italian car has a

problem with the engine that is waiting for parts.'

'Brylcream man was by now sensing a sale and getting cocky.

'Somewhere nice Madam?'

Kate's glare was enough. He waved an arm in the direction of a new lemon coloured 'Ford Consul Capri.' 'This new model is lovely. This would suit and serve you well for many years and at only £915 on the road, is excellent value too. We can arrange hire-purchase and have it on the road by next Monday.'

Resting her hand on his arm in a firm and restraining gesture, 'you are a dear man and I'd love to buy that one, but, you need to realise this. I'm not looking for the future, I'm looking for now! Right now! I want something that I can drive out of here, this afternoon.'

The salesman pulled a 'fish that got away' face, 'oh I see.'

He was dithering so Kate took charge. 'Haven't you got any pre-loved ones to show me?'

'Pre-loved?' He was now pulling an even stranger face.

'Sorry, it's my Sicilian upbringing, I meant second-hand vehicles.'

'Ah yes, I see what you mean, follow me.' He led her through the showroom, past his desk and out into the yard at the back. Once outside, Kate wasn't listening to the 'patter,' she was scanning round the yard for something to leap out. Amongst the White Zephyr, the red Consul, two Populars and an Anglia, something caught her eye in the corner.

'What's that,' she enquired of the host.

'Surely you don't mean the Thames van? I see something far more ladylike.'

She interrupted again… 'I'll decide, thank you. Is it for sale?'

'Well yes I suppose so, with conditions attached.'

'Conditions?'

'I can't sell it to anyone who lives within a thirty mile radius of Bradford, because…'

'That's fine I'm from London, but why?'

'That van Madam, is a 1961 Thames 7 cwt., high compression, top of the range with all the extras. It was purchased only 18 months ago by Flash Stan the Sponge.'

Bored with the sales pitch, Kate's patience and flirty charm was wearing thin. 'And this is relevant…?'

'Yes. He loved that van more than anything, until he reached too far for a 3rd floor skylight, a couple of months ago and landed in…'

'Basta, basta! Sorry, I mean please stop, I don't need graphics!'

'Anyway he was stone dead. His widow asked me to take the car and made me promise that she wouldn't ever see it being driven round Bradford. She can't bear to see it again.'

Kate had a thought. 'Does it need one of those silly handle things to start it?'

'No Miss. Thankfully Stan opted for the electric start option, because he was fed up with the number of times a day he needed to crank up his old van.'

'Ok, ok. I get it. Well if I take it, it'll be hundreds of miles away by tomorrow. How much do you want for it?'

'It's a steal at £290'

'All right Mister. If you can have its fluids, oil and stuff, checked and topped up for me and ready to drive away by five today, I'll give you cash.' She handed him ten five pound notes. 'I'll give you the rest when I come back.'

'Thank you Madam,' he said taking the money. 'I'll have the paperwork ready for your return. I'll need your name and address,' he said picking up a pen.

'Si si, of course you do. It's Mrs Domiziana Johnson. 142 Addison Road, Kensington.'

'Ha, it sounds like dominant.'

She gave him the stare. 'For good reason.'

He swallowed hard and showed Kate out to the street.

She returned to the Hotel, calling in on the bookmaker, who by now owed her £260. Not the amount she had just agreed to spend, but, 'owt's better than nowt', as they say in Bradford. Back in the room, she gathered her thoughts and her things together, including the details of the phone call, she needed to make.

Because the main station was just up the hill from the Hotel, Kate elected to make the call from there. It meant collecting as many pennies together as she could, but it kept her in control of the call. Her independent side was getting fed up with 'helpfully' being put through by Hotel staff.

'Hello operator. I would like to find a number in Fraserburgh, Aberdeen, please. The village of Strichen in fact. Yes, it's the home of the Scott family. Yes, I've got a pen.' Kate took the Waterman and the notebook from her bag. She repeated the words in her ear. 'Fraserburgh 5 7 7 3. Thank you. Can you put me through? Yes I know I have to press button 'A' when I'm connected.'

When she heard the Highland accent, she pushed the metal protrusion until she heard the coins drop into the box.

'Fraserburgh 5773' said the lady in Scotland.

'Hello,' said Kate. Is that Betty?

'Yes dear, it is. Who's that?'

'This is Claire Reeve. I'm a friend of Denis. We met in London at Christmas and he told me to ring you if I'm ever in Scotland, to see if he's home?'

'Oh I'm sorry dear, he is supposed to be on leave this week, but he hasn't come here yet.' She paused for a moment. 'And I haven't heard from him either. Do you want me to phone the Barracks and see if they know where he is?'

'Thank you for offering Mrs Scott, but I'm on a tight schedule this week. If he was there with you, I would have come and said hello, but if he's still in Aldershot or even en-route to you, I won't have time to come back later.'

'Ok dear. If I hear from him I'll tell him you called.'

'Please do and tell him I'll catch up with him one day. When he least expects it.' The receiver made a strange sound in Kate's ear. She guessed her money had run out and the call was going to end if she didn't put some more in. 'I think my money's......'

The GPO's equipment didn't let her finish the sentence. Betty was gone, along with an opportunity. She likened the disappointment she was feeling to that of an angler who doesn't quite manage to net his fish.

22

Kate

E mma grew up quickly. She excelled at my old school, the convent and it was strange seeing her in the old uniform. The school wasn't as strict as it was in 1980 when I started there, but Sister Geraldine was still there and remembered me well. We hugged as I took Emma for her first day and the memories came flooding back. She couldn't hide her disappointment about Cambridge, although she tried very hard, bless her.

The years passed, as they do. I loved my work and resisted applying for promotion. I liked the face to face work with the offenders I dealt with and didn't want to spend my days pen pushing and attending meetings. I was still on the coal face and loved the fact that no two days were the same.

Home life was peaceful. Emma was always on the lookout for a date for me and tried to persuade me to join a dating website. I wasn't interested. To me, men were a waste of time and energy. I had dated a couple of people from work over the years, but we just ended up talking shop and there was no spark. I felt like I had eaten the finest dinner, so wasn't going to settle for a burger. No one could match up to Jackson and I made the comparisons early on. It was a dangerous game. I was denying myself the chance to be happy, by my own expectations.

Emma was my life. I tried not to be one of those mothers whose whole life is centred on their 'baby.' I knew it wasn't healthy. I had my work and my friends, particularly Bridget who had a baby son at this time and we would swap stories and advice. She went on to have three more children, so I wasn't the expert for very long.

Emma and I travelled as much as we could. I wanted her to experience the world and realise that there was more to life than London. The availability of cheap flights meant we could visit places like Poland and Romania, as well as Paris and Barcelona. She loved the forests in Romania and the castle belonging to Count Dracula. She loved new experiences and devoured books and culture as if she was starving. Paris was delightful. We stayed in a small apartment for a week, taking the metro around the city, to galleries and exhibitions. Returning home tired and elated to cook a meal on our small stove in the Parisian kitchen. She made me crepes on the last day, with fresh raspberries from the market.

We travelled to Morocco and Turkey and hunted through the souks for bargains to take home. Emma furnished her room with her finds and had an eclectic mix of old and new. She painted with James and her walls were covered with her work. Stars focussed heavily and she was influenced by Picasso and similar modern artists. She had talent and she loved expressing herself in this way.

Where did the years go? Soon it was time for Emma to leave school. She opted to do her A-levels at a local sixth form college. She loved the convent, but was aware of its limitations. She was brave and soon had another new group of friends. Weekends were spent at Camden and Portobello markets and she developed her own style of dress. Part gothic, part vintage she looked amazing. Francesca had a fit when she dyed her hair a vivid shade of purple, but eventually got over it.

I waited for the teenage tantrums and moods to arrive. She wasn't perfect, but apart from the odd spot and moody moment, she sailed through adolescence and her teenage years. By the time she was ready to go to University, I was happy she would cope. She could cook, she could sew, she could paint and she could make those around her laugh and want to know her. What more could I do? She was her own person. I didn't like some of her boyfriends, but they didn't last too long. I don't think anyone would be good enough for her in my eyes.

We talked about her father. Before she went away, we argued a lot about him. She wanted to visit him or look him up, but didn't quite have the courage. Like me she was frightened of rejection. I should have encouraged her, but I didn't and I will have to live with that forever. I didn't want her to get hurt. Jackson was now an internationally famous scientist and had married a woman in New York. She was beautiful. Why would he want to know us? A woman he could barely remember from university and a wacky daughter he didn't know existed. No, let's leave things as they are.

She started University in Newcastle upon Tyne. She quickly adopted the Geordies and loved the student life. Partying in the local bars and clubs, she was in demand. Her studies didn't suffer, as she was a girl that could burn the candle at both ends, often working through the night.

She loved Newcastle and took up a house share with three others, in a terraced house near the University. I met her flatmates for the first time when I went up to see her for a weekend. Alex was a lanky medical student who had moved from Glasgow and I found it difficult to understand what he was saying.

Greg, a philosophy PhD student, was more my scene, as we argued about various theories of the universe, after a few too many glasses of red wine.

Sarah was a loud, strikingly attractive girl from Wakefield. Her voice grated on me after a while, but Emma became friendly with her and they often went out for nights in the Bigg market. She was allegedly studying English, but didn't ever actually seem to do any studying.

Emma on the other hand blossomed. She liked her independence. I hadn't become the clingy mother that at one time I feared I would. I left that weekend feeling everything in the garden was rosy. My little girl had flown the nest. Life was good. How wrong could I be?

23

Friday 24th May 1963

K ate turned the van off Edwards Lane and came to a halt on the hill of the orange brick council estate. Her target was a semi-detached, three bedroomed house, four doors from the corner behind her. She had planned the escape route carefully in case this didn't go well. She would be escaping downhill to the van and if it should fail to start in the normal way, she would be able to roll down the slope and drop the clutch, whilst in second gear, to 'bump' it in action. It was like the reserve parachute of a free-faller. Parachutists never contemplate the failure of the reserve. Kate didn't either.

She looked at her watch. It was twenty past three. It was very dark and very wet. The rain bouncing off the hollow van roof was deafening. She couldn't have slept in the van if she had wanted to.

She had set her alarm clock for quarter to midnight. It should have been about an eighty minute drive from the Midland in Bradford to North Nottingham. However, in driving rain, in a car with poor quality windscreen wipers and headlamps that could be outshone by a couple of tallow candles, it had taken more than two and a half hours.

She was thinking to herself, what the hell I am doing this for? The week had always been ridiculously tough in prospect, but things hadn't exactly gone as well as she had hoped. 'The best laid plans of mice and men,' as Bridget's father Joe used to say. She wasn't dressed for the weather and there were no dustbins lined with plastic bags in 1963, so a cheap rain proofing solution wasn't available.

Between three thirty and four o'clock in the morning was usually chosen as the optimum time for surprise raids by the police. Kate had done her research. The human body clock and core temperature are at their lowest ebb, sleep at its deepest. This was about to be tested. She shut her eyes and breathed deep. The exercise was to calm and focus her after the draining journey. There wasn't going to be time for a full meditation. It was now after three-thirty and Kate wasn't waiting any longer.

She had planned to be blonde for this 'job,' because at night it would show up better and any witnesses would be wrong about the colour of her real hair. However, there was absolutely no point ruining a perfectly good wig in a rain storm. Her own hair didn't look great, but in less than half a minute, out in the weather, she'd look like a swimmer anyway.

She pulled it from her head and put it in the glove box, after she had taken out a long bladed screwdriver, with a hickory handle and robust looking shaft. Strong enough to force open a low tech wooden door with a single lock. The joy of breaking and entering in the pouring rain was that the noisy weather would mask the sound of a forced entry.

She left the van unlocked and ran to the back garden gate. A phone call to the boy's school by Elizabeth Starling, in a Scottish accent, to check the address that afternoon had been fruitful. What she was planning was bad enough. Scaring the wrong family would be more unforgivable. As expected, without any security checks, the school administrator had been happy to confirm that the wrong address had been given and more than willing to provide the correct one. To be fair to the school, Elizabeth was convincing. She knew the boy's name, date of birth and she knew too much detail about the health of his mother. It was a plausible enough to get a result and for that she was grateful.

She reached the back door of the house quickly, but was already soaked through. Screwdriver poised to squeeze between the door and the jamb. She lent on the handle for support. As she did the door opened and how she didn't fall straight through it on to the kitchen floor, was a miracle.

She steadied herself instinctively by sticking out the arm bearing the screwdriver. Her forearm struck the frame and it was just enough to break the impending fall.

It would have been prudent to check first she thought. Then she would have entered the house in complete silence. It could have been worse if the door had opened further. It would have struck a Formica covered unit and she might as well have knocked on the front door.

Kate shut the door quietly and waited. She didn't breathe at first. Listening above the sound of the rain, she was waiting to see if she had disturbed the occupants from their sleep. Blissful silence. Five minutes later she made her move.

In the time she had waited her eyes had adjusted to the gloom. She could now see enough to move around the small room without incident. She looked at the kitchen cupboards. Not many, how did people cope with so little storage she mused, recognising the mind can often focus on the mundane even when faced with such a task? Where was the medication? 'A dying woman must have medication,' she thought. She couldn't have got that wrong, surely?

The search of the kitchen proved fruitless. It was time to try another room. She had invested too much to give up easily. Besides, one of Kate's qualities was resilience. She needed it on this occasion.

The next door down the hall was open. This seemed to be a trend of the time. Open doors.

The dining room wasn't yielding much. The dark stained sideboard, comprising of three drawers and three cupboards didn't contain any drugs either. Papers and bric-a-brac filled the drawers and a china dinner service in the cupboards. 'That probably comes out at Christmas,' Kate thought. She flashed back to her childhood and pictured Francesca with her bone china service that was cleaned more often than it was used.

She went further down the hall. The door at the end was almost closed. Remembering there was a trick to stop hinges squeaking, by opening the door in jerky movements, she held the door tight and pushed firmly until it was open enough to peer in.

Even in the dark she could make out the shape of a single bed against the far wall. She held her breath again. Looking closer she could make out a shape under a heavy crocheted blanket.

Mother was downstairs. Hardly unexpected given how ill she was. The toilet was on the ground floor and if Mrs S wasn't completely bedridden, it would make sense to be nearer to it.

A flash lit up the room. 'Damn,' thought Kate, 'not now please.' Thunder and lightning would wake even the heaviest sleeper. While she was contemplating her retreat, her sub-conscious managed to deliver two delayed messages to the front of her head. The first one was brain saying that in the brief illumination that lit the room, there was something of interest on the mantelpiece.

The second realisation was that almost twenty seconds had passed before the faint rumble of thunder had caught up with the flash. A reprieve she thought, but if the storms heading this way it's going to get louder. She had to act fast. What had the back of her brain noticed above the hearth?

Taking no chances, Kate got on her hands and knees and crawled slowly towards the chimney breast. The woman's breathing was shallow, but constant. Not a sign of good health, but thankfully she was in a deep sleep.

Reaching the tiled, feature mantelpiece, Kate reached up for the objects on the top. There were several boxes of different shapes. White ones, with hand-written labels. Kate lowered them all to the carpet and lying prone on the floor, opened them one by one. There were pills in most of them. Two of the boxes' contents seemed more interesting. One was a bottle of liquid. The other was a packet containing three glass syringes with integral needles, with small protective rubber caps.

With a box in each hand, Kate made her hands and knees journey back to the hallway.

Through the door, as she stood up, another flash lit up the glass pane in the top third of the front door. She started counting. Mississippi one, Mississippi two…, …until Mississippi sixteen was followed by a slightly louder crash than before. The storm was getting nearer.

It was too dark in the hall. She shut the kitchen door quietly behind her and turned on the light. Blinded at first, when her irises settled she read the label on the liquid's bottle. 'Diacetylmorphine.'

She opened the box and removed the cork-topped

vial. It wasn't full, but there was still plenty in it. Even without nursing training, she could work out what was needed. Thank God for the internet.

The syringe poked through the cork. The plunger pulled back to draw up the colourless liquid. Without knowing why, she pointed the needle skyward and pressed until the drug emerged from the point in a faint spray. She must have seen it in a film, but realised it was to expel air. Air bubbles injected into the blood stream can be dangerous. The irony would have amused her if she hadn't been so tense.

She turned off the light and opened the kitchen door once more. Creeping down the hall, she reached the bottom of the stairs. With a syringe in one hand, Kate used the free hand to steady herself on the moulded wood bannister rail and crept upstairs.

She knew how to place her feet as wide as possible on the treads, touching the strings in fact. That way, even the creakiest staircases wouldn't make much noise. Two at a time, she climbed. At the top she had a choice of doors again. Fortunately, all ajar. Eliminating the bathroom and the box room, left a choice of two.

Lightning flashed once more, she didn't bother to count this time. The storm wasn't the most important thing in her mind at that moment. In the second bedroom, the unmistakeable odour of a teenager's room. Clutter too, that confirmed it. She had found him.

It might have been atrocious weather, but it was warm enough for the youth to be sleeping with both arms and his chest outside of the blankets. It didn't matter which limb, so Kate chose the nearest one to her, as she approached the bed. The chances of hitting a vein were slim, but the end result wouldn't be different. It was just a matter of how long.

There was no point waiting for another lightning event. Even if his veins were visible, it would still be a tall order for the untrained Kate, to make her first injections into a 'patient,' in the dark, a success.

No time for doubt or hesitation, the thunder was getting louder. Kate grasped the boy's wrist with one hand and with the other, pressed the needle into his forearm and squeezed more morphine than was necessary, into his body. The yelp of pain and the spasm that made him sit bolt upright wouldn't haunt Kate, but it was the look he gave her that would. His eyes had opened wide and they stared at her face, in a silent scream.

He looked down at his arm and looked back at Kate. He repeated the action two or three times, in disbelief. Perhaps he thought he was in a nightmare. Who knows?

She had stayed too long. It was time to go. Not silently down the stairs. Kate almost jumped down the entire flight. By now, the boy had pulled the 'sharp' from his body and was awake enough to realise he had been attacked.

She could hear him get out of bed and follow her to the top of the stairs. It was clear to her she'd misplaced the injection. If she'd found a vein or artery he wouldn't be pursing her. It could now take several minutes for the lethal drug to take its effect.

The noise of Kate's escape and her pursuer had woken his mother.

'Freddy! What on earth is going on?'

Kate took her opportunity. 'Say goodbye to your mother Harold.'

He stood for a moment, confused at what he was hearing, but he was intelligent enough to realise at this point, what her words meant. His body continued to move towards her.

She threw the kitchen door shut behind her, to buy a few seconds more escape time. Then she lost time fumbling with the back door lock. She pulled open the door and jumped the two steps into the rain soaked night.

He was close enough behind her to feel his breath on the back of her neck. A strange noise escaped from his mouth. Kate turned. Lightning flashed. Harold's eyes glazed over, but not from the light and he crumbled to the floor. He went down face first, his limbs heavy with the weight of death.

She didn't stop to check his pulse. Kate knew and was grateful for whichever power had saved her.

Soaking wet, panting hard and now feeling the familiar nausea, she drove the first five miles with the window open.

24

Kate

I read Emma's many emails with amusement. She loved writing to me. Although we spoke frequently on the phone, she would generally email me every night before she went to bed to tell me about her day. They mainly consisted of events at college, complaints about Alex eating everything in the fridge, including the last bit of cheese she had been saving for a sandwich. She spoke of her nights out and her flatmate Sarah's boyfriends. Emma didn't have a boyfriend yet.

I suspected she was harbouring a crush on one of her lecturers. It was Mark this and Mark that. Mark Chappell was a lot older than Emma, so I hoped nothing would happen there. I had heard about lecherous lecturers and their students whilst I was at Cambridge, but most of the staff were old enough to be my father, or grandfather.

She started to open up about her emotions a bit more. Maybe it was easier on paper than to talk to me face to face. She fell out with Sarah, who she felt was obsessed with sex. She had slept with many men at the house and Emma was fed up with finding strangers in the kitchen after a heavy night. She didn't want to judge, but she liked her own space.

She also spoke about her father and a re-kindled desire to see him. What had brought this about? Mark Chappell was still mentioned regularly. She had coffee with him, discussed her essay. He had praised her for an assignment. They had gone for a beer. She seemed to be playing down their relationship. Did she see him as a father figure, perhaps that's why she had started thinking about Jackson again? Or was that just a mother being too suspicious. Not suspicious enough as it turned out.

Friday was a normal day for me. I went to Wandsworth Prison to interview a prisoner on remand for a horrific burglary, committed on the home of an elderly couple. His attitude stank. He showed no remorse. He needed the money for drugs. As he tried to justify his actions, I started to think maybe it's time for a change of career. I found myself switching off, as his whiney voice continued. He would be locked up for a few more years for this crime and to be honest, he deserved to be. Some people can't and won't change I guess. What had happened to that idealistic girl many moons ago? She had grown up. I understood a lot about people, it was my job to. I could analyse their actions and their risk to society.

Psychopaths were born not made. There was a big group of serious offenders whose personality disorder was fixed and part of them. They didn't have the capacity for change. Sad, yet true, they had to be contained. Luckily the Probation Service had moved with the times and Public Protection was paramount. I like that part of the job, working with the Police and analysing risk. I felt I made a difference and the world a bit safer. Of course you can't always predict the future can you? Risk assessment is effective, but it's not an exact science. There will always be a maverick, someone you could never predict what they are capable of.

I was pondering this as I caught the underground train back to work. My phone rang, it was an unknown number. I paused before going down the steps to the underground, as the phone signal would cut out. A man's voice said. 'Is that Kate McLean?'

'Yes,' I replied, hesitantly.

'This is Northumbria Police. Are you in a position to talk?'

My stomach turned over. As he told me the news, I crumpled on to the floor and rolled down the steps.

25

Friday 24ᵗʰ May 1963

It had been a long night, driving north from Nottingham. The M6 wasn't complete yet and the way to Scotland had been a mixture of quick sections of new motorway, interspersed with old trunk roads, through towns and villages.

If Kate hadn't been so exhausted mentally and physically, she might have enjoyed the Lake District and lowland scenery. However, it was now more than six hours since she killed the teenager and she needed food, a bath and lots of sleep. If tomorrow came up to expectation, she was going to have an equally exhausting day.

In the final stretch approaching Paisley, Kate looked for somewhere to park the Thames van for the night. Thinking ahead, she had earmarked a couple of streets, away from the town centre that would leave a walk of only about half a mile, to the Hotel.

The booking, in the name of Smith, had been made from a phone box in Bradford. She had been very specific. A double room, with brass bedstead, for the nights of Friday and Saturday.

Kate parked the van, took her bulging suitcase and struggled, manfully at times, the last half mile. When she reached Orr Square, a discrete sign outside meant she had finally made it to the Ashtree House Hotel. A fine Georgian House turned into a very comfortable hotel, in 1883. Blonde Kate entered and approached the desk.

'Good evening Madam,' said a soft Gaelic voice, owned by the smart, fair-haired, middle-aged duty manager.

'Good evening to you too, I have a reservation in the name of Smith.'

'So you do, Mr & Mrs Smith for two nights. Is Mr Smith parking the car?'

'No, he's been delayed on business and won't be joining me until tomorrow. Oh and we don't have a car!'

'Very good Madam, Thomas will show you to your room.'

With a single press on the bell, Thomas the 'hop' appeared and took hold of Kate's case.

'Room 17,' said the manager. Thomas took the key and escorted her to the main staircase and up to the first floor. He opened the door with a deft movement and stepped back for her to enter. Once inside, Kate scanned the room. A not unpleasant, cosy looking room, with solid oak furniture and chintz fabrics. However, her expression changed when she saw the bed. It too, was a heavy piece of oak, with a wine-red cover and cushions.

She turned to Thomas and said. 'I'm sorry this won't do at all. I specifically asked for a brass bed and was told that is what I would get.'

The bell-boy's expression, said 'what's the fuss about,' but his mouth said, 'I see Madam, if you wait here, I will sort this out.'

Kate replied. 'Please do, my husband has allergies.' She didn't really know how that would make a difference, but she figured it would emphasise the point. 'No-one would argue with a medical need,' she thought.

True to his word, Thomas was back in the room in less than five minutes. 'The duty manager sends his utmost apologies. You did indeed ask for a brass bed.

However, this room was available and being larger and more spacious, he thought you'd be more comfortable in this one.'

'That's quite all right. He meant well, I can see that.' Kate had softened.

'And,' said the charming young Scot, 'he will make a suitable reduction to your bill, at the end of your stay. Now, if you'll follow me, I'll take you to room 31.'

It was one floor up and at the back of the Hotel, with the noise from the kitchen bubbling up from below. He was right, number 17 was a nicer space, but this one was perfect. Purpose before style! She pressed an English pound note into Tom's hand that had put her case on the luggage support. He thanked her and closed the door gently behind him.

'Damn,' she thought, forgetting to ask about dinner. She opened the door quickly and called him back. Tom must have been thinking, 'now what?' But being the soul of discretion, appeared instantly and said. 'Yes Madam?'

'I'm very hungry, Thomas, is the restaurant open?'

He looked at his watch. 'Dinner in the Dining room is from seven, Madam.'

'On second thoughts, could I just have something quick and easy sent up here, before the evening rush? Please ask chef if he can manage a cheese and tomato omelette, with salad and potatoes, maybe? I'm so tired that it would suit me not to have to dress formally?'

'Very good Madam, I will go and see him now.'

Shoes off, she wasted no time getting on to the soft mattress. Her sleep was disturbed by a sharp knock. Attentive Tom was back, with a silver tray with a large dome over it. 'Your omelette, Madam.'

'That was quick, thank you.'

'Chef's very sorry, he had no salad, so he hopes

sautéed new potatoes and fresh Scottish white asparagus will tempt you.'

'Tell him, he's an angel. In fact, you're all angels,' and gave him another pound.

'Thank you Madam, we appreciate it!' With a polite nod, he was gone.

Kate lifted the lid. 'Bloody hell,' she thought. There must have been four, free range bantam-laid eggs, whisked into that thing. Six plump, butter covered, sprigs of asparagus and a mound of fattening, but delicious, potato. Thinking, 'I'll give it my best shot,' she did. There wasn't anything more than fragments left on the plate when she put it down. Tiredness was taking over. The sandman was in the room and as with babies, her dinner was having a soporific effect.

She was going to sleep, when her subconscious reminded her of tomorrow's visitor. She had only had a stand up rub down with a damp flannel that morning and her personal hygiene was at unusually low ebb. She would have to bathe before retiring. She had to keep the room fragrant and inviting.

The water couldn't come out of the taps fast enough. Modern high-pressure plumbing this wasn't, but it was hot, wet, deep and inviting. When she was in it, she could have slept right there.

26

Kate

The following days were a blur. I barely remember my father driving me up to Newcastle with my mother. I recalled the phone call however, word for word, spinning around inside my head. 'I am so sorry to tell you that your daughter is dead.' 'NO!' I screamed inwardly when I came round. I had fainted in the tube station.

I think I went slightly insane. Not the insane that needs to be locked up in a ward and restrained, but the sort of insane that sits in a chair, gazing through the window, dribbling and uttering meaningless sentences. My mind could not take in what had happened, so it simply shut down. My mother and father took over, their strength made me ashamed.

As I entered the mortuary, the cold air hit me, like a rush of blood to the head. I sucked in the air along with a medicinal smell of disinfectant that I feel will haunt me forever. Calm words are uttered in a low tone by the woman in white, who is looking at me sympathetically. I didn't hear a word she said, as she uncovered my daughter's body, but I wished with all the heart I had left, that it was me who had died.

She lay there looking ethereal, with her white porcelain skin and long curls framing that face. Her eyes were closed and she looked as if she was sleeping. I had seen her like this so many times over the years. I would gently wake her, though I never wanted to, she looked so peaceful. Today I wanted to wake her. Please God, let her wake up. It's been a mistake, you haven't taken her, why would you. I could feel a scream in my throat that would never be released.

The purple bruising around her throat, the angry red welts glistening on her neck, told me that I was wrong. She would never wake up. She would never finish university. She could have set the world alight. She would never fall in love. She would never get married. She would never feel her own child in her arms. She would never be old. She was gone. She was truly gone. I knew that because I couldn't feel her presence within me.

My brain registered a sharp pain that felt as if it was lodged between my shoulder blades. It was followed by a surge of anger that I could never have envisaged. Red rage tore through my body. Who had done this to my baby? I will hunt them down myself. My beautiful baby girl had been ripped from me and her life cut short. No words can describe the feeling unless you have lost a child in this way. It's not nature's way or any God that I could recognise. Dark forces hung in the stagnant air.

I don't remember the funeral. There were hundreds of people there. Teachers; friends from school, college and university; family; and the Press hovering like flies around the packed church. They would do anything for a story. I hate them and their lack of respect. Let her rest in peace. Don't make it worse. And yet, can anything be worse than this?

The answer was yes. Whoever stole my daughter's life, her hopes, dreams and her future, didn't crawl somewhere and die. They didn't see her picture in the press and think. Oh my God what have I done? They didn't hand themselves in to the Police, remorseful, unable to live with the reality of what they had done. No not at all. They carried on.

Two more female students were killed during the following five months and each death was more gruesome than the last. Their killer had become bolder, encouraged by success. There were no clues or forensic evidence. Two more precious lives were snuffed out like a candle.

Panic set in at the University and staff sent out leaflets advising students how to keep safe. That's not how students live is it? They should be carefree, away from home for the first time, broadening their horizons and spreading their wings. No one wanted to live in fear. Lock your doors. Make sure you don't stay home on your own. Report anything suspicious. Parents responded by taking their daughters back to the suburbs and the safety of the bosom of the family. I didn't blame them. It was too late for Emma. Feisty, funny, brilliant Emma. I was lost in a dark place and couldn't find my way back.

I couldn't work, I couldn't eat and I couldn't sleep. My life became a waking nightmare. I spent hours in her room lying on her bed, or looking at her paintings and the clothes she'd never wear again. I breathed in the smell of her and it felt like acid eating into my soul. Why would I go on? My life was meaningless now. I had failed as a mother. I hadn't protected my little girl. Her father didn't know she had existed, I had failed him too. He could have enjoyed seeing her grow. I know he would have loved her. Why did I make excuses? My own selfishness and pride got in the way.

For the first time in my life I couldn't levitate. I couldn't leave myself behind and go to another place. I wanted to so badly. Anywhere, but not here. Any life, but not this life. How do people bear this? To lose a child is bad enough, but to have your child murdered and snatched away from you? No one should bury their child and it's a cruel heartless God that allows it to happen.

I stopped attending church. Father Dominic had visited me and Francesca many times to offer prayers and hope. He failed to convince me and although I didn't want to upset my mother, I couldn't listen to any more advice or platitudes. Confession was meaningless. I blamed myself for Emma's death. I talked to my father. No one else could get to me. Bridget stopped coming after a few weeks. Her four healthy children were a reminder of what I had lost. What Emma had lost? Sorry, it wasn't her fault.

They were expecting me back at work at some point. I couldn't face it. I could never sit face to face with a murderer or sex offender again. Why would I want to work with those people? They create victims. They leave a path of destruction and damage. Let them rot. Work colleagues and friends called to see me. They were obviously shocked at my deteriorating appearance. Curvy, happy, caring Kate had been replaced with a skinny, hollow, bitter and twisted shell. They didn't stay long.

27

Saturday 25th May 1963

S he opened her eyes. It was light, very light. Birds were chattering on the roof, out of sight, but noisy nonetheless. Kate had no idea of the time. She hadn't asked to be woken, she wasn't wearing her watch. Half asleep, she groped round the room until she found it. Eight thirty-five. Still time for breakfast she hoped. The omelette, good as it was, was long ago and today was another day when fuel was important.

In record time, she made herself pretty presentable and entered the dining room at ten to nine. She needn't have panicked. Nine thirty was the deadline at the weekend. Kate managed most of a full Scottish breakfast before heading back upstairs. Then she had another quick bath to freshen up, before the task of deciding what to wear. Seductive, but not too tarty, was the brief she gave herself. Mini-skirts were not the norm yet and to be honest, weren't always complimentary to a lady of a certain age.

She chose a floral patterned, cotton summer dress, with a short, but not unflattering sleeve. It also had a neckline low enough to gain attention. Light tan stockings and black shoes with a heel still practical to walk in. She looked at her hair. Which one? She decided to stick with the 'Marilyn Monroe' look, after all 'Gentlemen prefer blondes.' Though the man she was looking to meet was no gentleman.

The day manager, she didn't know his name, had been tasked with ordering a taxi for eleven thirty. She

141

added that she would need him for at least a couple of hours, to show her all the sights, maybe three. She tidied away her things into the suitcase and buried it in the bottom of the wardrobe. Checking her watch, she locked the door and went down to the lobby at twenty-five past. Her driver was already waiting out front and with a cheery smile and a 'good morning', held open the back door of an unrecognisable saloon. Hamish, introduced himself and asked, 'where to?'

'I don't know,' said Kate, 'I haven't been to Glasgow before. Show me anything interesting. The docks, the university, the parks?'

'Ok lady.'

'Oh and I'll reward you well.' She still had handbag full of cash, so didn't worry how long it took to find what she came for. Kate had been to Scotland and Glasgow, several times before, but let Hamish chat in his clipped vowel way about the history of his home town. Kate's intense gaze was searching beyond the various monuments she was being proudly led to. She didn't hear much of the commentary, her mind was elsewhere. In deference to her host, she politely said 'yes', 'really' and 'I see' a lot, hoping her affirmations would be, more or less, in keeping with the conversation.

After an hour of traversing the city, she called out from the back. 'Stop a minute!' Thinking he'd missed a light or signal, the driver pulled up sharply, throwing her forward in her seat. Straining to see out of the back window, she persuaded Hamish to do a U-turn and go back the way they had come. As she passed the stationary vehicle she got a good look. 'Damn,' she said quietly. It wasn't him. This man was too old. Certainly in his thirties, maybe forties. His hair wasn't dark enough and his face was all wrong. 'False alarm.' A very confused Hamish needed an explanation and he pulled a face.

'I'm so sorry. I thought I saw someone I know, which is silly of me. Why would I meet a friend five hundred miles from home?'

'Strange things can happen in this life,' said a sagely voice from the front.

'Ain't that the truth,' said the Londoner in the back.

Another hour passed, along with numerous bridges, ships and old buildings. Kate was bored with, what seemed like a fruitless exercise. 'What about the parks?' Kate offered.

'Aye, we haven't seen those yet,' and he drove to Richmond Park's entrance.

'Isn't there a larger one south of here? Begins with a 'P', I think?'

'Pollok Park's south west of here, right enough. It's quite a way out of the city though.'

'What the hell, let's go anyway.' 'In for a penny, in for a pound,' she thought, patting her handbag.

'You're the boss,' said her obedient chauffeur and turned the car again. Fifteen minutes later they were on Pollokshaws Road, approaching the park's main entrance. Looking ahead Kate saw something that could mean the end of her search.

'Stop here please, Hamish.' He obliged and brought the car to a halt, about fifty yards short of the gates. Just in front of them was a small queue of families, waiting, not for the park, but to buy ice cream. Kate asked Hamish to wait. She left the car and walked to join the back of the line. As she got closer to the window, she smiled. It was him. A stocky, dark-haired young man, with unmistakeable features.

Kate wondered what she was going to say.

Although if her information was accurate, he wouldn't need much encouragement. 'Hello,' she said brightly, 'is Mr Whippy your real name?'

'It's Fred,' said the ice cream seller, in a west country accent. 'What are you after, miss?'

'Call me Kate and I suppose I'm too early for a 99?'

'99?' Fred repeated.

'Ten years too early I'm guessing. It's an ice cream with a bar of chocolate in it.'

'I've got a choc ice if you want chocolate.'

'Don't worry. I'll just have one of those swirly things in the picture here.'

Mr Whippy dutifully coiled a large amount of soft ice cream onto a cone and handed it to her.

'Do you want anything else?'

'Have you got a collection of whips you could show me, Mr Whippy?' She said boldly, not knowing where her cheek was coming from.

'Are you a policewoman or something?' He leaned out of the window and peered round to see who she was with. 'You ask a lot of questions.'

'Good God no! I'm a writer. We're a curious breed. It's how we get our material for our stories. I'm up from London and I'm bored. I thought a handsome young man like you, might brighten up a dull trip.'

Fred, was visibly swelling with pride and was about to answer when Kate added.

'But, if you're not interested, I won't keep you any longer,' and she turned to go. Deliberately and as slowly as she could, she bent over in front of him, to adjust her shoe. Mr Whippy took the bait!

'I didn't say that,' he called after her, 'wait a minute!' Kate turned back to face him. 'Where are you staying?'

'Paisley,' she replied.

'That's funny, that's where my depot is and I have to return the van there later.'

'What time's that?'

'Well, I can work until ten if I want, but I can finish earlier.'

'Do you know the Ashtree House Hotel?'

'Of course I do, it's in Orr Square,' said the young man with a grin. He was being reeled in, hook, line and sinker!

'I'm in room 31. Tell them you are Mr Smith and they'll show you up. Come at seven and bring your whips!' She walked away. She could feel Fred's eyes boring into the back of her. She couldn't resist moving her bottom, just in case he needed any more encouragement.

Hamish woke up from a snooze as Kate opened the door. He didn't seem to know or care what she had been up to. 'Home Hamish, or should that be hame Hamish?' Her driver laughed at the mock Scottish accent and turned the car in the direction of Paisley. She looked at her watch. Nearly three o'clock! 'No wait! Can we go via a department store? There are some things I need before going back.

'Very good, m' Lady.' He sounded like Lady Penelope's Parker, but he couldn't have known it. Thunderbirds wouldn't be shown on screen for another two years. With the car parked outside, Kate ran in and grabbed some stuff. More clothes, shoes, underwear and more toiletries. She came back to the car and put the six bags onto the back seat, beside her. Hamish was awake this time. 'Back to the hotel?'

'Not quite,' said Kate, 'could you drop me at Paisley station, I want to check the train times for my journey back.' At the station he offered to wait, but Kate thanked him and insisted on walking back. She made him take twenty pounds, even though he had asked for eleven pounds ten. When the blue Sunbeam was out of sight, Kate walked to her own van and put her department store purchases under the blanket, in the back.

Back at the Hotel, she greeted the evening receptionist and explained her husband would soon be arriving. She went on to tell the man in uniform, that her latest husband was considerably more youthful than herself. With a wink she added. 'Being rich does have some advantages. I hope I can rely on your discretion.'

'It's my middle name,' he said in a cultured Edinburgh accent.

28

Kate

Days turned into months and eventually a man was arrested and charged with the deaths of five students, in Newcastle and Durham. The Police rang me before the news hit the headlines and the relief I expected to feel didn't come. They had always assumed it was a stranger rape. A homicidal predator on campus, preying on the vulnerable. Well he was a predator, but when Mark Chappell was arrested he was smiling at the camera, enjoying the attention.

He had spent weeks planning each murder meticulously, grooming his victims by praising their work and building their confidence. He was known by all the victims and they let him into their homes. He would then make the crime scene look like a break in. Having made sure they would be alone, he took the ultimate power and control over their lives. He was caught because he was disturbed by the last victim's flatmate, who had returned early because he wasn't feeling well. Chappell panicked and ran, but was soon caught by the Police.

He had apparently always wanted notoriety. An average student, a failed PhD, he entered the world of the academic. He worked his way up from junior lecturer. Always the charmer, the narcistic qualities that hid his sadistic nature and his dark soul. When he was fourteen, a girl he had been friendly at school with disappeared, never to be found. No one was ever charged with her murder. At puberty he had probably offended for the first time, locking in a pattern of behaviour he could not help but repeat.

He had no remorse. As I sat in the wooden pews at Newcastle Crown Court, he glibly denied all the offences. He had an alibi for Emma's death. A gaunt, weary looking wife who eventually admitted he had forced her to lie for him. She spoke of their marriage. As a prosecution witness he glared at her, trying to intimidate her from the glass dock. She found her voice and began to describe how he had broken her, her confidence and then the violence. He had kicked her down the stairs when she was six months pregnant. She lost the baby, but didn't report him. He was her husband, she looked up to him, he was clever and she was not. She lived in fear. Any small thing could upset him. She learned how to please him, however it was never enough. She was willing to lie for him. After all, he couldn't have hurt those girls could he?

As she told the Court the truth, I looked over at Emma's killer. I wanted to scream, I wanted to shout. He stared back at me and then a smile curled around his lips. He knew he would be convicted. He didn't care anymore. He thought he had the ultimate power, that of life or death. Mark Chappell. His name would go down in history. 'The Campus Killer.' That was enough for him.

People talk to me of closure. What does that mean? Does it mean you accept something at last and put it to rest? Somehow your subconscious mind has come to terms with the unmanageable truth. It doesn't stop hurting, but you learn to live with it. Maybe? It was a relief to know that Mark Chappell would take no other lives. He would spend the rest of his life in prison, but was it closure? I don't know. It was a slow process.

I decided to carry on living. It was a conscious decision. I had considered the alternatives often, but that would be another victim for Chappell. My parents would have buckled under the weight of more grief and sorrow. I would look for a reason to live. I found one, eventually.

Work no longer held any meaning for me. I left the Probation Service for good. I think they understood. All my morals and principles had been eroded by my grief. I could not care for others. I could not care for myself really.

I found a job in a 'wholefood' café. The owner Beverley nourished my body and my soul. She was a caring eccentric. Worn down by her job as a social worker, or burnt out as it is known in the trade. She had decided to live an alternative life. She baked her own bread, grew her own vegetables and could cook delicious food for the tiny café that people would travel from other parts of London to pick up. She couldn't cook and serve at the same time, so when I had gone in for a coffee and started chatting one day, she hired me on the spot.

She didn't ask questions. She knew something had happened to me, but she didn't pry. She encouraged me to eat her food. She nurtured me. Her food nourished my frail body. She had a motherly quality that had served her well in her career and her soul was as old as the hills. There wasn't much in life that she hadn't seen and she was able to make the grumpiest customer smile. Her easy warmth and caring nature was exactly what I needed. I enjoyed the job. At least it gave me a purpose.

I started to swim. Every day before work, I would move up and down the pool. Powerful strokes, blocking out the voices that still haunted me. My body and mind became stronger. God works in mysterious ways you know.

Anyone who has lost anyone will know this fact. Birthdays, anniversaries, dates that mean something somehow lock into your brain. On those days I would wake up with a heavy feeling, a sadness weighing me down. I couldn't actually move sometimes. On Emma's birthday I stayed under the duvet until the day had passed. It was a physical sensation.

As I went about my business in London, on my way to work on my old bicycle, recently trendy again, I would see a flash of hair, a hood pulled up. Her red suede boots would belong to someone else, but for a split second I would think it was her. A split second of happiness. It wasn't enough.

29

Saturday 25th May 1963

Once upstairs, Kate had an hour and twenty minutes to ready herself. A perfumed bath was running while she used the man's electric shaver, she had bought in Selfridges. Lady shavers and razors hadn't been invented yet, but it was no reason to go hairy, she thought. As long as she did it daily, a man's one would do the job. Also, it vibrated more than a modern battery one, so wasn't an unpleasant experience at all. When she was smooth enough all over, she got in the bath. Clean, fragrant and smooth. How could her young buck resist her? Make up, with lots of rouge on cheeks of her face and her chest. Strong red lipstick, said 'hooker,' but on it went.

It was time to dress. The ivory silk & satin, jacquard-weave, corset wasn't the easiest garment to put on, she thought. Thankfully though, it laced up at the front, so could be done without assistance. She particularly like the bullet-bra cups. Even though she would never see forty again, they gave her the breasts of a twenty year old! The corset stopped at the hip and had four long, shiny satin suspenders, hanging from it. A pair of ivory nylon stockings were pulled up and fastened to the waiting clips. French knickers went on over the top and when the shoes were on, she looked and felt fantastic.

She unwrapped six pairs of black, nylon stockings and loosely laid them in the top drawer of the chest of drawers next to the bed. She placed with them, a large silk scarf and a long round handled curling brush. A double edged, six inch bladed knife with a particularly sharp angled point, was then hidden under two hand towels, from the bathroom.

Originally, her plan A was the knife, purchased in an Army surplus store in Oxford that she had spotted on the drive to Cheltenham. However, over the last few days she had started to feel guilty about the mess that would be left by such a bloody killing. It was bad enough to leave without paying, even worse to leave a corpse in the room for the Hotel to sort out. To leave the room in need of redecoration and new carpet and soft furnishings, didn't seem fair at all. It was still plan B though. There was a chance the new plan wouldn't work, so it was in the drawer too, as insurance.

It was now quarter to seven. Happy that she couldn't prepare any more, she sat on the bed to do some meditation and breathing exercises to help keep her calm and her heart rate manageable. After what seemed far too long a wait, she looked at her watch. It was nearly ten past seven. 'Damn,' she thought, 'he wasn't hooked at all.'

She paced the floor, wondering what she could do. Nothing was coming to mind. Besides, she was hardly dressed to go anywhere public. Her thoughts were interrupted by a knock on the door. When she opened it, there was a red-faced and almost breathless Fred.

'I thought you'd stood me up Mr Whippy. Come in and have a drink, you look as if you need one!'

When he was in the room and had composed himself, he explained that his boss had insisted on going over the holiday rotas and days off for June, even though Fred had said he had a reason to be in a hurry. It sounded deliberate.

'Anyway, you're here now. Have a beer while I run you a bath to relax you and make you a nice clean boy.' Kate let her dressing gown open slightly to give Freddy a sneak preview of the after-bath entertainment. He sank into the armchair with the beer, poured into a toothbrush glass. The thirsty boy had finished it by the time Kate had turned the taps on.

'Boy you needed that didn't you?' She reached for another bottle and the opener. Handing him the second one, she said, 'don't relax too much tiger. I need you to stay on your game for me.'

She could see from his face and stance that he wasn't that relaxed yet. 'He might need another couple,' she thought. She went back to the bathroom, fiddled with the taps a bit and thrashed about to make bubbles on the top. She opened another bottle and left it at the end of the bath. Taps turned off, she went back to the room.

By now Mr Whippy had already taken off his shoes and half his clothes. Kate offered him her hand and led him to the bathroom. She pushed him gently inside. Closing the door, she told him not to come out until he was feeling and smelling better. He seemed to be happy to be 'mothered.' Kate knew why, but she drew the line at washing his back.

Ten minutes later, he re-entered the bedroom with a bath towel round his middle. 'Here goes,' she thought and handed him beer number four. She needed a drink herself, but a clear head was more than slightly more important. He went to sit in the chair again, but Kate steered him to the bed instead. She left him to his drink and went into the bathroom. Disrobing from her gown, she adjusted her hair, put some blusher on her cheeks and the top of her chest and returned to her young admirer.

He was now lying with his hands behind his head and his feet up on the mattress. The sight of Kate in her lingerie transfixed him. He liked older ladies, especially this one. His eyes followed her round the room. 'Good,' she thought, 'this will be easier if he's keen.'

'You're gorgeous,' said the boy from Gloucester.

'I know,' she replied, 'and we're going to play a little game. My turn first and then you can do whatever you want with me!' A movement from Fred's towel answered for him. 'Now it's time for me to tease and please you.'

She opened the top drawer and took out the stockings. One limb at a time, she tied her victim to the four solid brass corner posts of the bed. She had practised knots for weeks that would seem gentle enough, but would tighten if pulled on. When his arms and legs were suitably secure it was time for Act 2.

Kate slowly slid the silk cami-knickers over the suspenders and clips and let them fall to the floor. She stepped out of them in front of him and bent slowly to pick them up.

It was almost certainly Fred's first sight of a hairless lady and it was too much for him to bear. His bath towel had been opened by his erection, which now pointed toward the patterned glass light fitting, in the centre of the ceiling. She couldn't resist teasing him some more. Holding on to one corner of the silk, she approached him confidently from the feet end and walked toward his head. As she did so Kate let the garment work a slow trail up his body, letting his sensitised genitals feel every fibre. Onward towards his head, belly, chest, neck and finally she left it to rest on his face. His nose was now inhaling the faint, but unmistakeable aroma of Kate's womanliness. Even though his eyes were covered, he must have been hypnotised. He either didn't notice or care, when she used a pair of stockings tied round his head as a blindfold.

Act 3. Lifting the panties, she gently pinched his nostrils together. Needing air quickly, due to his increased blood flow, Fred opened his mouth. As he did so, his captor pushed the silk material into his open mouth. He almost choked there and then and with muffled anguish, he tried to loosen himself to free his airway. He couldn't get loose, but had overcome his gag-reflex enough not to choke on his own vomit.

Finale. While Mr Whippy was thrashing around trying to escape, Kate retrieved the scarf and the hairbrush from the draw. With as much speed as she could manage she double reef-knotted two of the ends together, forming a loop and slid the woven silk circle over his head. She pulled the knots toward her, inserted the hairbrush into it, up to halfway. With a deep breath she began turning the brush like an old plane's propeller. By now, young Freddy wasn't enjoying the game anymore. He was sensing danger at last. Lots of it. He bucked and pulled like a shark on a forty pound line.

'If there's ever a time when you don't want stockings to ladder it's now,' she thought and kept turning for all she was worth. The tourniquet was now a solid column of silk all the way to his neck. The remaining scarf was cutting in to the flesh and she didn't think he could possibly breathe any longer. Time seemed to go so slowly. Minutes passed and he was still fighting for life. 'How?' As Kate fought to hold on for what seemed like an eternity, she noticed a slow, but definite change in his complexion. The colour was slowly draining away. He was dying, at last.

The strength of his fight went with the colour and soon he was motionless. Kate was not taking chances. If he'd got free, it would be her that would be on her way to the mortuary. She waited at least ten minutes after he was still and his skin was a strange shade of blue grey. She let go of the brush. She went to the bathroom and was as sick as she'd ever been in her life.

When she came back to the room, he was as she had left him, but looking colder. She took off the corset and stockings and dressed for a cold evening. Trousers, two jumpers, coat and driving shoes. Before leaving the room, she cut two lemons and used the halves on all the hard surfaces she had touched. She didn't want to leave unnecessary fingerprints, in case the police somehow found her before she was home.

She put on the kid gloves and gathered her bag. Turned off the light and locked the door. In the lobby, she told the night porter she was going for a walk while her husband was taking a rest. He wished her a pleasant evening and held open her exit.

After walking briskly to the van, she turned the key. The faithful old flat-four engine growled into life. For the first time in over an hour she breathed normally, after the sigh of relief.

As fast as was safe, she drove to England.

30

Bridget

I started to lose Kate when she went to Cambridge. We were like an old married couple in some ways and it was difficult to part and go our separate ways. She sat her Oxbridge exams and accepted a place at Cambridge. That was never going to be my world and part of me felt some slight resentment, if I am honest.

My dad was most surprised that Kate, who liked to think she was a staunch socialist, was 'selling out' and becoming part of the establishment. He was also secretly proud of her I think and she was like a dog with two tails when she found out she had a place. I tried to be happy for her. I knew deep down that she was more conventional than she made herself out to be and this choice probably confirmed that notion.

I was worried I would lose her friendship though. She might have more in common with the Cambridge lot than with me. She might join 'footlights' and change in to someone I wouldn't recognise. As a working class girl, I imagined the place to be full of people that I might cross the street to avoid, but this was Kate, we're talking about. She surely wouldn't change that much.

She was going to study Law, I was going to York to do Business Studies. My parents were struggling financially to help me and I knew it wouldn't be easy. It seemed to me, looking back that we both had our own anxieties about the changes in our lives. Cambridge certainly changed Kate, but not the way I thought it would. Not 'our sensible Kate,' never in a million years.

She rang me regularly at first and emailed me with her news. The course wasn't quite going to plan and she was questioning her choices in terms of Law.

'It's so bloody dull,' she wrote, 'and the men are oafs.'

She started to think she had made the wrong choice.

'Bridge, I should have come up to York with you, this isn't me at all,' she lamented.

Then something changed. She sent me a text, at about two o'clock one morning. Late by Kate's standards, she wasn't usually up at that time. She might go the bar or a party, but by midnight she had usually turned into Cinderella. It read

'I am not drunk, but I have just met the man who will change my life. I can't tell you all now, but he is everything. Is this love, Bridge? I feel sick. He is lying next to me and we have just had the most amazing sex. I know, don't say it.'

Kate, what the hell? This was not the Kate who left London. Sensible Kate, pragmatic Kate. Kate who had a plan for her life. It all changed in an instant. I couldn't reach her most of the time, either emotionally or physically. She didn't answer her phone, it was often switched off. I sent her long texts, asking all sorts of questions she didn't answer. I nearly rang James and Francesca because I was so worried, but I had to consider Kate's feelings. She wouldn't have thanked me for interfering. My own work suffered, as I struggled to understand what was going on. I eventually realised. She was in love and nothing else mattered. Her studies, her friend, her parents all took a back seat during those mad months with Jackson.

We were both due home for Christmas. I was

desperate to see her and find out what had happened. Who was this man who had changed my friend in an instant? I wanted to see her, see the light in her eyes and for me to understand. I wanted to keep our friendship and share the secrets in the way we had done in the past. She had sex before me and I was naïve enough to want to know all about it. It was as if we were on a journey and she had suddenly galloped ahead and left me behind.

I heard the news from Francesca. I had arrived back in London a week before Christmas and had been ringing Kate on her mobile. She hadn't answered, so I rang the landline at home. Francesca said she hadn't heard from her recently, but was expecting her back in a couple of days. I heard nothing, then Francesca rang me and invited me for lunch. I assumed that Kate would be back and maybe it was a surprise thing.

I arrived on the 23rd December as arranged and was greeted warmly by my best friend's parents. I accepted a glass of mulled wine and sat down in my usual position at the end of the sofa. It felt like home, a second home anyway.

'Where is she?' I said looking around for signs of Kate. The place looked eerily tidy. Francesca had her own cleaner by now and as she insisted on cleaning up before she came, the place was extremely clean. Usually, my friend managed to leave enough of her things lying around, to take away the impression of a show-home. There would be at least two books on the go, magazines, cans of diet coke and often a bowl of popcorn, Kate's ultimate favourite snack. There was nothing. I was starting to get a bad feeling about it all.

'She's not coming home for Christmas, Bridge,' said James looking directly at Francesca as he said it. They began to tell me what she had said. Kate had been honest at least and told them that she had to stay in Cambridge with Jackson and felt she couldn't bring him home yet. They were clearly upset, but trying hard to be the progressive parents they believed they were and allowing their daughter the freedom to make her own choices. I felt a lump in my throat, which was ridiculous. She was happy. She was in love. It would all be ok.

James had made a fabulous curry and spread of Indian delicacies. I tried to eat, drink and be merry. It was like the saying about the elephant in the room, though. They were interested in my course, my life in York and just about everything really. Francesca knew York quite well, so was especially interested in discovering my impressions of the city. We all frequently glanced over to the chair where Kate would normally have sat and all felt the loss. Still, there would be other Christmases when the four of us would be together again and life had to go on.

We exchanged gifts and said our goodbyes later that evening. Kate had rung home and we all spoke to her, albeit briefly. I could tell she felt guilty. It was our Catholic thing and we both easily detected it in each other. She was torn. She had made up her mind though. When she did eventually return home, everything had changed.

I was home for a long weekend for a family wedding when she rang me and asked me to meet her. We decided on a small coffee shop near our old school. I asked her why she was home, during term time and she wouldn't tell me over the phone. I realise why now.

I found it hard to comprehend what she was saying. She was clearly distraught and found it hard to get the words out. Jackson had returned to the USA and she was pregnant with his child. 'Oh Mary mother of Jesus!' She had dropped out from Cambridge and would get a job.

'It would all be alright,' she said. 'Plenty of people are single mothers these days.'

As she said this, it all sounded plausible in one way and I wouldn't have worried, if there hadn't been tears flowing down her cheeks, at the time.

Kate became a mother and it all happened so quickly. Well, so it seemed to me, away at University and quietly feeling relieved that I hadn't made such a monumental mistake as my dearest friend. When Emma was born. I rushed to the hospital with a bottle of champagne and a hamper of treats for Kate.

I looked at baby Emma and looked at my friend. She was holding her baby girl and staring in wonderment at her. For a split second I envied her, she was in her element. I plucked up courage to ask her what she was thinking.

'I wish Jackson was here,' she said, simply.

It was complicated alright. I just couldn't get the Jackson thing. Why couldn't she just call him? Forget her pride and all the other things stopping her. He has a daughter, he deserves to know. I am ashamed to say I pressured her a bit. It didn't work though. I knew that Kate wouldn't change her mind now. She was becoming a force to be reckoned with. She had grown up overnight it seemed and now she was a mother. Emma came first.

The next few years changed us both. I graduated from York University with a first. My mum and dad were extremely proud and at least I felt that their sacrifices had paid off. I was taken on by a City bank and returned to London to live. I had loved Yorkshire with a passion, but it didn't offer the opportunities of my home city. Besides, I was a Londoner first and foremost and had missed my family. My sisters were growing up quickly and my brother had just joined the Army. It was good to be home.

I loved my job and I made some serious money for a while. It was an obscene amount really, in terms of salary and yearly bonus. Enough to pay back my parents and buy them a caravan in Clacton, where they would disappear for weekends with the girls. I was aware that Kate and I had swapped lives in some ways.

I had a flat in Canary Wharf and she would visit with Emma. The chrome and glass furniture wasn't very child friendly though and I would worry as she headed towards the sofa with a pack of crayons. It was stressful and I realised that I had changed as well. I was becoming fussy and liked my expensive lifestyle too much, for a girl from Hackney.

Then my life changed. My lovely, kind, homely mum was diagnosed with breast cancer. I was thrown into chaos and questioned everything about the world and my own life. I took her to chemotherapy at her local hospital and she remained remarkably upbeat and cheerful. She praised the NHS for her care and brought a smile to everyone's face on the ward. It made me ashamed of my bad thoughts and dark days. My dad was a tower of strength to the family and kept everything going at home.

My mum had been admitted one day, as the treatment took hold. She was dehydrated and looked as pale as a ghost.

'Bridget love, I would like you to meet someone,' she said. I looked up and saw an extremely handsome young doctor holding my mother's arm as he adjusted her drip. He was tall with blonde tousled curls, resembling the hair of a toddler rather than a grown man. He smiled. She winked at me and I inwardly winced, realising it was another of her plans to set me up.

'He's just like Dr Kildare,' she joked, 'and he's Irish.'

I laughed at this point. There was nothing subtle about my mother when she was in matchmaker mode. It worked this time though and we were married within four months of our meeting. Mum's treatment worked, thank God and she remains in remission. She is a fighter my mum and she kept her sense of humour, as she introduced Michael to the rest of the family by saying, 'it was worth being ill to see our Bridget settled.'

I have four beautiful children now. No job in the city anymore though. With four children so close in age, it wasn't feasible to stay on. It wasn't really me, anyway. I had to take advice from Kate initially, when my first child Francis was born, as I didn't have a clue. Emma was seven by then and Kate was happy working for the Probation service. She joked about me becoming an earth mother, as the babies started to arrive. We would meet up for coffee and chats whenever we could, although it was often easier for her to come to me, as my family increased in size. I started an internet business selling baby clothes. It was easier than trying to find a job and Francesca gave me some good contacts in the buying world through Harrods. I started to make a regular income and things became easier. Mum and Dad retired to Frinton-on-Sea, which was great for the kids, when we could get down there.

Life had a groove now. I was a busy mum of four. Kate had her job and Emma and we stayed close despite our hectic lives. Kate didn't get over Jackson though. She kept photos of him and whenever I moaned about Michael, who was generally a good husband most of the time, I could almost see the scenario she was imagining.

Did she envy me with the large family, large mortgage and large dog? She has always said she would have at least three children. It didn't happen for Kate though. I even turned into my mother at one point and started to try and find her a partner. I arranged dinner parties with 'spare males,' usually found by Michael at the hospital and perhaps not really quite up to 'Kate's standard'.

This was an expression from the past. Kate's 'bar' was set very high. Intelligence and humour were top of the wish list, followed by spiritual, sensitive, hard-working, loyal and strikingly good looking. Of course she was describing Jackson and he was the benchmark. No one could reach it or get even close. Adrian the psychologist was clever and kind and funny. They dated for a while, but he looked a bit like a short sighted version of that guy in the film, Groundhog Day. What's his name? Bill Murray that's it.

She met a musician called Will. He was good looking, funny and they had a few good nights out. But when she rang me from Glastonbury one year, knee deep in mud and grime, whilst Will's band blasted out in the background. I knew he was doomed.

'Bridge… Save me from myself, he is gorgeous, but he is so thick. I can't bear it. We were having a discussion about politics and he didn't even understand the difference between the parties. Wait for it, he actually said.'

'Labour, well, they labour don't they? Conservatives… well they conserve.'

That was it for a while. No more dating. Kate threw

herself into work and bringing up Emma. I always hoped she would meet someone and have more children. I hope I don't sound judgemental, but sometimes, only having one child, puts the focus well and truly on them. It seemed to me that Kate's life took a back seat to Emma's sometimes. Her guilt at not involving Jackson, added to the mix I think and made her want to be the best possible parent. If he had been around, maybe it would have been very different. It makes me sad to think about that now. Jackson and the two girls he would have adored. Life is cruel sometimes.

Emma's teenage years beckoned and I was still dealing with my younger children, so it was all a learning curve. She didn't really rebel though. She had some positive influences around her to deflect the tantrums. James was so laid back, he was able to discuss most things with her and although Kate was protective, she allowed Emma to be herself. What a talent she had. From a young age, she painted and by about nine or ten was making pots and bowls and other works of art. Kate was amazed at what she produced and James encouraged her to express herself.

Emma was more bohemian than either of us and we loved it. I encouraged my children to be artistic, but as they grew older I realised that Emma was gifted. I have to stop now. My throat is starting to close a little. Tears are welling up in my eyes. She wasn't my daughter, but I loved her. I wish I could say I knew what Kate was going through, but I didn't. I couldn't reach her.

The Kate I knew had gone. Who honestly knows what you would do if your child was taken from you, in that way. I like to think I wouldn't judge. It broke my heart to see Kate's broken soul. I can't even talk about the day it happened, but life was never ever the same for Kate. It was like looking at a ghost. She was there, but she wasn't there. A big part of her had gone.

I was a mother too, but my four, were walking and talking and breathing and laughing. That was the difference you see. Catholic guilt? Or is it survivor's guilt? Whatever it was, I felt it as strongly as a knife slicing through me when I looked at my friend. Emma was her life and her reason for being. Confident, independent Kate had morphed into Kate the survivor. Is that survival, maybe I would prefer the alternative?

There's no happy ending here, but let me tell you one more thing about Kate. She has a steely determination and her will to live would override any desire to end it all. Emma was too worthy and too important to be forgotten. Kate chose to live for Emma and slowly began to pick up the threads of a life.

I wish I could say we remained close, God knows we tried. Both of us did, but it became too hard for her to come round here. The house had the clutter that four children provide and the chaos of our family life. She couldn't bear it. One day maybe things will change again. She will always be my Kate and my inspiration for living.

31

Kate

2017 started badly. I hated New Year. It was a celebration I didn't want any part of. I took each day as it came, that was enough. Bridget rang me and asked me to go round to her house for dinner and drinks, but I declined and I could sense that our friendship, after so many years, was in jeopardy. Grief makes you selfish. You think everyone should understand. You hurt others to punish yourself, but it makes you feel more worthless. It's a vicious circle. I loved Bridget, but you wouldn't have known that from the way I treated her.

I had channelled my limited energies into my undemanding job. I also joined a support group. I surprised myself. I had always hated organised groups. Self-satisfied people, usually with good intentions, but not my kind of thing. I wasn't a joiner. Even at school, I hadn't been in any clubs, apart from the sports' ones. I saw myself as an individual. I would deal with my grief as an individual.

Sister Bernadette collared me in the café. She was relentless in her pursuit of saving my soul. She hadn't been brushed off by me, like so many of my friends. She came bouncing back each time and wouldn't take no for an answer. She sat in the café with her book, like a presence from a previous time. Beverley loved her and encouraged her, through cake and her homemade flapjacks. They were certainly better than anything Sister Bernie had ever produced and she could make good food when she put her mind to it.

I think they ganged up on me, but in the kindest and more thoughtful way they could imagine. I still resisted, but couldn't help but smile at their efforts to help and support me. Sister Bernadette turned up on New Year's Day clutching some leaflets. My heart sank. They were titled.

POMC... We understand.

It was a support group based in North London. Parents' of Murdered Children. No Sister Bernadette, you would have to take me kicking and screaming. What could be worse than sitting around with other people, comparing the death of your child and hearing other similar or even worse stories? It equated to another Dante Circle of Hell, as far as I was concerned.

I underestimated Sister Bernie. I did go, when she had finally worn me down. The first meeting I attended was at the home of Gillian Brown. I had seen her on TV a few months earlier, campaigning against Knife-crime. Her son Toby had been killed at his school, by an older gang, who stabbed him after he refused to give them any money. Gill was a force to be reckoned with. As she spoke to me about how she felt after his death, her grief, her guilt, I started to shake. These women and they were mostly women, were an inspiration to others. They campaigned selflessly to change laws and something they all had in common, was that they didn't want their child to have died in vain.

I started to attend the fortnightly meetings and looked forward to the warm and comforting atmosphere, created in the homes of these people, whose lives were devastated like mine. I couldn't see though, how I could do anything for Emma. A serial killer like Chappell couldn't have been predicted. He was an individual. I could see that his wife was a victim of his violence and she could have reported him. Would it have stopped him killing? Probably not.

I supported their causes with as much enthusiasm as I could muster. It gave me a focus, a purpose in life. When a man was arrested for killing his baby daughter, we went to the trial and supported the baby's mother. We were a visible force, reminding the public that terrible crimes are committed on a daily basis. Was it helping me? I can't answer that. It made me protective of those women and I would make a change, but not in the way they thought. Would I be a saviour, or just a sinner? That's a rhetorical question by the way.

I was working online at home, doing some admin for the group, when a message appeared in my email box. The sender was 'mazey@outlook.com' and my heart stopped. At least that is what it felt like as all the muscles tightened in my chest. No! Not now. What could he want? I couldn't open the email. I just stared at the screen.

Two weeks passed and I still hadn't opened the message. I had changed my email address years ago, but I suppose in 2017 it's not that difficult to find someone is it? Why did he want to find me? I took a deep breath and opened the message.

32

Sunday 26th May 1963

K ate and the Ford van arrived in Gorton and coasted to a stop, slightly ahead of a white Mini-van, at just after five-thirty, that Sunday morning. It was light already, sunrise was half an hour ago, but the street was deserted and silent. She put on black gloves, good quality kid leather and thin enough to be a second skin. She reached into the back of the van, for the flat-blade screwdriver and pliers, she had prepared in the back.

Kate's father always said that he could open any of his old cars' locks with a screwdriver. Well now was the time to find out! She quietly let herself out of the van and walked back the few paces to the Mini Traveller's back doors. She placed the screwdriver's tip into the lock and gripped the handle with her left hand. Using the pliers in her right, she gripped the screwdriver just where the shaft joined the handle. With a sharp downward push on the pliers handles the lock was forced violently through ninety degrees. The resistance it had offered was minimal. Kate placed the tools on the ground and turned the back door's lever and pulled it open.

Rummaging as quietly as was possible, she searched inside. It didn't take long to identify the long canvass bag and she knew it wasn't a fishing rod. She kept searching, she'd got the rifle, but where was the revolver? She thought they'd be together. After what seemed like an eternity of looking, she concluded that the vehicle wasn't hiding it and gave up the quest.

Closing the doors she took the tools and the rifle shaped bag back to her own van and placed them carefully under a burgundy Midland Hotel blanket.

Before departing the scene of the robbery, she had one more trick up her sleeve. Kate broke a quarter-inch piece from a matchstick and removed the dust-cap from the nearside front wheel. She pressed the soft wood into the tyre's valve until she could hear the unmistakeable hiss of it deflating. In the dawn silence the sound was deafening and she had to put the cap back on, loosely, to slow the process and dim the shrill note.

Five minutes later and the metal rim was touching the ground, so she screwed the cap back on, firmly this time. The weather was going to be fine and sunny on this particular Sunday, deliberately chosen, to make it more likely to be a Motorbike day, but she hoped that the flat tyre would further deter them from using the van. Kate called it massaging the odds and it was becoming a habit.

It was still not six o'clock and far too early for a stake out, so Kate let the car roll further down the road before turning the key. The high-compression side-valve engine wasn't quiet or smooth. Hopefully, she thought, she was far enough out of earshot of the crime to not wake anyone. She would wait elsewhere.

Kate drove up the A672 and across the moorland on an early reconnaissance mission. The bleak, dark, peaty landscape was even more desolate before they built the M62 motorway across the moor in 1970. In Bradford, a few days before, Kate had bought the 1963 equivalent of satellite navigation. She opened the Ordnance Survey map across the passenger seat, after she had parked in a lay-by, not far from Shiny Brook. She studied it to ensure she was in the place of interest.

She drove further, to check for places to park, hidden from view. It wasn't really possible to hide her bulky vehicle on the main road and impossible to drive on the undulating moor itself. She found a place just after the Ripponden Road, three and a half miles from Oldham. It had a perfect view of all the traffic going toward Saddleworth.

Kate was pleased she had come early enough, to not only observe, but to re-plan the plan. She was happy when she had plans A; B; & C, firmly locked in her head. She shivered momentarily at her own thoughts. She had been lucky that day in Bingley. Peter had almost committed suicide for her. Lady Luck should be graciously greeted when she comes your way, but never taken for granted.

It was nearly eight thirty and time to get back off the moor. At the village shop, Kate bought the Sunday Express, even though she felt she had read bits of it before. Not really hungry, but knowing this could be a long day, she scanned the shelves. The vacuum-packed, pre-prepared BLT sandwich wasn't going to be in stock for another thirty years, so she settled for cake. As Marie-Antoinette once said, 'there's nothing wrong with cake when there's no bread!' A Madeira and a Dundee, too much for her moderate appetite, but she couldn't decide. She paid seven shillings and eleven pennies for her goods and got back into her metal office on wheels.

Planning to hear mass if she had time, Kate looked at her watch. She needed to pray for forgiveness for what she had done and even more so for what she was going to do. If she hurried, she could get to St Mary's in time for the nine o'clock.

Even though she had looked it up in advance, finding the church in Union Street and parking, proved more time consuming that planned. Father Corry had already started without her, when she slipped in the back of the church and quickly took place in the last pew. The first thing she noticed was it was being celebrated in Latin. Kate was too young to have heard Mass regularly said in the language. Once a Cardinal had come to her childhood parish and he had used the Latin format. She understood nothing that day and she was struggling with it again. The only clues being the visual standards of the preparation of the gifts and the sermon was thankfully in English. Ironically, whilst Father was in the pulpit delivering the only part of the proceedings that she could have understood, her thoughts were so far away, she had no idea of the subject.

She spent the next half an hour, not really paying attention. Her mind was rehearsing the rest of a busy day. Her concentration was broken by the words: 'Pater noster qui es in caelis…'

The 'Our Father,' Kate knew that much, her mother had had the prayer hand written by a calligraphist and framed on the dining room wall. She had seen it a thousand times and knew it by heart. She also knew that if the service had reached this point, Communion would quickly follow and the bustle of parishioners going to the Alter to receive it, would divert attention from her early exit. Only a Catholic could feel guilty at leaving early she thought. She wasn't alone, a pessimistic man in a belted raincoat, held his head shamefully low and briskly made his way out into the waiting sunshine.

The Sun was well and truly up by now and should encourage the pair to go to their favourite spot. Kate started the engine and headed back down the road she had used to arrive.

173

33

Jackson

Kate,

Do you remember me? I hope so. Perhaps I am kidding myself. We spent the happiest eight months of my life in Cambridge in 1995. Where did you go? I spent so long searching for you. I bugged your friends, your tutors. I called you more times than I can remember. In the end I turned up at your place, but they said you had left. No one would give me your London address.

I had to accept you didn't want me. Part of me couldn't accept it. I knew we were meant to be together. You were the part of my heart that was gone and is still missing.

That was a long time ago. I buried myself in my work. I have to share something with you. I can't rest until I do. I don't even know why. Do you remember when we looked out at the stars on that little balcony? That telescope you bought me. I made you a promise. I told you one day we would travel through time. You laughed, but I've done it. I have done it Kate, for you. You were my inspiration. You always will be.

I hope this finds you happy and healthy. Did you marry? I expect you have a family of kids around you now and a beagle. We always said we would get a beagle. I was happy with Nostradamus, that old black cat that adopted us.

I was married, briefly, a few years ago, but I'm now divorced. The usual story. Too much work and no play made Jackson a dull boy. She was a lovely woman, but she wasn't you.

I have said too much already.

I am now in London, working on the project I have told you about. I am at the Birkbeck Institue, part of London University You can reach me here any time, if you want to. If not I'll understand.

Jackson

34

Sunday 26th May 1963

Plan A involved waiting patiently beside the road at the chosen spot, between Oldham and the A672. She parked, with Manchester behind her and using the paper and tape she had bought earlier, she covered the back windows of her van. With the engine still, she waited. Kate's lack of patience throughout her life was legendary and when she felt time-pressed, it got worse. She picked at both cakes and read a couple of less familiar stories in the newspaper.

She fidgeted away the next two hours, the van's rising temperature, even with the window open, added to the discomfort. Moving wasn't an option, they must be coming and as time passed, their arrival became more imminent. Whether it was nerves, or the real lemon lemonade she had bought and drunk, she didn't know. She cared only that she needed to wee and soon!

Casting round her surroundings for a private place to go, wasn't offering any answers. The rolling landscape gave little shelter at the spot she chosen to park. There had been scarcely a car go by in the time she had been waiting, but the Law of Sod says, as soon as you pee in public, someone will find you!

An idea came to her. She re-parked the van at a forty-five degree angle to the road. It stuck out a bit, but not enough to completely obstruct this quiet A-road. She went to the passenger side and opened it. This would shield her modesty, should a car return toward the city, at the wrong moment. Fortunately, because of the warm weather, Kate wasn't wearing a coat or a jacket. A light crew neck sweater was not in the way, finishing a couple of inches below the waistband of her black slacks. She unzipped the side opening trousers and slid them down, together with her white cotton briefs, to her ankles. She crouched facing the van's interior and relieved herself into the verge. 'Hurry up,' she thought to herself, as it seemed to take far longer than usual, until she was re-clothed.

She heard the sound of an engine behind her. 'Shit!' The indignity of her act was bad enough, but now she had launched herself in to the van with her knickers only half way up. She'd been in more embarrassing situations in her life, but she couldn't remember when. The noise got louder and passed, on the wrong side of the road, to avoid the front wing. Kate had her face pressed into the driver's seat in an effort to be invisible. She hadn't had time to shut the passenger door and the vehicle had an abandoned look about it. 'Please don't come back to investigate.'

Kate's heart rate must have topped two hundred when she lifted her head, to see the maker of the noise. The motorcycle was sixty to seventy yards ahead and it wasn't slowing down. The glint of bright blond hair, contrasted by the black half-helmet, of the pillion passenger, looked familiar. It was them!

Zipping up her trousers, she listened, until the engine note faded into the distance. There was no need to rush now. She had a fair idea where they were going. Kate re-positioned the van, but left the engine running. When she felt enough time had elapsed, she moved off, slowly behind the bikers.

Not quite two miles further, she saw their bike in a lay-by, polished and shiny in the midday sun. Kate paused at the sight, a hundred yards or so short of the machine and making a five point turn, faced back the other way. She moved slowly and stopped a quarter of a mile away on the left hand verge. She turned off the engine and gathered her thoughts. The plans in her head were checked once more and it was time.

She took the rifle from its case and the ammunition that she had found in the mini and looked closer at what she had. The 'rifle,' as it turned out, wasn't one at all. It was a single barrel and felt like it was a Ladies' shotgun and the brass cased cartridges probably buck-shot. Not exactly deadly, unless fired at very close range and aimed accurately. Another question formed in her mind. 'Had they brought the revolver?' If they had, it would be able to shoot six times and her own weapon, only once. She didn't like those odds much at all.

She replaced the gun in the back and locked all the van's doors. She re-tied the laces on her black sensibly flat-soled shoes and walked back toward the lay-by. As she got to it, she could see the bike, but not its owners. A couple of hundred yards up the slope from the road was a hillock with a tree and a stone monolith, about the size of a small car, underneath it. It didn't need Kate to be a genius to work out, this was their place.

There wasn't any sign of them on the surrounding open moorland. As Kate started to traverse the lower part of the hill, to see if she was right, a shot rang out from behind the rock. Kate's heart rate climbed again, at the knowledge that they had brought the gun and she had left hers, a quarter of a mile away. That seemed foolhardy now, though she had thought, walking up the A672 in broad daylight with a gun in her arms wasn't sensible either.

She should have turned back. She didn't know

why, but something drove her on to get a better look at the shooter. A second shot made her jump again, followed by a man's voice bellowing, 'come here with that thing!'

By the time Kate had positioned herself where she could make out two figures, under the tree, the noises had stopped. 'Why?' Kate got as close as she dared, forty or fifty yards, no more. She could just see the back of a bleached blonde head, moving rhythmically up and down and it dawned on her why the shots had stopped. 'At least the lovers are distracted enough not to see me, she thought and gained some confidence at the relief.

Voyeurism, or was it safer to keep the enemy in view? Either way, Kate watched for a while longer, half-expecting a full on love session. It wasn't to be. Clear to see from his expression and movement, it was over already. Next, the two fumbled in a backpack they had brought and two bottles and two glasses were laid out on the grass, beside them. From the motion that followed, it was obvious that a cork was being pulled. 'Wine? How very continental for the 60's.'

Wine and a motorcycle don't mix, Kate moralised and it gave her an idea, somewhere between Plans B & C. If you'd drunk that much alcohol, it wouldn't take much to lose control of it, particularly on twisty roads, would it?

Like a Ninja, Kate left her vantage point on the hill and made her way, quickly, back to the van. The new twist on the idea needed a bit of preparation. Sitting in the driving seat once more, she realised that wing-mirrors in those days, were small and mounted on the wing, not on the door. Frankly, they were useless. Trying to see anything approaching from behind, let alone accurately judge its speed, was impossible. Rethink.

She went to the back of the van and removed the paper, covering the rear windows. A noise made her rush back to the front seat. A green Triumph Herald passed without incident. Kate started the engine and drove to a section of road, where a longish downhill section of road, turned into a dog-leg left. At the bend, the right hand verge sloped down, toward a water-filled ditch. She smiled and muttered, 'excellent.'

She took the gun and blanket and put them in the front, next to her. She took two more of the lead-filled cartridges and put them in each of her slacks' side pockets and started the engine. Thankfully, she had filled the tank with petrol that morning, 3d a gallon cheaper than London. Mr Brylcream had topped up all the other fluids before delivery, so she should be able to keep the car running, long enough. She eased the van forward until she was parked about sixty yards from the bend. Adjusting the rear-view mirror, she was able to see through the back window, anything approaching from behind.

Nervous anticipation and the rising temperature of van's interior, made her wish she'd packed a more modern deodorant, to keep fresh. Never mind that, concentrate on the task, there will be work to be done, soon hopefully. As the minutes dragged by, the bright sun and the constant need to stare in the mirror, had caused her head to pound. No ibuprofen in her bag she thought, or anywhere. How did people cope in this era? Aspirin doesn't quite hit the spot.

Movement on the reflected horizon made her forget the headache. A single head-lamped, narrow vehicle was gaining ground. 'Here goes!' Clutch depressed twice, she rammed the Ford gear stick into first and accelerated the van forward. She tried to get the timing right, too quick and he would tuck in behind. Too slow, he would pass before the bend.

After thirty yards she lost sight of them. They were in the other lane and attempting to overtake, she hoped. If so, it's perfect. 'Now,' she said to herself and braked hard, turning the wheel to the right to serve into the path of the bike. So much so that she nearly drove herself over the edge and she fought with the big wheel to stay on the road. As she did so, she sensed the shiny machine passing her on the right. One of the two young people on-board was screaming as it left the road.

By the time Kate's vehicle had skidded to a stop, the motorcycle and riders were halfway to the Brook and the man in front was losing his fight for control. Taking the gun, Kate left the van, crossed the road and onto the moor. As she reached the verge, she saw the front wheel suddenly drop at least a foot down. The violent stop, that the gulley or ditch had caused, was enough to throw both passengers in differing, but similar trajectories. The girl travelled further than the man. Weight difference, or catapult effect? Who knows or cares, but it wasn't necessarily a fatal crash.

As she ran down the bank behind them, Kate could see the male had landed, skull first, on a stony outcrop and was lying motionless and bleeding from more than one part of his head. Her attention turned to the other victim. She too had landed badly, but on her side and on softer ground. She was rolling and screaming in pain, clutching her right arm. Although without medical training, Kate knew a dislocated shoulder when she saw one. Someone less tough would probably have blacked out with the pain, but not this one.

She didn't see Kate until she was only a few feet

away. When she did, rage overtook pain.

'You stupid cow, look what you've done!'

Kate didn't speak. She lifted the gun and moved closer. A new expression formed on the casualty's face. Rage gave way to terror. Her subconscious must have been saying… 'Revolver in backpack' to her, because the one-armed woman grimaced with pain as she tried to reach behind her with the remaining good limb. As she did so, the right one fell limply, further from its socket.

Screaming again, she stopped trying and moved to support the stricken arm. Kate thought that maybe to shoot this sorry creature, was too good for her. Suffer longer maybe? Being Catholic, or not, didn't influence her decision. She needed to move quickly, sooner or later someone would stop to investigate the accident.

She looked at the woman, girl really. She looked younger than the photos. Make up badly applied, but still a face that could belong to a teenager. She thought of Emma. She moved forward.

She brought the barrel to within three feet, of the roaring, platinum-haired fiend and squeezed the trigger. Two ounces of lead vaporised in the chamber and the roaring stopped. Kate had shut her eyes as she fired and had turned away before re-opening them, so she never saw the mess she had made of the familiar features.

Kate moved briskly across the five or six yards of moor, towards the male, broke the gun and reloaded. Surprisingly calmly she closed the gun and put it behind her prey's right ear. Closing her eyes again, she whispered, 'this one's for the children' and squeezed a second time. Her ears were still ringing as she tossed the weapon into the Tarn, some hundred yards away and returned to the road. She had to pause to be sick at the side of the road, not at the sight of what she had done, but at the thought of the sight of what she had done.

Before removing the kid gloves for the last time that afternoon, she tossed the remaining ammunition out of the open window. 'Get the Hell out of here,' she urged herself and headed back toward the city.

35

Kate

W as he mad? I checked the address. It seemed genuine. My heart was racing. I started checking the internet. I hadn't looked him up for a long time, long before Emma went to University. Wikipedia had included a photo this time that stared down at me, hair still curling around his shoulders, eyes just as bright, a few laughter lines around his eyes, but there he was, still Jackson.

His CV was impressive. He was a Professor at the Birkbeck Institute of London University. During the last few years, he had been given awards for his work in 'Movement of Time' research. What the hell? Surely if he had managed that feat, it would be all over the papers. People would be queuing up to go back in time. Visit their relatives, see Elvis perform. You couldn't keep that sort of discovery quiet. Could you? His email intrigued me in more than one way. I was desperate to see him, but how could I? I would have to tell him about Emma. I will break his heart for a second time. By the way Jackson, we have a daughter. Oh yes, but you can't meet her she's dead. She was murdered. Sorry.

Hours passed, memories flooded back to me. I felt as if I was on automatic pilot. I decided to go to his office. I couldn't keep away. I couldn't think of anything else. I didn't tell James and Francesca, they wouldn't have approved. I didn't live with them anymore, I had my own flat now, so thankfully they wouldn't find out. They still believed Jackson had deserted me in my time of need. I didn't correct them. Another lie. Layer upon layer, how subtly we change the truth to suit ourselves.

I dressed carefully, although I didn't quite understand the occasion. After so many years apart it couldn't be classed as reconciliation. Just two old friends, meeting up? It felt more somehow. I had my own agenda. You probably know that.

This meeting could change everything. Change the world.

I allowed my unruly curls to make a return for the day. How would he remember me? I slipped on a white tee shirt and jeans, hang on who was I kidding. I'm forty-two not twenty-two. I threw the clothes aside and slipped on a dress I had bought for a party that I didn't attend. It was olive green, hugged the right places and was as classy as anything I owned at that time. Grief doesn't work as a fashion statement and it was a long time since I'd been shopping for clothes. I pulled on a pair of black leather boots, found a scarf belonging to Francesca that I had borrowed at some point and made my way to the tube.

I rang the University's main number and asked to speak to him. A female voice said, 'hang on I will put you through.' I hung up. He was there. I entered the building. It was glass and chrome and very impressive. Money didn't mean anything to Jackson. Well it didn't in a previous life. He was on the top floor. I took a deep breath and walked through the reception doors.

Is it possible to see Jackson Maze please? I haven't got an appointment. Yes, my name's Kate McLean. How this could be a University, there was obviously money for research these days. How times have changed.

He hadn't changed as much as I envisaged. A little older, but the years could have been crueler. He looked taller than I had remembered, despite my heels. His eyes, still the same piercing blue, smiled at me in genuine pleasure and mine returned the compliment. 'How have you been Kate?' He said in the slow southern drawl that I recognised so well.

I couldn't speak. The words were stuck in my throat. Cool, calm collected Kate had become a gibbering wreck in his presence. I pulled myself together. 'Where do I start?' I said, almost shyly.

We went to a small Trattoria, a few streets away from the sterile offices. Over a glass of house red, I began to relax. Wanting to pinch myself, I felt as if I was seeing a ghost. As he started to tell me about his life and his work, his hand closed over mine and I felt the warmth of the man that I had loved for so many years.

He told me about his return to the USA and how he had tried so hard to find me, returning to Cambridge, desperate to tell me how he felt.

'I made the biggest mistake of my life, leaving you there,' he declared, 'and yet, if I hadn't, I don't know if I would have made the discovery that is my life's work.'

Honest to a fault, that was Jackson. He told me.

'Our love was all consuming, I couldn't think of anything but you, but maybe it wasn't healthy? I don't know?'

I made noises in agreement. I had to hold on to my pride in this strange situation. I had planned my speech, but as I began to say the words, I wondered if I was making the worst decision in my life, again.

'Look Jackson, it wasn't your fault. I didn't want to be found. I couldn't be the person you wanted anymore.'

I gulped as I told him that after he left I received some devastating news. My mother Francesca had died, tragically in a road accident. Leaving James and I bereft, in a pit of grief and despair. Well that part was true anyway, but not for the reasons I was telling him. The plan I was formulating had formed in my head, the minute I began to take in the contents of his letter.

'Oh my God baby. Why didn't you come to me? I would have been there for you.'

I felt sick with the lies that were pouring from me in a torrent. 'I couldn't face anything, Jackson. I just wanted to curl up and die. My beautiful talented Francesca had gone and part of me had gone with her.'

I told him I had spent years getting over her death and my emotions had simply dried up with grief. I had nothing to give him. He seemed to accept my explanation, his own mother had passed away two years ago and the empathy he felt, seemed genuine. I didn't deserve it. What kind of cold hearted bitch was I? What about Emma you are thinking. Please believe me when I tell you there was a motive to my madness. A slow burning spark of hope that was building with everything he told me.

We looked at each other over the table. A waiter brought us plates of spaghetti. Neither of us could eat a mouthful. The emotions were overwhelming, hanging in the space between us. Where do we go from here?

Trying to appear normal, I asked Jackson to tell me about his work. He changed, his voice changed and I sensed how important this was to him. Professor Maze, the Nobel nominated physicist was talking and I was mesmerized by what he was telling me. Over the past twenty-odd years, he had spent all his waking moments on his theory of time travel. He started to explain to me, the basis of the whole experiment. I was careful not to let my eyes glaze over and feigned understanding of all that he told me.

He explained that whilst working on Quarks & Hadrons at the 'Collider,' under the Swiss countryside, they (the team) had proved the existence of the elusive 'Higgs-Bosun' particle. By now that was common knowledge, but apparently two years later they discovered particles so infinitely small they weren't visible to any equipment. They also had some strangely unique properties. Almost in ghostly way they could pass through anything, even the traditional barriers like lead and concrete. They could travel wherever they were directed.

They needed a name for them. One of the researchers came in excitedly one morning, saying that the word 'Obilium' had come to him in a dream. When it was checked into every search engine, it turned out that the word didn't exist in any language or form, worldwide. So the 'Obilium' was born.

Jackson went on to explain that whilst the other researchers were just happy to make the discovery, he was looking for uses. A life-long student of the works and teachings of Nostradamus, he decided this could be the way to test the 'concentric circles of time' theory. Although Jackson thought that time might be more like spherical layers, which he described to my non-scientific mind as being like the skin of an onion.

After leaving Switzerland and taking up the post in London, he no longer had two and a half billion pounds worth of (seventeen mile long) tunnel to play with. It took him over a year to develop the linear accelerator. An electro-magnetic equivalent of a ruby laser, it was capable of firing a beam of particles without the need for such a large circular accelerator.

That was the breakthrough moment. He then built a three metre high, Cheops pyramid in Glass and mounted the new devices in each of the five corners. The idea came to him when he remembered something that he had read as a twelve year old, in Dr Lyall Watson's amazing book, 'Supernature.' The Cheops shape has mystical properties when used in conjunction with a plinth, inside it, at a height of one third that of the pyramid's height.

Vaporising objects into Obilium wasn't difficult. The hard part was harnessing and directing the resulting particles into a usable beam. I'm going to spare you the lengthy explanation, mainly because it was at this point that my ability to follow the science left the room.

The short version is that Jackson solved the puzzle and began sending fruit-flies back in time, by firing the fly's DNA encoded Obilium into the earth's crust. The early experiments were only for a few minutes, but because of the precise life cycle of the insect it was possible to be surprisingly accurate. Plants which had had their growth monitored were sent back and retrieved to further test and calibrate the experiments.

The early retrievals didn't go too well. Missing leaves and other imperfections, meant long hours working on encoding and decoding programmes. They're a sort of organic, Zip and Unzip type function. I could grasp that bit. To make Jackson's life a bit easier, he discovered that that strength of beam's output was directly proportional to the amount of time traversed.

Eventually it became precise enough to send and retrieve items perfectly to any time in history. I was elated.

The clever gorgeous man had cracked it.

36

Beverley

The Kate that I met, sitting in my small cosy café, was probably not the Kate that you know. When I talked to others about her, particularly Sister Bernie, it was hard to connect the contradictions. I didn't see the confident Kate, the Probation Officer, the academic, the mother. I saw a woman who had lost her way.

Her eyes haunted me and I recognised instantly that the life-force had literally been taken from her. What was left was a shell. Despite her frame, she looked frail and as she ordered a coffee and sat down to read a book, or a paper, it was clear that she wasn't taking anything in. She was going through the motions of a life. A life not worth living, it would seem.

I know that feeling well. I could recognise a kindred spirit when I saw one. She wasn't quite a zombie, but there was nothing for her to connect to. She was clinging on to life by her finger nails. They would have been polished a shiny red and manicured beautifully at one time, I guessed. Now they were bitten to the quick and made nervy movements, as she tried to relax.

I needed to know her story. The desire to sooth, to comfort and to understand is an intrinsic part of my makeup. I have tried to change, harden up and look after number one, but somehow it has never really worked. I can't help myself. Kate looked like a wounded animal, one I would have rescued from the shelter, given the opportunity. She drew me in and I began to understand.

I was always one for a lost cause, even as a child, when I was growing up in a part of London, not yet gentrified, or easy on the eye. To be more precise, it was a rough council estate in Leyton. I could see the poverty that surrounded me, I could smell it. Poverty has a strange odour if you are not familiar with it. It's a combination of unwashed clothes, cheap food cooking on the stove and cigarette smoke and it never seems to leave.

You can scrub the floor, bleach it even, wash your clothes and yourself, but it hangs around like an unwanted visitor. My parents worked hard to get away from the estate. There was a stigma that was attached to you when you mentioned where you came from. The crime and the drugs were destroying what had been a working class community.

Eventually we moved into our own house, a few miles away in distance, but a million miles in reality. I couldn't forget where I came from though, it shaped me into wanting to help, make things better and I suppose gave me a sense of who I was. It wasn't a bad childhood by a long stretch and I appreciated what I did have. Solid, stable parents that loved me and wanted the best for me. Their values separated them from some of our neighbours.

I saw other families, at close range, where this wasn't the case. I could hear the arguments, the screams, the flying and then broken crockery. I saw the next day the bruises, the downcast eyes and the embarrassment. It made me feel sad inside.

There were friends' homes that I wasn't invited to, under any circumstances. They were too ashamed. Some were unable or unwilling to escape their destiny.

Unwanted pregnancies, more poverty and history repeating itself. Only a few had enough fire in their bellies to get away and made their mark on the world. Quite an accomplishment given their adversity.

I was always described as a bit eccentric and even at a young age, I stood out. My secondary school demanded a certain type of dress, accent and behaviour, in order to cope with the social setting that it provided. I was a hippy born too late. This was a time before the Goths, the radicals and the free thinkers that are more prevalent today. You needed to fit in to avoid being labelled a 'freak' or a 'weirdo.'

My clothes came from Oxfam before it was fashionable to shop there. Vintage didn't quite exist in East London in the seventies and I didn't want to be a Punk either. That scene seemed too aggressive and too violent for my caring nature. I would listen to Pink Floyd and Deep Purple whilst my friends were screaming to the twanging guitars of The Bay City Rollers. Still, there was Marc Bolan, which was a compromise.

I coped somehow. I wasn't a victim and had enough of a sense of my own identity to ward off the bullies. There are always bullies. You can easily spot them at school. Sometimes it's harder to spot them in the adult world. They can hide under a veneer of charm, confidence and control.

After we moved house, I continued to travel to my old school. I didn't want to change school at that stage because it was nearly time for my O-levels. It kept me grounded. I made some friends that are still in my life today. I continued to wear my embroidered trousers, my kaftan tops and my dangly silver earrings from Peru.

I am not ashamed to say it's a style of dress that I

haven't changed much over the years. I loved shops that imported clothes from India and suchlike, particularly if it helped the countries involved. I wasn't concerned if the clothes didn't conform to trend. Buck the trend was my motto and I was more interested in people and cultures, than fashion or music.

I wasn't perfect. It came to my parent's attention that the smell emanating from my bedroom was not patchouli, or any kind of joss stick. Whilst my friends were indulging in their newfound interests in drinking, through pubs and nightclubs, I was hanging around with an older group. They lived in a local commune, where the drug of choice was cannabis.

I started to smoke it when I was seventeen, deciding it was healthier than alcohol and I thought it helped me get in touch with myself. I liked getting stoned, sitting around with my group of drop-outs, discussing the topics of the day. Usually the issues were around poor housing, the Tory government's failures, the rise of feminism and women's rights and the move towards equality.

All the men in the group were political in some way or another. They had taken over the house in Notting Hill in the sixties after it had been left empty for some years. People came and went, but the house remained a squat, or commune as we preferred to call it. My eccentricity worked for me there and I felt at home. I didn't know what I wanted to do with my life and this was somewhere I could be without pressure.

Of course my parents hated it. They hated the very notion of it. Their belief was that you worked for what you had and that 'Thatcher' was right to sell off London's housing stock, to those who had the right to buy. I soon tired of arguing with my father and fighting with my mother about our choices of lifestyle.

I decided to leave home and move into the commune, full time. I had scraped passes at some A-level qualifications, but had no idea what to do with my life. They were outraged at my lifestyle choice. I started to feel that they had never understood me, or what I was about. Emotionally and physically, I moved away from them and from then on my life began to spiral in another direction.

I thought I was worldly and sophisticated at nineteen years old. How wrong was I? I had the self-belief of my youth and felt that I had made an alternative lifestyle choice that would set me apart from my dull and unadventurous parents, who were trapped in the 'system.' We could all look after each other and form an alternative society that wouldn't make the same mistakes. We would welcome people of different colours and religions and we would be self-sufficient.

I loved the garden in Notting Hill and the fresh vegetables that Robin, the designated caretaker of it, cultivated. Rosie who cooked most days, made bread and cakes and we all mucked in to complete our jobs. We would all be equal. I wonder where have I heard that before?

When I first joined it seemed idyllic. The first hot summer was spent in the gardens and I enjoyed the tranquillity of the private, special space within an urban setting that was such a contrast. We tie-dyed T-shirts and made alternative designs to sell at the Portobello's Saturday market.

I guess there was around ten of us when I joined. Everyone seemed to have a place, a role to play. Two of the guys went off to do labouring work, outside the unit. That brought in extra money for food, for clothes and for cannabis. We decided against growing our own, it was too risky. We knew the local police and residents were starting to resent our presence in the property. By the early eighties, property prices were booming and we were in a six-bedroomed house that would have been attractive to the wealthy buyers coming into the area. The council left us alone for the most part. We kept the house clean and well maintained and as the council regularly changed their policies, we were just one of many groups of squatters on their books that got overlooked.

The winds of change started to blow through the commune and although initially, the changes were slight, I began to sense major ones on the horizon. The sense of community slowly started to diminish. Some of the older residents, who were the mainstay of the place, moved on. To other places in Cornwall, Scotland or somewhere more rural and less chaotic. There had always been a stable foundation for the commune, created by the true free-thinkers and more altruistic members, but this was now threatened.

Cannabis, always prevalent, was joined by ecstasy and then cocaine. The place became somewhere to use drugs and latterly, to buy drugs. John and Grant came into the commune from prison. We had agreed to give them a chance. They needed somewhere to live and start their lives. Eventually they were joined during most of the days by other like-minded people, who didn't want to work at all and saw the place as a chill out zone.

I continued to work outside in the grounds and helped in the kitchen, but I started to resent some of the others, who treated us like second class citizens. It seemed as if the women were doing the work and men were watching them do it.

I was still a loose cannon in many senses. I had no ambition and didn't know what I wanted in life. Smoking cannabis regularly didn't help. It left me more lethargic and lacking in motivation. I had a short relationship with a man from Kingston, Jamaica. He was living with his brother in a nearby property and we met at a party, at the squat.

He wasn't good for me. At first he made me feel incredibly special and different. He would listen intensely to what I was saying and for a while I started to believe it might be something lasting, but after a few weeks of intense sexual liaisons, he moved on. He didn't break my heart, but he hardened it. Men were all a waste of space.

Six months later I gave birth to a baby boy. I was twenty four and by then I was using cocaine, to stay awake. Everything went into free fall. I tried to be a good mother, but the only friends I seemed to have left at that point were fellow squatters. We were held together by circumstances, rather than true friendship.

The pain never goes away. My son died when he was ten months old. The authorities said it was a cot death. They said it with disdain, as they looked around my living conditions and at the wide eyed vacant young woman that I had become. Had I left him too long? Was I high on something in the other room as he took his last breath? I will never know.

That's when my life changed. It had to. Alongside my grief and hysteria at Ashley's death, I could see the stark reality of my life; claiming benefits, living amongst liars and thieves, blotting out my problems with cannabis and cocaine. I had brought a small life into the world and he was dead because of my lifestyle and the problems that were of my own making.

I woke up in a bright hospital room with the glare of the fluorescent lights blinding me. I was alive. 'Fuck,' I thought. I can't even do suicide properly. I saw my mother's face at the door as soon as soon as she realised I had woken up. 'Bev, you're coming home with me.' And I did.

I went to the local Polytechnic and did a social work course. I sorted out my life as best I could. I then spent the next twenty five years helping those people whose lives had spiralled out of control, just as mine had. I worked with drug addicts in South London, giving out free needles and advice. I worked from clinics and hospitals and tried to make a change.

I had some respect from my clients, probably because they sensed I had once been in their shoes. My passion became people and I saw my only purpose in life was to help others and to change their lives.

As a community social worker, my eyes were opened wider than I believed possible. I sometimes worked a twelve hour day, as emergencies, usually unpredictable, could take you into the early hours. My parents were finally happy that I'd made something of my life. As I collected my CBE from Queen Elizabeth for my work in the community, I realised that in the end, it was myself I'd been saving.

Neighbours of a Stockwell squat had rung the centre to say they had heard a baby crying, but when they knocked on the door, no one answered. I went to the property with a new colleague, Sonja, who had only started in the job a few weeks before. She was still training and she still had the naïve enthusiasm that she would soon lose. The front door was locked, but I looked under a nearby flower pot and found a rusty key. The door opened and we entered the house.

As we walked into the front room, the all too familiar aroma of strong 'skunk' stung my eyes, as they squinted to focus on something moving in the corner of the room. The smoky room had recently been occupied I guessed, but the sight in the corner made my eyes sting with another emotion entirely.

In a dirty, wicker dog's basket with a grubby blanket, lay an infant, probably about eight months old. His screaming had reduced to a hoarse whimpering, as I picked him up. The smell of urine permeated his silky brown skin and his eyes looked into mine, with both fear and hunger.

'Phone the Police Sonja,' I barked.

I looked down at the little boy. It dawned on me at that moment that I couldn't do that job anymore. I had to get out.

You can guess the rest, or at least you can guess how I felt. I wanted a second chance at motherhood. I wouldn't throw it away a second time. I wanted to take that little man and run. And never come back. To give him the life he deserved. Instead, I handed him over to the authorities and the next day I resigned from my job. I started fostering children, but found it so hard to let them go. It was too late to be a mother again.

I borrowed some money from Barclays bank and opened the café. I had always been a vegetarian and the area was becoming affluent. It was the right place and the right time.

I poured all my energies into the project. I loved getting up early and baking the bread. Before I met Kate I was doing most of it single-handedly, apart from a few hours help I had, mid-morning. I couldn't afford anyone really. I was baking cakes and making some vegetarian savouries that I had been turning out for years. Business was growing and I needed someone I could trust. We started talking on the first day she came into the café, but it took her about fifteen further visits before she opened up to me. She and I both knew that the pain in her eyes came from her soul. When I eventually told her about Ashley, we cried together. I asked her to work for me. She agreed. It was a breakthrough.

After the first time we talked about him, I asked her not to mention my son again. It was too painful. I focussed on Kate and her healing. It gave me a purpose and I was able to find a group that I thought might help her. We spent hours in the kitchen and in the café talking and putting the world to rights. It didn't change anything, but it was a safe haven, as they say, in a heartless world. A cliché, but she needed something that I couldn't provide, forgiveness. Somehow she felt she had let down Emma. Kate, I know that feeling all too well. We can't forgive ourselves, so we just go on trying to make the world a bit better place.

Sister Bernadette, well she tried as well. We were a team trying to re-build Kate. It didn't really work, but she was and is always grateful for our support, our love and our friendship. Our sisterhood has given my life some meaning back too and I hope the same could be said for Kate.

Something has happened recently. I would like to think I am an intuitive person and I know Kate better than most. She has been back in touch with Jackson, I know that much, but that's not enough to explain the light that has returned to her eyes. I expect she will tell me eventually. In her own good time.

37

Sunday 26th May 1963

Since coming off the moors and heading south to Stalybridge, Kate had noticed a strange noise coming from the front of the van. It started as an intermittent squeak. Not a very loud or continuous one at first. She hoped it would go away. It didn't. The noise worsened to a constant squeal. By the time she reached Hazel Grove, there was a problem developing. The steering felt strange and the van felt as though it wanted to crab sideways. Kate's mind rewound back to Saddleworth Moor. She remembered that when turned to the verge to force the motorcycle over it, the front offside wheel hit the grass verge. Had it been hard enough to damage something?

It seemed so. Kate was getting anxious. The problem had got worse over the last twenty-five minutes and she still had more than two hundred and fifty miles to go.

London wasn't a whimsical destination. She had to be there today, even if it was late evening. Monday's plan was vitally important to her whole being. She couldn't let a spot of car trouble interfere with it. Her mind was racing. If she had gone to Manchester she might have been able to catch a train to London, but she was in the wilds of Cheshire. Piccadilly station was almost thirty miles behind her and Crewe was too far ahead to guarantee arrival in a sick vehicle. What if it stops all together? The AA and RAC didn't have recovery vehicles yet. She was feeling tense now. She had owned a mobile phone for almost thirty years. What would she give to have one now.

Passing Poynton Park on the London road, at a sedate thirty miles an hour, the steering was just about manageable. Something on the right hand side of the road caught her eye. It was the end of a runway.

'A runway?' Back of brain was screaming at the frontal lobes. Runway means planes. Planes mean transport, long distance transport. She couldn't ignore the signals.

Kate turned the van round carefully, so as not to make things worse and drove back to have a better look. Sure enough there were buildings, hangers and planes dotted around the apron. Decision made, she went back to the last crossroads and turned left into Chester road. This time she noticed a small sign saying Woodford Aerodrome. Three quarters of a mile later she found the entrance on the left. The van limped into the site and stopped at the Car park area. Not a very big space, but there were only two other cars. A Wolseley and a Hillman.

Kate got out, taking her handbag with her. She needed it if she was to pay for a pilot. She scanned the field. The administrative block and offices seemed a good place to start. Empty, deserted and shut. 'Of course, it's Sunday, but surely those cars belong to someone,' she thought.

Further away at the edge of the runway, Kate could see a fuel bowser and a tall brick building with windows all round at the top. The control tower of course, if anyone's here they would be in there. She walked across the narrow concrete path.

When she reached the doors at the bottom of the brick edifice, she knocked. No answer. She opened it and called in. 'Hello, anyone here?' Still silence. Undeterred she climbed three flights of stairs. On the top landing was another door. Solid wood, with a plaque that warned:

CONTROL TOWER
AERODROME PERSONNEL ONLY

She had come this far and desperation drove her on. She knocked firmly on the door. Before she could knock again, it was opened.

A bespectacled man in his fifties, wearing a crumpled suit and tie said. 'Can I help you miss?'

'I certainly hope so,' she replied. 'I want to charter a plane.'

'I suggest then madam that you come back after nine tomorrow and see Mrs Perkins in the office. She will take a booking for you.'

'No, no, you don't understand, I mean today. Now in fact.'

'The man laughed. Today, that's impossible. It's Sunday afternoon. All the commercial pilots are at home sleeping off their lunch, I don't doubt and the private pilots haven't really started their summer Sunday flying yet. The weather's still a bit chilly at ten thousand feet. So unfortunately, I can't really help.'

Kate wasn't giving up easily. 'I've got money. Can't you phone someone? Ask them to name their price?'

'Look lady, I'm just a weekend Air Traffic Control supervisor. It's a hobby. I'm a librarian the rest of the week. I don't have the pilots' addresses or phone numbers. I just need a flight plan from them and I help them take off and land. We don't socialise together.'

Hopes were fading when a thought crossed her

mind. 'There were two cars in the car park when I got here. Whose are they?'

'The blue Hillman Imp is mine and the Black Wolsley belongs to Mad Hugh Evans. Why?'

'Well, I can see what you're here for, but why is Mr Evans on the airfield'

'Oh I see what you mean. Yes. He's working on an old Autogyro that he's restoring.'

'Is that why he's mad?' Kate enquired with a puzzled expression.

'Yes and no. That thing he flies is the maddest thing you'll ever see in the skies, but his nickname goes back to 1944. He volunteered to fly a hedge-hopping mission in Holland, to photograph German emplacements round the bridge at Arnhem. He was the fourth to try, the other three never came back.'

'Really?'

'So I suppose he might just take you. He still likes an adventure.'

'Can we ask him if he'll take me?' She had pleading face on.

The man laughed again, even harder this time. 'You can if you wish, but I can't leave my post up here until seven o'clock this evening. But know this. I wouldn't get in that thing of his with him, even if you offered me a thousand guineas. He's mad and his plane or helicopter thing is even stranger than him.'

He was still chuckling to himself as Kate shut the door behind her and started descending the stairs to ground level. Her mind was racing ahead. She'd been told where to find Mr Evans and she made her way over to the hanger. When she got there the huge doors were open a few feet and she went in. Inside she could see a number of different flying machines, but no sign of life.

A noise from the far end, like a metal spanner being dropped, focussed her attention towards the left hand corner of the room. When she got there she couldn't believe what she was looking at.

The strangest looking machine she had ever seen lay before her. It was a museum piece. It had wings, but it had another appendage. What looked like helicopter rotary blades were stuck on the top of it. It was as if it couldn't make up its mind about its identity. She could see why a thousand guineas or even twice that, might not entice anyone less than a complete lunatic.

Kate hovered on the spot. She was weighing up whether she was lunatic enough. A quick glance at her watch told her it was twenty past three and the day was running away from her. She decided yes, she was lunatic enough.

'Hello,' she called loud enough for an echo to come back from the building's metal walls.

A head of dark wavy hair and a ruddy complexion poked out of the fuselage.

'Are you wanting me?' The voice was more welsh than 'Sir Tom.' Kate stopped herself from saying the mad word. 'I'm looking for Hugh Evans.'

'That's me and who might you be?'

'My name is Rebecca Grant and I'm in need of rescuing. I've been told that you are my very best hope.'

'I don't think I've ever been called that before.' He answered in a Valley's lilt. 'Best hope of what?'

'My car is making strange noises and I've got to get to London…. Tonight.'

Mad Hugh laughed. 'Being laughed at was getting depressingly familiar,' thought Kate.

'If I'm your best hope you could be in trouble young lady,' said the man she guessed to be in his mid to late forties.

'Please help,' she implored. 'I'm desperate for someone to take me. My daughter is emigrating to Australia in the morning and it's my last chance to see her before she goes.' It was the best thing she could think of to play on the welshman's heart strings. Just to make sure, she added. 'I'll pay whatever you ask.'

By now Hugh had climbed down to floor level. He paused, pulling a face that looked a bit like he was chewing a toffee. Kate tried not to fidget. If she pressured him the deal could be off. Before Hugh could speak Kate cranked up the charm offensive another notch. 'That is the finest flying machine I have ever seen, what is it?'

Hugh wasn't saying much up until this point, but Kate had clearly hit the 'proud aviator' button at exactly the right moment.

'It's an ex-army Avro 671 Rota MK1 designed by the late great Juan de la Cierva. It's got a seven cylinder.......'

Kate interrupted as gently as she could. 'Why does it look so different?'

'Well', Hugh was winding up for another history lesson, 'the design combines the stability of fixed-wing flight with the versatility of rotor-bladed lift capability.'

Kate stared.

'That means you cannot stall it. You cannot spin it and it's easier to land because you can come down from any height, without having to perfectly judge the ground.'

'Genius,' said Kate.

'Certainly if he hadn't died so young, there would be thousands of Autogiros buzzing around.'

Trying not to think of how he may have died, Kate

smiled and said. 'I would be honoured if you would take me up in her.'

'Do you mean it?' He had a quizzical tone. 'Most people laugh at her.'

'I most certainly do mean it,' said Kate crossing her fingers behind her back, 'please take me to London.'

Hugh looked thoughtful. There was hope. 'Whereabouts have you got to go?'

'As close to West London as you can get me.'

'I used to fly down to Hanwell Airpark for Autogiro events until they closed it. I know the way well enough, but I won't get permission to enter West London air airspace, now that Heathrow Airport has got so busy.

'Oh,' said Kate looking disappointed.

'I would need to file a flight plan days in advance and for better reasons than a leisure flight, to get them to agree.'

'Where could you take me?'

'Don't know yet, I haven't a lot of fuel in the tanks.'

'I saw a fuel truck on my way over to you. Can't we fill her up?'

'Maybe, but I'm supposed to put in a requisition and wait for ground crew to do it.'

Kate looked at him with pleading eyes. 'I'll buy you all the petrol on the truck if you do this and give you enough to spoil Mrs Evans when you get back.'

'I'd have to find her first and…'

'Oops,' thought Kate. 'Change the subject.'

'Would a hundred cover it?' She opened her bag and started to count out five pound notes.

'Cover it! ' Hugh said in disbelief. 'It's not that thirsty. A few pounds worth would fill her up. Mind you, even when fully fuelled she will only have a range of about three hundred miles. That's not enough for a round trip.'

Kate looked around the hanger for inspiration. 'What if we filled up a couple of those?' She pointed to a couple of olive-green, military type, jerry-cans. The never say die Kate had an answer for everything today. She was starting to feel confident that her mission was back on track. The lovely, but possibly mad Hugh Evans was putty in her hands. Well almost.

38

Kate

It sounded unbelievable, like something out of a science fiction novel, but I believed this man. I trusted him with my whole being. Surreal as it may have been, I knew I'd found the answers that I was looking for.

As he paused to look at me and smile again, I asked him the question that had been on my lips for the previous hour and a half. We were the only couple left in the restaurant by this time.

'Have you tried it out with a real person?' I knew the answer by looking at his face. Like a proud parent with the child he had created, his lifetime achievement.

'Yes of course baby, but if I tell you about that I might have to kill you.' He grinned. 'But if you agree to have dinner with me tomorrow night, I might just change my mind.'

I coyly accepted, not wanting to appear over keen. He turned up at the bar where we had arranged to meet, looking delicious in an exquisite suit.

'Get you in your fancy outfit.' I said mockingly, when I really wanted to say, 'let's skip dinner.'

'Do you like it? When I got nominated for the Nobel Prize and had to attend the ceremony last December, I went to my favourite Saville Row tailor and he worked his magic. I looked like a winner on the night, even if I was overlooked and they gave the award to an 'energy conservation project.' I wasn't too upset. I couldn't have published all my findings anyway. People have been killed for what for they know over the years and I still haven't decided if this should be made public knowledge.'

We took it slowly this time, no rushing to his bed with the irrepressible passion of youth. We both knew this was important and neither of us wanted to break the spell. I was terrified on two levels, one that my feelings would run away with me and I would have to tell him the truth about Emma. I couldn't risk it at this stage. Secondly that he would go away again, taking away the thing that I craved more than anything in the world. The secrets that he held in his laboratory could change my life and his forever.

I have never been a schemer, but I became one. I allowed Jackson to fall in love with me again. Somehow I just managed to hold something back. A part of me that I thought had gone forever the day my daughter died. I would one day be able to allow Jackson into that part of my heart that was sealed more tightly than the secrets in his journals. Together we had created a child, but individually, he had created a miracle. A breakthrough that could change everything. One day, I thought, not too long now.

We sat in his high-ceilinged loft near the University. It was winter now. Miraculously a log fire burned in the grate and warmed the air, despite the size of the building. We curled up on the massive sofa, he had purchased in my honour. I think previously he had sat in a big old chair and worked into the night. We made the loft into a home. Our home, our life together had started again.

We had just eaten lobster, drank a chilled bottle of wine and started to talk about the concept of time travel for the umpteenth time. What could you do? How could you change history? Would you want to? Would it be dangerous? We mused about history and the power of the 'pyramid.'

He was the scientist, I was the philosopher. It made a heady combination. He could take me where I wanted to go, but he hadn't worked out in his mind if it was ethical. Had he created a monster? He was such a moral guy, he cared for people. If he hadn't created 'the time-machine,' he would have looked for a cure for cancer. He only wanted to make things better.

He was well aware that in the wrong hands, his creation could cause havoc. Some power-crazed dictator could easily take over the world, without a moment's hesitation. Supreme power, in the hands of a humble man, from a farm in California. Life is strange isn't it?

I kept up the pretence of being obsessed with my mother's death and its impact on me. It wasn't hard. I just kept thinking of Emma and twisted round the scenario. I wasn't faking my feelings though. The emotions I was expressing were genuine. 'Forgive me Francesca,' I whispered to myself and to my mother.

On Christmas Eve, we made love for the first time since Jackson had left Cambridge. He cried tears of joy, of love and peace. I lay next to him hearing and feeling his heart. It was the happiest moment I had felt since I lost Emma. The guilt overwhelmed me, I hadn't allowed her to see her father and how could I be lying here with him, bathed in a glow of love. I turned to face him. As I kissed his face, he looked up to me. 'Did you keep the telescope?' I asked him.

'What do you think?' He winked as he said it.

We gazed up at a new night, a new beginning, the stars hadn't changed and they were the same stars we had looked at, on our last night together in Cambridge. The truth in our stars, destiny had played a part in our reunion. I hadn't planned that miracle.

'Let me go back,' I whispered. He looked at me. He didn't have to ask why or where at that stage. He knew me so well. Would he want to risk losing me again? Would he think I was a mad woman? His voice was slow and deliberate.

'Your mother,' he said.

'Yes I sobbed. Let me see her. Let me tell her the future. I can tell her to stay home on that fateful day. Please Jackson.' I implored him.

He looked at me intently. 'I can't Kate. I can't risk losing you again. The only human I ever sent back in time stayed there.'

My face and heart sank. 'It killed him?'

'No he's still alive today. He'd got put in Jail for wasting Police time and he missed his retrieval.'

'Oh how unfortunate. Is he OK?'

'Thankfully yes. I found him by using Internet searches and went to see him to ask if he wanted me to arrange another go.'

'And,' I said.

'He wouldn't. He's having a 'golden' life on his yacht in Florida. He made a fortune predicting 'Superbowl' scores, so now he wants to stay there.'

My mood lifted. 'So it's not dangerous then.' I pressed the advantage.

'Seems not, but there is always the possibility of missing your return and that would be problematic. Besides, I've just got you back after all these years and selfishly I want to keep you in sight.'

Silence is powerful when used in the right way. I learnt that, years ago. I didn't speak. I just gave him the look that I knew he wouldn't be able to deny.

'I'll think about it,' he finally offered.

'You have to,' I replied. 'I will come back to you. I have every faith in your invention. You have to have the same faith in me.'

He held me tightly in his arms, his breathing was shallow. I held my breath, as if my life depended on it, which in a way it did. 'When would you want to go to?'

'1963,' I replied. 'It has to be during the month of May, but after the nineteenth. It's important. I can't tell you why at this stage, you have to trust me, but it has to be then.'

'And you have to trust me baby,' he replied. 'I will move heaven and earth for you, because I can. Whatever I decide to do with the 'pyramid,' I will do this for you.'

And so it was done.

Jackson kept his promise. He spent three weeks programming and preparing the equipment. It wasn't a quick process. He was so paranoid about something going wrong, he checked everything a dozen times. And then he checked everything again. It was a long laborious process and he did it with love. We spent the days apart and the nights together when I would tell him of my plans. Not my real plans of course. I had to work twice as hard to make my mission plausible. He wanted to meet my father. I had to prevent that meeting, so more lies were told. My Catholic guilt kept me awake at night, long after Jackson fell into a peaceful slumber.

1963, was a year to remember for those old enough. The 'Profumo Scandal,' dominated the papers. I scanned through the computerised copies with a diligence and tenacity that I didn't know I possessed. We planned how I would manage for money. We laughed together as we looked up the horse races for the seven days I would be there. I would survive and I would return.

He already knew that we could change history. His

previous experiment had proved that to his satisfaction. I can't tell you about that now, but safe to say, that Jackson for a few hours had the whole world in his hands. The guy he sent was a saint. He didn't know for sure it would work. He was willing to risk his life to find out. Like me though, it turned out he had nothing really to lose. He didn't come back though, but that really is another story, for another day.

I started to levitate again. It was a sign to me that things were changing. The black cloud that had hung over me like a weighty blanket had gone. I had a spring in my step. Bernie and Beverley put that down to Jackson and his re-appearance in my life. I didn't dissuade them. It was true, but not necessarily for the reasons they thought. Time travel, Bernie would have laughed out loud. Her faith was absolute. No one should have that power apart from 'Him.' Science shouldn't interfere with the natural order of the world. Should it?

I visited my parents. They noticed the change in me and they were both touched by it. I couldn't mention Jackson, but I said I had been seeing someone who made me happy. That was enough for them. They loved me unconditionally. I didn't need to tell them my every move. I told them I was giving up work at the café. I would maybe go back to college, but needed to think for a while. That was fine by them. Francesca secretly hoped I wouldn't settle for another menial job. They both appreciated that the café and the serenity there had been all I could cope with. In their eyes I was moving on. And so I was, but in order to go forward, sometimes you have to go back.

During the day, I rented a car and planned my route. I travelled to the British Museum and researched everything that I could about the era I would be visiting.

Currency, habits, travel, trains, cars, you name it. Would it cover every eventuality? Probably not, but I needed to be confident that I could achieve what I had set out to. I studied my victims with the sort of intensity that would have made any researcher proud. It's amazing the things you can find out on the internet. I scoured the book sites for old copies of out of print biographies and newspaper articles. I could do this, I knew I could. With courage and a sprinkling of luck.

39

Sunday 26th May 1963

The man with the glasses in the control room had agreed to help. He'd tried to locate the keys to the 'Bowser,' without success. He had however, helped push the 'AVRO' out of the hanger and close enough to the fuel truck for the hose to reach. He took ten pounds as a fuel deposit and noted how much went into the machine and added ten gallons to the slip for the two cans. They were duly stowed in the fuselage.

To ward off hypothermia, Kate put on the leather flying hat and bomber jacket that the boys had dug out of a forgotten closet. Without knowing too much about her, Kate felt like Amelia Earhart. Or at least looked like her.

Time was tight. Hugh pointed out that there was less than four hours of daylight left and even at full throttle, London was almost two hours away. David, the ATC's real name, helped fuel and load the aircraft. Kate had taken her things from the van and put them in the cockpit. She was helped to climb in and strap herself up. Hugh got into the pilot's seat and did the same. They were ready for the off.

David pulled the propeller firmly clockwise like a man who had done it many times before and the seven cylinder rotary engine coughed into life. Hugh let the revs settle into a rhythm for a minute or so, while Mr Controller returned to his position in the tower. Once he was up there, the two men exchanged a thumbs-up and with increased throttle the magnificent flying machine eased off the apron.

When they were at the end of the runway, Kate estimated its length at about seven or eight hundred yards, but when he gave it full throttle and the rotor-blades moved faster into a blur, the runway was hardly needed. The metal bird took off almost vertically. Moments later they were above the trees and into the clouds.

The noise was deafening. The engine, propeller, rotors and wind noise combined into an orchestrated assault on her senses. Kate was more used to the almost silent hum of a Ryanair 837. She didn't know if she could take two hours of this.

Communication with her pilot would be difficult, so it had to be with hand signals. He had a radio and earphones, but she didn't. The pre-flight agreement was that if time or fuel became an issue, he would land somewhere as close to a station as he could manage. That way it would be possible for her to continue her journey using an early evening train into London. They had levelled out and her pilot turned and gave her the sign asking if she was ok. She replied with the thumb and fore-finger circle and three raised finger sign for OK. She had learnt that, scuba-diving in Egypt on a holiday with Emma. Pushing the memory aside she focussed on the task in hand.

Kate started to forget her deafness and was enjoying her new vantage-point. It wasn't so cloudy that she couldn't admire the view of the beautiful peak district from the air. Hugh had worked out a heading to follow and had remarked that it wasn't windy enough, even at eight thousand feet, to worry about vectors, crosswinds and other stuff she didn't understand. Apparently that would help flying time and fuel consumption.

Just over an hour and a half later, something distracted her from her enjoyment of the view. The engine note changed and there was something troubling about it. It was misfiring on one of its cylinders. Hugh throttled back, but still it continued. He increased the revs and it made no difference. Her pilot made a signal, he was going to land.

Kate could sense him looking all around for a suitable course of action. A minute or so later he banked and turned left, as the plane leant over she could see why. He had found a railway track and started his descent. It was clear he wanted to get down, soon. She felt the 'autogyro' losing height more rapidly than before. The ground was almost rushing up to meet her. 'Jesus,' she thought, 'this is going to hurt.'

The plane came down at a ridiculously steep angle and what seemed to be far too fast. Just as she braced herself for impact, the skilful pilot pulled out of the dive and lowered them gently the last few feet to the ground. Only fifty or sixty feet later they had stopped and turned round to face for home. The engine was relaxed to idle speed, but not turned off. She then learnt that the trouble had started over Luton and by the time he had found a suitable field near to a station they were in Bushey.

On the ground Hugh caught Kate's bags and then helped her off the wing. While she removed her jacket and hat, almost taking her hair off with it, he explained that it appeared one of the cylinder plugs had broken and he would have to limp back. He left the engine idling while he put the fuel from the cans into the tank. He then told her the best way to walk to the station and said, 'Goodbye Rebecca,' with a broad welsh grin. 'Thank you for being the prettiest co-pilot I've ever had the pleasure of flying with.'

'Bye Hugh, this has been an experience I will never forget.' She kissed him on the area of his cheek not covered in leather and said. 'Promise me something.'

'What?'

'Listen carefully. You've put yourself at risk for me today and I'm going to reward you. The Epsom Derby is only a few days away. Put your money on a tri-cast or whatever they call it these days, when you put the first three horses of a race in the correct winning order. The winner will be the favourite Relko by six lengths. The second will be Merchant Venturer and third will be Ragusa. The money you will win will allow you to fly this baby well into your retirement.'

He looked puzzled.

'Don't ask me how I know. It would take too long to explain. Just trust me. And when the time comes, don't believe the things people will say about me. I am not what they think. Just believe that. Please.'

He couldn't think of an answer. As she turned to go she said. 'Oh and the van's yours, the keys and log book are in the glove box.'

Mad Mr Evans waved and with a hint of sorrow in his voice, mumbled, 'take care.' She had touched him and he was sad to see her go. She didn't hear him. The Avro's 6 good cylinders drowned him out. It was half past six and only twenty-seven miles from London. She bought a ticket to Euston Station and as she sat waiting for the 6.45 train she afforded herself a smile. Everything would be ok. Her wild weekend was over. Her work here was nearly done.

40

Kate

The small church of St Joseph's, hidden behind a parade of smart shops could tell you a few stories. I felt as though I had attended the Sunday morning mass there for as long as I could remember, excepting only when ill, or on holiday. Though we still had to find the nearest church to wherever we stayed when we were away from home. That was Francesca's rule. James rarely attended other than special occasions and although he sometimes made the effort, it was more for Francesca than for God.

As a young child, I liked the solemnity of the occasion. The repetition of the rituals was comforting and it became a kind of sanctuary from the outside world. However badly things were going in society, Father Dominic would be waiting to greet you and somehow he would put things into context. The world somehow seemed a less scary place. The Priest was diminutive in stature, but his presence filled the room.

Francesca was a traditionalist, like her own mother. She literally put her life in God's hands and believed her faith would see her through the hard times. 'He' would take care of her and her family. She had me, her miracle baby. 'He' had answered her prayers. Her comfortable life, a loving husband whom she adored and a successful career meant she was truly blessed.

I can remember Sunday mornings with warmth, but not necessarily connected to God. It was the time of the week I got to spend with my mother and we would start by deciding what to wear. It was a tradition. I would sit on the end of the bed whilst she sat at her dressing table putting on her 'face.' It was important to her that we looked good. Sometimes she would tut embarrassingly loudly when she spotted a member of the congregation dressed too casually, or God forbid, in a pair of jeans. 'No respect,' she would mutter under her breath. I couldn't see the problem personally, they were there to worship, not to win a 'Best dressed in Pew' award, but I humoured her anyway.

I would sit in church in my smart tailored dress and high shoes feeling like Audrey Hepburn. The heels were a big problem to me. I've always loved the look of them, but somehow the pain and suffering involved, just didn't seem worth it. I would squeeze my size five, slightly broad foot into the delicate shoe and feel immediately like a giraffe whose body was always slightly off balance. I was taller than my mother by the time I was fourteen, but I didn't inherit her grace and poise. I didn't complain. I suffered in silence and looked forward to feel the delicious warmth of the hot water that I would immerse them in, when I got back home. Pain and church will somehow always be interlinked in my mind. My perseverance though, would pay dividends in later life. By my late teens I could chase a number 27 bus wearing stilettos and be still sure of catching it.

So Sunday morning was mother and daughter time. We would chat about our week on the walk to church and Francesca would gossip about people at work, who had upset who and why and I felt I knew most of the staff through her anecdotes.

James would stay home and cook lunch. It was his quiet time, listening to the Archers on the radio and playing some of his old vinyl from the sixties. Sometimes we would return to Frank Zappa blasting out, the smell of lamb and rosemary wafting from the kitchen and we would look at each other and smile.

Back in church, we would whisper to each other as the familiar faces walked in and we'd stop our conversation to nod a greeting to the people whose movements were so commonplace that we could quite accurately time their arrivals. However, because of its location, the church was also an open door to various people staying temporarily in the area, tourists and Father Dominic's waifs and strays. Homeless people, some with drug and alcohol problems and some to whom life had been especially cruel. We tried not to judge, we could see the wider picture, but the desperate souls with their hollow eyes and haunted expressions moved us and reminded us of how lucky we were. The mix of people was never entirely predictable and was part of the church's particular charm. No one was ever turned away.

Father Dominic was a constant. He was a short, wiry man with a shock of gingery red hair that would eventually fade with time. His green eyes, always bright and always interested would never change. He had a wit to match his intellect and his fan club of ladies of a certain age, hung on his every word. He had been raised in Dublin, in a large family, of eight. Most of his siblings still lived there, but he had been seduced by London after leaving the seminary, learning his craft in the gritty and deprived areas of a city that on the surface was energetic and prosperous.

He was given the responsibility of his own church at the tender age of twenty nine and he had remained in London, throughout his Priesthood. His life was a true vocation in my eyes. He could communicate with people at any level, without being patronising or officious. I am sure he regularly disagreed with some of the doctrines of the church and told my mother about his 'heated discussions' with Bishop McKenzie. It made him more human in my mind. Like me, he was a 'thinker' rather than a follower.

Francesca adored him. She knew his welcome was genuine and that the warmth he generated in the small church came from his heart. Despite her busy life, she could be relied upon to help out with any of his causes. It amused James no end when she returned home and told him she had been helping out on the 'soup run' for the homeless, as one of his regulars had been taken ill. She didn't exactly clothe herself very well on that October evening and to her horror, she was forced to wear one of Father Dominic's old jumpers, it was so cold. With her perfect hair and excessive jewellery, she stood out like a sore thumb. Francesca didn't do 'dress down,' so after that she stuck to the Jumble sales and fetes, to which she was more suited.

Father Dominic and I had an odd relationship in some ways. As a child I looked up to him and listened very carefully to everything he had to say. By now you know what an inquisitive, questioning child I was. You can probably imagine how it was as I got older that Father Dominic sometimes got the brunt of my frustrations, as I sought to find sense within the teachings and sermons he delivered.

I would deliberately ask him questions I knew he couldn't answer or would refuse to answer. My mother would despair, but I often viewed our discussions as a kind of sport. Perhaps secretly, so did my adversary?

I would argue with him about women's rights and

equality and the fact that the Catholic Church still wouldn't ordain female priests. I would get firmly on my soap box and question him on the child abuse scandals, the hypocrisy of the sacrament of confession and anything else I was feeling strongly about at the time. He never lost his sense of humour though, I'll give him that.

His worst memories of me almost certainly involved the weekends when Bridget was staying over and he would have the two of us to contend with. He usually tried the tactic of deflecting us from the subject matter, under the guise of wanting our help with one of his many projects.

One recollection I have of our 'help' remains firmly in my mind. We were eighteen and had just finished our A-level exams. He asked us to accompany four trainee priests who were staying with him to gain experience of a large city church. They had come from a small village in the West of Ireland, where the most exciting thing to happen was finding a missing cat, or finding out that the village church silver hadn't been polished properly.

Our mission, which we had whole heartedly chosen to accept, was to show the priests the sights of London before they returned home. To this day I am not sure why he trusted us with that task, he obviously imagined that we would be tourist guides of the highest level, both being born and bred in London. Perhaps he expected we would be whisking them round the Houses of Parliament, Big Ben and the Tower of London with the appropriate historical content.

Instead, we decided on a more appropriately cultural day out. We started at Harrods and were confident we could discuss the effects of consumerism on the masses and provoke some interesting conversation with the slightly dull group of young men. Things livened up in Soho and after a pub crawl in the West End, their eyes were certainly opened to the 'real' London. Maybe not in the way Father Dominic had wished, but we were young, foolish and full of life. I think the priests enjoyed their day out too and probably still talk about it, as they go about their business in a gentler part of the world.

Father Dominic was delighted when I got my place at Cambridge. He hoped it would 'calm me down,' as he put it and the structure of University life would guide me to the right career. I am sure there were many discussions between Francesca and Father Dominic, as to the direction my life would take. Not so, as it turned out in reality. He tried not to show his intense disappointment when I returned home in 'disgrace.' A seldom used word in the nineties, but true nevertheless. I was forced to deal with my mother's frequent glances when she thought I wasn't looking. It was different with Father Dominic. His eyes would look directly into my soul, the green brightness dulling slightly, as he told me how I had wasted a fantastic opportunity. He was old school and in his view anyone could get pregnant and have a child, but he had expected more of me. I'd had a good education, how could I make a mistake of such immense proportion?

I didn't see it quite like that. I was a woman now, not a child and in control of my own destiny. At least that's what I thought. How dare he? He was living in the dark ages. I could still have a career. At least I didn't argue with him about the outcome. He knew and I knew that I would never consider an abortion. He welcomed baby Emma into the bosom of the church, when she was born and eventually baptised.

He didn't ask too many questions about her father. I had by now stopped going to confession. It confused me too much. What was I supposed to be confessing to? Falling in love? Having sex? Being pregnant out of wedlock? I didn't feel guilty about any of those things. Perhaps it was a sign of things to come. I had already learnt to justify my actions and to resolve my 'sin' to my own satisfaction. You may be surprised to know that I did feel guilty about Jackson, about my refusal to tell him about the pregnancy and about not giving him the chance to do the decent thing. In reality my pride wouldn't let me make the call. In answer to your question, yes, I always knew deep down I was wrong and God knows, I've paid the price.

Subtly at first, I turned my back on the church and on Father Dominic. After Emma's birth I gradually stopped attending Mass with Francesca. I had a baby at home to look after now didn't I? I needed to breast-feed, the church wasn't a place for a young infant. I convinced myself that my life had changed and the church had not. Somehow the feelings I had about the physical place changed. I felt judged and somehow I was lacking.

I justified my behaviour, telling Francesca that the regulars would be whispering in the way we had whispered together. Don't get me wrong, she was initially devastated when she heard the news that I was pregnant and had had her own battle coming to terms with it. Her loyalty to me though, outweighed her negative feelings and she became a proud grandmother. She held her head up high and if anyone expressed any comments she didn't like, the 'look' would return. She would pull herself up to the tallest she could maintain in her heels and the person offering an opinion would visibly shrink in her presence. She was a contradiction in terms, but her love for Emma and me outweighed anything else.

As a concession, I attended occasionally and as Emma got older we would sometimes go as a threesome. Francesca also took Emma without me and it eventually became their time together, as it had once been mine.

On the day before I was to be reduced to vapour and hurled through 'shells of time,' I felt an urge to do something that I hadn't done for a very long time.

As I entered the church, my blood seemed to run cold. The enormity of my assignment and its possible outcome weighed heavily on my whole being. It felt as if my heart would burst with the intensity of my feelings. Was I having a panic attack? I had experienced panic attacks regularly after Emma's death and at times, wished that I'd been having a heart attack, preferably a fatal one.

This felt different. I couldn't breathe properly. Although I was just about catching my breath, it was such a strange sensation. Normally a meditation session and breathing exercises would calm me completely, whatever I was doing or experiencing. Today, I couldn't clear my head or control my lungs. My whole body felt as though it had been filled with concrete, or some kind of entity. What was happening to me? Had my sins really found me out? For the first time in a few weeks, the euphoria I had felt at the thought of accomplishing my mission had dissipated and I was left with an overwhelming feeling of sadness.

Nevertheless I continued towards the confession box. I couldn't allow anything to change what I was about to do. A cough from the other side of the heavy wood panelling made me jump. My nerves were on edge and I tried to control the feeling of terror rising in my chest. I had to overcome these feelings. Like a mantra, I repeated 'mind over matter' to myself.

The noise of a chair slightly scraping on the tiled floor brought me back to reality. I heard Father Dominic's slightly laboured breathing. He was over eighty now, should I be telling him my intended sins? Was it fair? No it wasn't, but I reasoned that I had to tell someone. Just in case, God forbid, I failed to return. I took a deep breath and entered the confessional and knelt on the hassock.

'Forgive me Father for I have sinned. It has been fifteen years since my last confession.'

I heard him whisper, 'nearer twenty.' Not much gets past him.

'Please forgive me for the sins I have committed and the one's I am about to commit.'

As I started to talk, there was a strange silence from the other side of the grille. His breathing had become even shallower and at one point I feared he was having a seizure. After a lengthy pause, he began.

'So child, you are telling me that you are about to travel back in time and murder nine people, some of whom are children? Do I have that right?'

'Yes Father,' I mumbled looking at my hands.

'What are you expecting me to say to you? That's fine? Go ahead? I'll give you absolution.' It was Dominic the Priest talking, not the man.

'Perhaps you believe that I think you're totally unhinged? Bereavement can do that to a person. You know that better than anyone. Am I to think, ah the poor girl has lost her mind?'

I swallowed. A lump was forming in my throat and I was struggling speak through it. Unwanted tears were welling from the corners of my eyes that couldn't be blinked away.

'I need to tell you Father. I am confessing to the crimes I am going to commit in 1963. There is a very strong possibility that I won't get back and if I don't return I need you know some of the answers. My mother, my father, Emma's father and perhaps even Emma herself will have questions, many questions.'

If the most unexpected moment of my life had been that fateful day when I found out my precious girl had been taken from me, the answer he gave me was the most puzzling.

There was a pause, even longer than the last, before he finally spoke again.

'I know child,' he said, in almost a whisper. 'I've often wondered what became of the 'brown bear?' But she was here the whole time.'

41

Bernie

When Kate told me that she had applied to Cambridge and had been accepted, I felt like a proud parent. When she finally went off to University, she came to see me before she went. We both shed a few tears and appreciated that things would change. Not in the way I thought as it turned out. She didn't write as often as I did and when she did, her letters seemed perfunctory, almost out of duty. I don't do faxes or emails. I am a bit of a dinosaur, I am afraid, so we were limited to pen and paper. I started to worry that things were not working out. Perhaps she was not coping with the work? Or maybe she didn't feel she was fitting in? Kate came from a lovely home, but she wasn't wealthy or royal, like many of the other undergraduates. No stop it Bernie you old fool. Kate has the social skills to adapt, anywhere. I have seen her in different situations and she can always perform as an actress, if she has the need to. She will be fine.

She wasn't fine. When she arrived back home the following year, she was a different person, harder somehow. She had fallen in love, but it hadn't worked out and she had let him go. No actually that's not true. I don't think she gave him a chance really. He was a clever man by all accounts, a scientist. Bridget had said he was crazy about Kate, but the silly girl wouldn't call him, write to him or make any contact, once he returned to America. Too much pride there, I think.

She came to see me a few days after she returned to

London. We sat on our favourite bench. The summer was over and it was getting colder. She looked tired. I felt my eyes prickle with tears as I looked at her intently. She told me her news quickly and without emotion, initially.

'I'm pregnant Bernie. I'm going to have a child and I'm not going back to Cambridge.'

Somehow, her words were not the ones I'd expected to hear. I tried reasoning with her and we spoke at length about it, for the next few weeks. I encouraged her to go back, with the baby. She could still carry on her education. Surely there would be crèches and other help? What about Jackson? Why didn't she contact him and give him the opportunity to be a father.

This was Kate at her most stubborn. She had decided that she was now an adult and could make her own decisions. Part of it was almost martyrdom. She would leave Cambridge and embrace motherhood. She couldn't be the best Barrister so she would be the best mother. I felt she was almost punishing Jackson for leaving her, even though it was only supposed to be temporary. She denied this, but in the years to come I think she realised what I was saying at the time was true. By then though, there was no going back.

I tried not to be judgemental. My religious beliefs had moved with the times and having a baby out of wedlock wasn't the sin it once had been. I worried for Kate and her unborn child and wished that she would change her mind and get in touch with Jackson. I thought about contacting him myself, but couldn't bring myself to interfere to such an extent. Kate would hate me. I would lose her and I couldn't risk that. She was the closest to a daughter that I had.

When baby Emma was born and I saw her in Kate's

arms, I began to understand. Emma was truly a gift from God and she brought joy to those around her. Kate's parents adored her too and this allowed Kate to start a career in the Probation Service and provide for Emma. I think she worked part time for a while, when Emma was very small. I had the joy of seeing her grow and would babysit for Kate, if Francesca or James weren't around. When Kate decided to send her to me, to teach at the convent, I was overjoyed. Our bond could not be broken and I was happy to be part of Emma's life, as much as Kate's.

The next few years were busy for all of us. I started to feel my age and probably looked it. I was still teaching, but only a few days a month. I still worked at the refuge and this was something I didn't want to give up. I met a social worker there called Beverley, who was visiting one of the women. Over time we struck up a strong friendship. She had had a tough life, but had turned things around and was a great inspiration to me. I was so proud of her when she received her CBE from the queen and it restored my faith in human nature.

Bev eventually left social work and opened a lovely 'wholefood' café, locally. I started to help her out when I could, although I have to say that my cooking leaves something to be desired. I didn't mind washing up and cleaning up though and we always had some good craic.

I kept in touch with Kate and her family and I was pleased when Emma was accepted at Newcastle University. I had long since stopped telling or advising Kate what to do and Emma had grown up to be a loving young woman that seemed to have a sensible head on her shoulders.

Sometimes in life, time just seems to stand still. When Kate's mother Francesca rang me to tell me about

Emma, I can barely recall the conversation or how it ended. The world stopped spinning on its axis, at that moment and I couldn't believe what I was hearing. Was there really that much evilness in the world? I was a silly old woman who still believed in the goodness in people. The last time I felt that angry was when I held my mammy's hand as she slipped away. I couldn't do anything this time. The worst had happened already.

You know the rest of my story. Kate eventually allowed me in, but the hardened shell I had seen when she returned from Cambridge had turned into concrete, this time. She literally lost her world. She lost herself. Bev and I tried to give her some love and support. It has taken her time, nevertheless she is starting to live again.

Kate told me something a few days ago. She told me that Jackson and herself were making plans for the future. It made my heart soar, but I can't tell you anything about that just yet, because she said she was going on a journey and will tell me all about it, when she gets back.

Apparently, she has to go on her own. I will be here when she gets home with my arms out wide. God bless you Kate.

42

Sunday 26th May 1963

K ate still felt exhilarated from the flying experience. She fleetingly thought of Hugh, he was a lovely man. Would his experience with her taint his life? Would he become notorious as the accomplice of a murderess? She hoped he'd take her advice and make the bets, then at least he could move somewhere far away and people might leave him alone. A twinge of guilt surfaced, she quickly pushed it away, an ability she had developed very adeptly during her mission in 1963.

She recognised that she was an emotional woman and she had spent many hours planning how she could suppress her feelings, for long enough to get the job done. Was she callous? Not really, she was almost the opposite of that, she cared too much. This was an exercise in self-discipline and control.

She compared herself to a soldier and not to a serial killer. Soldiers have to focus on the task in hand, being told it's for the greater good. Her mission was to rid the world of people who had destroyed numerous lives and had shown the worst side of the human psyche. They had also shocked and saddened all those who knew of their crimes. Minimisation and denial are states of mind that she had often witnessed in her previous line of work. Criminals are very competent at this, in order to live with their crimes and indeed themselves. Kate wasn't a hypocrite, but she was well aware of the paradoxical nature of her thoughts.

In 1963 the world would be asking some pertinent

questions. Killers like Kate, were always subject matter for psychologists, psychiatrists, newspapers, books and articles. They scrutinise their backgrounds, their personalities and their childhood experiences, in order to explain why they turned out to be people who could kill and continue to kill, without remorse or care. They try to find a 'modus operandi' or 'MO,' as the police abbreviate it. They try to link victims in an effort to discover patterns. Sometimes there aren't any. Sometimes, as with Kate's cases, they would never establish the link. Not through incompetence, but because the link was in a future era. 'And you can't see into the future, unless you're Nostradamus.' The thought made her smile, even though it was no 'smiling matter.'

As the stations between Bushey and Euston passed uneventfully by, they were outside her consciousness. She was too deep in thought about the things that would be said about her. 'The strange mystery woman, who doesn't appear to be unhinged, or mentally challenged.' 'She meticulously planned her seemingly motiveless crimes.' As a woman she would be judged even more harshly, she knew that. Women were nurturers, mothers and carers, not murderers.

She couldn't dwell any longer on the subject. Kate the serial killer had a final task to perform and she needed to stay mentally strong. A different Kate had emerged during that week in 1963. A person to be reckoned with, she wasn't a victim any more.

A platform porter knocked on the window and distracted her from her thoughts. She opened her eyes and peered through the glass. The maker of the noise was pointing at the sign above his head.

'EUSTON STATION.'

Kate nodded her thanks and gathered her bags.

Once she was through the barrier and on the main concourse of the station, she looked around. Her subconscious was guiding her actions and Kate was following. She entered a phone box, took six pennies from her bag and dialled the operator.

'Please get me the Crown Hotel in Paddington.' When she was connected she had requested a comfortable double room in a quiet part of the hotel. 'I'm on my way, but I might be a while yet,' she told the receptionist. Assured that she could arrive as late as she needed to, her room would be ready, she collected the unused pennies and opened the bi-fold door.

Though it had taken time, she was eventually getting used to 1963, almost affectionately. On her first day she couldn't have imagined how she would feel by the end of her week. It had all been too strange and her excitement and curiosity had been stifled by the reason she was here. Her full concentration was needed to ensure that she was able to complete her mission. She had unconsciously taken in her surroundings, as she moved around the busy London streets.

Jackson had given her this gift, a uniquely real experience of a bygone age, but to Kate, it had felt like a film set and she was playing a part. As the week had progressed she'd become a 'sixties' woman and she'd never be the same again, on so many levels.

She pulled herself together as she approached a tired looking, uniformed man, pushing a yard wide station-issue broom.

'Excuse me, can you tell me where the nearest Catholic church is please.'

'I afraid I can't darling, I'm a heathen,' he replied with the raspy breath of someone who smoked thirty

'Players Navy Cut' every day. 'Luckily for you Lady, I know someone who can answer your question.'

Spotting the station toilet attendant about to descend the steps to the underground 'Public Conveniences,' he called out.

''Ere Marjorie, you're a 'rock-cake,' where's the nearest one of your churches?'

The good natured, grey-haired woman turned at the sound of the familiar voice and walked back.

'Praise be,' she said. 'Alf, you've finally found the Lord. I told you it was never too late!' The wry smile gave her charade away. She turned to Kate and said.

'I'm guessing the answer's meant for you love, 'cause this old fossil won't find religion 'til his death bed.' Kate nodded. 'Turn left out of the station and then left again. Walk up Seymour Street, take third on the right and the church is on the right in Clarendon Square. You can't miss it, it's got St Aloysius in large roman script above the columned entrance.'

She found the church fairly easily, with Marjorie's precise instructions. Despite her years in London, Kate couldn't remember ever having seen it before. Like a lot of churches, she supposed, unless you were in need of one, you could quite easily pass by. And Somer's Town is one of the quieter areas of the Borough of Camden.

It was eerily quiet as she opened one of the pair of large, heavy, ornate doors. The creaking and the sound of a small bell ringing in the distance reminded her of the recent encounter she had experienced at her own church, just over a week ago, but in some ways a lifetime away.

She made her way through the nave of the church looking for any sign of the confessional. She noticed by looking at the large board outside that there was no evening service. She wondered if she was wasting her time.

The confessional's booth was in the gloom of the fading light, situated in the annex on the right hand side of the church. It was in a place where the stained glass windows couldn't lend anything and she couldn't see a light switch. Even with her new found confidence, she didn't want to stride about looking for one, or even impose herself on a weary priest, who was probably preparing for bed. She turned around to leave, thinking that she should have stuck to her original plans, when a voice came out of the darkness.

'Have you come to pray, confession finished ten minutes ago?'

Kate felt very uncomfortable. A strange feeling of déjà vu was rising from the pit of her extremely anxious stomach. Yet she was sure she had never been in this church in her life.

'Forgive me father for I have sinned. It has been eight days since my last confession,' she started to blurt it out, before either an invitation or being in the confessional itself. She stopped, realising her mistake.

A soothing and young sounding Irish voice replied. 'Come then and tell me, I've got time.' His tone and intonation was strangely familiar.

She began with the most incredible part of the confession. He wouldn't believe her of course. Time travel to a Priest in the sixties would take an awful lot of convincing. She didn't have the time. He didn't say much as she told him about the killings. Her own voice sounded hollow as she explained why she was there. She then told him what her 'victims' would have gone on to become. In her heart she didn't expect him to believe her.

'Why are you here in this church? Are you genuinely sorry for what you have done? You know I can't absolve without real remorse.'

She paused for thought. Was she sorry? She couldn't answer the question honestly. She didn't know how she felt at that moment.

'I don't know Father. I'm sorry that I've killed them, but I'm not sorry that they're gone.'

He might possibly have heard about as many as four of the murders, by now. She had avoided looking at the news stands' posters while she was at the station. Perhaps that had been short-sighted? Perhaps the Police were on their way, right now? Perhaps even in the 'redhead' wig, Mr Broom-pusher might have recognised her? Time might be short so she pushed on.

'I had to tell you why, Father. My conscience wouldn't let me go back to 2017 without explaining my actions, whilst I'm still in 1963. I know you can't possibly believe me, but it's all true. I am from the future. My time here and my mission isn't yet complete and I won't have time to come back tomorrow.'

She told him about her daughter, about her life, about what had happened to her. She didn't use any names, but as the story unfolded the young Priest was as intrigued as horrified. Was this the ultimate sacrifice, was it a mother's love or the tale of a deranged woman. His short 'life experience' had never brought him into contact with anyone like this.

'I couldn't do anything Father,' she sobbed. 'I should have protected her, I let her go... It was my fault... I will do anything to let her live, this chance for me to come back in time was as if another outcome had been granted to Emma. I had the power to change things, it had to be fate. God brought her father back to me, to bring her back. Didn't He?'

During her moving monologue the young priest's mind wandered back to a programme he had listened to on the radio, a few days before.

The female Brown Bear would protect her cubs from anything. She could fight and fend off, adult male bears, sometimes twice her weight to save her cubs. Male bears take no part in the parenting process. Worse still they practise 'infanticide.' They kill the cubs, either to eat, or to make the female receptive. She might die in the process, yet more often than not, somehow the mother bear would find strength from somewhere that she didn't actually possess.

This woman, in his confessional, reminded him of that story. What was happening to him, he was starting to understand her? Of course he couldn't condone what she was doing, but somehow he understood.

Father Dominic hadn't been working on his own very long and had heard only a handful of confessions a day for the last few months. This was one he'd never forget. It blew his mind. He was young and he knew that he didn't know all the answers. He had read the papers and he guessed who was in front of him, but she was convincing and she seemed of sound mind. What about her soul? Could it be saved?

It was slowly dawning on him that if she was telling the truth, her mission had not yet finished.

As he went through the motions of absolving her mortal sins and gave her the penance of 'the stations of the cross,' he wondered why he had been chosen to receive this confession. It had challenged his spirit, emotion and intellect. However, his faith would see him through and he would use his experiences to inform his work in the years to come.

He couldn't tell her what he was thinking, nonetheless he prayed for her. He left her in the church and went for some quiet contemplation in his private rooms. Kate started at 'Station One,' saying the four prayers at each of the fourteen 'stations,' until her 'conscience' would let her leave.

When Kate was outside once more, there were no Police cars. No flashing lights. She took a slow walk back to Euston Square and felt as if a huge weight had been lifted from her. Nothing had changed, but she knew she would get through the next twenty four hours. She hoped the gentle young priest would recover.

In front of the station, she got into one of the three, waiting black cabs.

Before being asked where, she said. 'The Crown Hotel Paddington, please driver.'

Her chauffeur moved out on to the Euston Road to head west. As he started to chat, it struck Kate that a Hackney cab with its partition between driver and passenger is like a mobile confessional. She was 'confessed out' for one day.

'Sorry driver, I'm not good company tonight. I've had a very wild weekend.'

He politely slid the privacy glass shut.

Somewhere on the journey, Kate started piecing together the evening's events.

Then a thought struck her like a thunderbolt. An image of a bear mothering her young flashed across her mind.

She was 'the Brown Bear.'

43

Kate

Jackson and I spent our last night together before my journey. I had prepared my outfit bought in a vintage shop. Thank God for retro. Everyone loves it. I borrowed a handbag from my mother that had been my grandmother's.

Jackson and I visited a coin dealer where we bought a couple of old fivers. I tucked them into the jacket pocket of the suit. We were like two children about to embark on the biggest adventure of our lives, but Jackson couldn't come on this journey. He would need to have faith and he would need to ensure that everything was aligned. He couldn't trust anyone else with the task. He had some assistants, but none of them knew what the time-machine was really capable of. He wouldn't take the risk. It was his Kate, he couldn't take any chances.

'You will be fine baby,' he whispered as he kissed me with the kind of passion we had re-kindled over the last three months. I wasn't worried. Was I anxious? Honestly no. I had looked death in the face before and I knew if I didn't come back to this time, I would have done everything in my power to achieve my goal.

God forgive me. Good and evil. To fight evil, you have to become evil. That's the sacrifice. What ever happened I would never be the same Kate. I felt like I was about to be re-born. It wasn't too far from the truth.

'I love you Jackson, more than you will ever know. You won't understand some of this, I know, but you must promise me you won't do any searches of 1963 until I am back.' He looked puzzled.

'What do you mean Kate? Have you changed your plans again?'

'Trust me,' I said, 'please trust me. Let's do it.'

Jackson opened one of the triangular sides and helped me up onto the plinth. I felt like I should have been strapped in. He closed me in and I blew him a kiss before he turned to the computer that would 'obilium' me...

44

Monday 27th May 1963

K ate's alarm went off at six-thirty on the last and most important of all days. She was in a comfortably grand room at the Crown Hotel, next to Paddington Station. She had taken a taxi from Euston the night before and forgetting that she had rung the hotel, told her cabbie to wait in case there was no bed for her. She needn't have bothered. Such a large Hotel always had space in those days. Kate knew it as the Mercure Hotel and approved of the refurbishment it had undergone.

It was clean and tidy enough and very close to where she needed to be. Nothing else mattered. After a bath she needed to meditate. The demanding morning ahead required a clear and calm mind. She was getting better at it during the course of the week, even without her phone app. Twenty minutes was enough she felt. She could do anything now. She dressed in the suitably sober tweed skirt-suit and cashmere sweater, purchased in Glasgow for the occasion. The look, inspired by the Gloucestershire headmistress, could do with pearls she thought as she put dull shades of make up on her pretty features.

She opted for the red wig for the day's task. There's something about the look of it, pretty and feisty. People didn't seem to mess with ladies with red hair. Her paternal grandmother was a natural redhead and was a case in point. When Kate was ready and repacked, she went downstairs.

A light breakfast was the best idea, thought Kate. Poached egg on toast & coffee and quickly read the Daily Mirror. There was quite a lot of coverage of the 'Moors Murders' as they called it, but nothing about young Fred. She guessed that stories from north of the border take longer to reach Fleet Street.

When she had finished she asked at reception for a clipboard and explained that she was a writer researching the village districts of London. Today she was in Paddington and tomorrow would be Marylebone.

'I'm afraid I've misplaced the one I brought to use.' She told the girl on the desk.

'No problem Madam. We have one in office to check in deliveries from the Brewery.'

'I'll buy another and replace it by lunchtime.' Kate lied.

'That's fine Madam, we don't have any deliveries this morning, so there's no hurry.'

Kate walked up Praed Street for five minutes until she reached the Hospital, a shade after nine o' clock. She made her way through the entrance and into the main building. Signs led to various wards and departments. She searched impatiently for the only one she was interested in. Maternity was on the second floor.

Kate thought that the only way to approach this was brazen confidence. She wouldn't change her voice, this act was going to be hard enough without something else to concentrate on. She entered the double doors and before she got to the second set of doors to the ward, she found the office on the left. Clipboard raised to her chest, she marched into the room. A startled Staff-Nurse and an Auxiliary looked round. Before they could speak Kate said.

'Sylvia Collins. I'm an LCC Health Inspector. My department are responsible for making random and unannounced inspections of Hospital facilities. The aim is to check on and maintain standards, across the board.'

'Staff' wanted to speak, but the combination of surprise and Sylvia's 'bulldozer' manner had her on the verbal back foot.

The 'Hospital Inspector' continued. 'Please tell Sister that I am here, but that I am to be left alone until the visit is over. That way I will be able to draw my own conclusions without interruption.

'Very good Mrs ...'

'It's Miss and before I visit the ward, can you show me the way to the baby unit?'

'Staff' took her back through the double doors and across the corridor into the ward opposite. Another office, this time with two Nurses in attendance.

'Thank you 'Staff,' I'll take it from here, but would you be good enough to explain to your colleagues who I am.'

'Yes Miss.' She went into the office. Kate went through the two grey and glass doors to see the babies. Once inside, she found a largish room with twenty metal-framed cots, ten on each side. Fifteen had babies in. Some were asleep, some were gurgling, some were crying and some were staring silently at the shape moving around the room. 'Can they see properly yet? Can they focus?' Kate hoped not.

All the cribs had boards, like the one she was carrying, apart from the hooked top to allow it to hang on the bed-frame. She read each one in turn. When she had read them all, she read them all again. 'Sylvia' went in to the nurse's room. 'Can you now show me the other Baby unit please?'

'Sorry?' One of them spoke, but they both looked puzzled.

'The rest of the babies born in the last few days?'

The other nurse said. 'These babies are the only ones. We don't have a second ward.'

'Sometimes we don't have this many,' the first nurse joined in.

'That's impossible.' Sylvia retorted. 'I should know. My sister-in-law came in yesterday morning and the child was born before midnight!'

One looked blank, the other said. 'You do mean St Mary's do you?'

'What do you mean?'

'Well, only that it's quite likely that your sister went to Paddington General.'

'Paddington General?' Kate was having a 'light bulb' moment. 'Shit! I'm in the wrong place,' she thought. She recovered her composure quickly.

'Oh, possibly she is. I'll know for sure when I've finished my report on St Mary's. I'll go and see if I can find her there. I thought it was too coincidental that she was in the very place I was due to inspect today. By the way, my first findings are that you are wrapping the babies too tight. Some of them can hardly breathe.'

'Really?'

'It'll all be in my report.' Sylvia turned to go. 'I'm going back to talk to the mothers. Keep up the good work.'

'Thank you,' they almost said in unison.

Once out in the corridor, she turned towards the exit. She had wasted enough time here. Time was tight. She had to be back in Bloomsbury by twelve and she still had something to accomplish first. Outside in Praed Street she was so anxious she almost threw herself under an approaching cab. He pulled up short, but he wasn't best pleased.

Seeing the look on his face Kate said. 'I'm so sorry. I stumbled on the pavement into the road.'

Her driver softened. 'That's OK lady. Where to?'

'I need to go to Paddington General, quickly. I'm late for an appointment because I've come to the wrong Hospital. Then I need you to wait for me. I won't be that long and then I want to go to Malet Street in Bloomsbury.'

'Yup, I know it well enough.'

'But,' she said. 'If there's enough time I want to go via Dover Street in Mayfair, there's something I need to return.'

Ten minutes later they were in the Harrow Road outside the General Hospital. 'Sylvia' took the clipboard again, got out of the parked taxi and made her way through the main entrance. She found maternity easily enough. A different layout from the last Hospital though. The mothers were in a ward on the first floor. The babies were in a unit on the ground floor, at the end of a corridor in a quieter part of the Hospital. She used the same confident approach and the same story, but this time it was a Sister who was in charge of the infants. The ward was smaller this time. The room had only twelve cots and about nine or ten were occupied.

Kate, in 'Sylvia' guise, moved efficiently down the ward. She scanned each sheet at the end of each cot.

GIRL; GIRL; BOY – Baby Stevens; GIRL: She moved on. The next one made her stop and take her time. It read:

MALE

Born: 10.23pm on May 26th 1963
Weight: 6lbs 3 oz.
Name: Chappell; Baby A

'Baby A?' She dropped the board with the sheet on it. Regaining herself, she picked it up and put it back.

'A? Please God, no!' she thought and crossed to the next cot.

The sheet hanging on its end noted:

MALE
Born: 10.48pm on May 26th 1963
Weight: 5lbs 10 oz.
Name: Chappell; Baby B

Two tears splashed onto the page as she placed it back. How could this be? There had been no mention of him being a twin. She had read everything about the man. That could only mean one thing that the other twin had died. How? Her mind raced ahead, but in her heart she knew what she had to do. She tried to convince herself that the baby sibling had not survived in any instance. 'God give me strength,' she thought, as she approached the nurse.

'Sister!'

'Yes Mrs Collins?'

'Where's Matron?'

'She's in her office on the second floor, why?'

'There's something highly irregular here. I need you to go and fetch her immediately.'

Sister wanted to ask questions, but could only manage, 'Oh. Yes. I see. Of course, I'll go now. Will you be?'...

Walking her to the doors, Kate replied. 'Don't

worry. Take your time. I'll be fine here until you get back...

Epilogue

Y ou know the rest. You know the truth now. My name is still Kate and I am a Serial Killer. I have purged the world of people, you will now never have heard of. I chose carefully. They will be wiped from the pages of history. They will never go on to commit the terrible crimes that I know would have taken place. You have to trust me on that. On the other hand, you will never be sure.

Revenge, is that my motivation? No. I changed the course of history because I could. Was it to suit my own needs? Yes of course. I can't deny that. You know too much. I caused suffering to stop suffering. It was all I could do. As I said before, please don't judge me. 'There but for the grace of God, go I.' What would you do? Do you ever lie awake at night and think about it?

Look up at the stars. They will still be there tomorrow. They are infinite, as is the Universe. I am just a woman. A mother. I'm nothing special. I did what I had to do. Please understand.

I could write more. I could write forever about what happened to me in those seven days I spent in 1963. But I have told you all you need to know, for now at least.

The End. Or the beginning? However you want to look at it, the choice is yours.

We hope this book throws up some interesting discussion and debate.

If you have enjoyed it, please tell your friends, or be kind enough to write a review on which ever website you favour.

Your comments, reviews and feedback are always welcomed by Beatrice, at this email address:

Beatrice@BeatriceJames.com

Or tweet to: **@obilium**

Should you wish to be kept informed about future publications, send a short note to the above email address, or tweet to @obilium

Volume 2 of **THE RETRIBUTION FANTASIES** series will be published, during 2014.

Titled: **SENTENCE EXPIRY DATE**, it follows Kate McLean's new role at the Ministry of Justice and her investigations into the most bizarre set of events that have ever occurred, in the history of Her Majesty's Prison Service.

Notes for the Reader

'Rosemary'

Rosemary Letts was nine years old in 1963. A slow child of very low intelligence, from an early age she was struggling to escape the taunts of other pupils. Already showing sexualised behaviour, she was almost certainly abused by her father from a young age. She regularly endured his extreme violence, as did her siblings.

She became a bully at school, to defend herself from the hurtful comments made by fellow pupils, and became more aggressive in her teenage years, as her character began to form. The event in 1969 that would change the course of her life was meeting a man, twelve years her senior, who would shape her views of the world. His lawlessness and sexual deviance would influence and control her actions for years to come. Together they would create a distorted family that would be a haven for the most despicable and deviant acts. Together they validated each other's behaviour and normalised events, such as the death of their eldest daughter, with a chilling series of jokes and innuendo.

Rosemary Letts moved in with Frederick West at the tender age of sixteen. In fact, on the actual day of her sixteenth birthday. She initially looked after his two daughters from his previous wife, whilst he served a prison sentence for some petty offences. It is widely believed that Rosemary killed his step daughter Charmaine, then six years old, whilst he was away.

Charmaine was a stoical, yet happy child and it has been said that one of the reasons Rosemary continued to beat her was that 'she wouldn't cry.' This was her violent style of parenting that established how things would be in their relationship. Their shared 'secret' and Fred's role in disposing of the body, would establish a pattern for their subsequent crimes.

Rose West was convicted of ten counts of murder. One of the victims was her own daughter Heather. She was murdered by Fred after being abused by Rose. They told friends and family she had left home to work at a holiday camp.

The Wests occupied a house in Cromwell Street, Gloucester. Their typical pattern was to pick up girls standing alone at bus stops around Gloucester. They would imprison them in the cellar of their home for several days before killing them. No one knows the true extent of their crimes or what happened to the girls before they died. Fred West took 'the secrets of Cromwell Street' to his grave, rather than implicate Rose.

Although evidence was circumstantial, Rosemary was found guilty of all ten counts and given a 'whole-life' order in 1997. She was only the second woman in British History to receive such a sentence.

The 'whole-life order' is a court order whereby a prisoner, who is being sentenced to life imprisonment, is ordered to serve that sentence without the possibility of parole. The purpose of a whole-life order is for a prisoner to be kept in prison until they die, although in exceptional circumstances a prisoner can still be released by the Home Secretary, on compassionate grounds such as ill health. A whole-life tariff can also be quashed on appeal, by the Court of Appeal.

'Steven'

Steven Gerald James Wright was five years old in 1963. He is more commonly known as the 'Suffolk Strangler,' currently serving a sentence of imprisonment with a 'whole-life' order, for the murder of five young female sex workers during 2006. There would probably have been a sixth victim if the partner he shared a home with, had not come home early from work, one night.

Steven Wright was born in Erpingham in Norfolk. He left school in 1974 and joined the Royal Navy. He married three times over the next few years and there was an allegation of an attack on a sex worker reported in the eighties. He was never convicted, but his lifestyle consisted of gambling, heavy drinking and frequenting 'red-light' areas where he regularly paid for sex.

He was found guilty of murdering the young women around the Ipswich red light area. The women were themselves victims of heroin addiction and resorted to working the streets to support their habit. Despite overwhelming evidence to the contrary, he always denied the offences. He was also under investigation for other unsolved 'cold crimes,' where the evidence suggested he may be involved. One such case was that of the 'missing, presumed dead' estate agent, Suzy Lamplugh. Nothing was proven, but the link was that he knew Suzy from the time when they both worked on the same Cruise Liner and a connection was made. Some believe that he has committed other crimes and pressure has been put onto the Police to re-open the files of the 'cold-cases'.

'Peter'

In 1963, Peter William Sutcliffe was a month from his seventeenth birthday. Working as a gravedigger in Bingley Cemetery, he was developing his own morbid curiosity for dead bodies.

In 1981, Peter Sutcliffe was convicted of the murders of 13 women and the attempted-murders of 7 others. He had carried out his crimes over a five year period, creating a reign of fear and terror on the streets of Leeds and Bradford. The Police were particularly slow to charge him and interviewed him nine times before he was arrested. He worked as a long distance lorry driver and he was obsessed with sex-workers in the red light districts of Northern England.

At his trial he claimed 'diminished responsibility,' stating that he was guided by the voice of God. He had been diagnosed with Paranoid Schizophrenia, but the plea was dismissed. He was given 20 life sentences.

Despite an appeal in 2010, he was told he would serve a 'whole-life' tariff (order). His attempts to be released have angered the many families of the victims, who have lost their loved ones.

His crimes were vicious and often lethal attacks on lone women. They were vulnerable either by circumstance or by fate, being in the wrong place at the wrong time. Seven women had a lucky escape, but were left with life-changing mental scars and injuries.

'Denis' (the one that got away)

Denis Nilsen was a 17 year old serving soldier in 1963 and when Kate did her research, she was unsure whether or not he was on leave and spending the time with his mother Betty Whyte in Strichen, Scotland. He could have been at the Barracks in Aldershot where he was completing his training. In the end, he was in neither place. She could not locate him and had to abandon the search as she didn't have any extra time. Nilsen had a habit of going 'Absent Without Leave' for a few days and during that week in May that was exactly what happened.

Denis Nilsen was a serial killer and necrophiliac who went on to confess to fifteen murders of young, transient men that he invited back to his home in Muswell Hill. On February 9th 1983, he was arrested after human remains had been identified as the cause of blocked drains. Sadly his victims, young homosexual men had never been missed. He was able to pick up his victims at various gay bars and clubs in North London. They were killed in his flat usually by strangulation, after alcohol had been consumed.

He retained his victim's bodies for extended periods of time before dissecting them. This was attributed, by his own admission of wanting friendship and not wanting the men to go, or leave him.

He was convicted at the Old Bailey in 1983 and given a life sentence which was converted to a whole-life tariff. In 2006 he was denied any further requests for parole. He is currently incarcerated in HMP Full Sutton.

'Freddy'

Harold Frederick Shipman was seventeen years old in 1963. Known affectionately as 'Freddy' to his mother, who was by then in the last stages of lung cancer. They lived on a council estate in Nottingham and the local doctor regularly visited them at home to administer morphine to her. Shipman would apparently develop a morbid fascination for the subject of death and particularly the power held by the local GP.

Harold studied medicine at Leeds, graduating in 1970. Seven years after his mother passed away. In 1974 he took up his first post as a GP. A year later he was caught forging prescriptions of Pethidine, a very strong 'opiated' pain killer and was brought before the medical council. He was fined £600 and ordered to attend a drug rehabilitation centre. He became a practice GP in Manchester in 1977 and continued through the eighties. In 1993 he started his own surgery at 21 Market Street, Hyde and was a respected member of the community.

Harold Shipman was known as 'Dr Death'. He is Britain's most prolific serial killer, to date. Proven murders ascribed to him total over 250. He was found guilty in January 2000 of 15 specimen charges. He was also sentenced to a 'whole-life' tariff.

Many victims' families felt aggrieved as their beloved relatives, parents, were denied justice, due to the volume of the murders. Shipman took his own way out. He hanged himself on 13 January 2004, in his cell in Wakefield prison, West Yorkshire.

'Mr Whippy'

Frederick Walter Stephen West together with his wife Rosemary, became the infamous relationship created the uniquely unusual team of cruel and sexually sadistic serial killers.

Fred was of low intelligence, but with a cunning streak that would enable him to cope. Born into a family of farm workers, Fred's father allegedly had incestuous sexual relationships with all his sisters and other under-age girls. He said that his father taught him bestiality at an early age. It was also alleged that his mother began sexually abusing him from the age of twelve, although this was never confirmed by Fred West. After a motorcycle accident in 1958, he became prone to outbursts of rage. Added to his deviant sexual behaviour, it would prove to be a lethal cocktail.

In September 1962, twenty-one year old Fred West became acquainted with a former girlfriend Catherine Costello. She was known as Rena and had been working as a sex-worker, eventually becoming pregnant with another man's child, before she was re-united with Fred. They married and moved to Lanarkshire, Scotland. Charmaine West was born in 1963 and Fred alleged he had adopted her. Rena bore him another daughter, Anne Marie, in 1964.

The family together with Rena's friend, Anne McFall, moved to a caravan park in Bishops Cleeve in Gloucester, at the end of 1965. Fred feared for his safety as he had knocked down a young boy in Scotland, with his Ice cream van. Rena Costello moved back to Scotland due to Fred's violence, but Anne McFall who was eight months pregnant with Fred's child, remained with him and then went missing. Her remains were not found until 1994.

Frederick West met Rosemary Letts on her fifteenth birthday, in November 1968. Her parents disapproved of him, but she moved in with him as soon as she was legally able to, on her sixteenth birthday. They lived together in a caravan before they bought 25 Cromwell Street, in Gloucester, where the majority of the atrocities would take place.

Between them, Fred and Rose had eight children, though not all were fathered by Fred. Three were of mixed race. Rose had got pregnant whilst working as a prostitute from their home. Fred filmed himself raping one of their daughters and in 1992 this was investigated by social services. Nothing came of their investigations as the children were too afraid to speak. The Police continued to search for their missing daughter Heather, whom they had reported earlier as being 'missing from home.' After the sexual abuse allegation, some of the children said that Heather was 'buried under the patio.' A family joke, apparently.

The Police excavated the garden and found Heather's body, as well as the bodies of numerous other young women. Fred West was charged with eleven murders.

On the 1st January 1995, whilst still on remand, Fred hanged himself. The house at Cromwell Street has since been demolished.

'The Lovers'

Myra Hindley and Ian Brady were possibly the most identifiable 'victims' in the book. The infamous child killers, the 'Moors Murderers' were covered by the Press on a worldwide scale in the sixties.

The Moors murders were carried out between July 1963 and October 1965, in and around Greater Manchester. People say that they changed history in the sense that children would never roam the streets, or play outside in the same way again. They preyed on children and their victims were five children between the ages of ten and seventeen. At least four of the five were also sexually assaulted.

Myra and Ian met at work in an office in Hyde, Manchester. They started a relationship that consisted of driving over the moors, listening to Hitler's 'Mein Kampf' on tapes. They became sexually obsessed with each other and the possibility of snatching a child. They planned crimes long before the first abduction and it was chillingly clear that their actions were truly pre-meditated. The only element of chance would be who would be unlucky enough to encounter them and be taken in by Myra, after all, no woman would hurt a child - would she?

Their crimes are forever remembered by the British public. Hindley has been frequently described in the press as the most evil woman in Britain, accompanied by 'that photo.' The mug-shot of the bleached blonde, hard faced murderess. Always judged as a woman, rather than a serial killer she was universally and venomously hated.

No one who was alive at that time would ever forget hearing about the tapes, played in Court, as Hindley pleaded not guilty and the case went to trial. Little Lesley Ann Downey was recorded by the sick pair, pleading with Hindley for her life. Although Ian Brady was a sexually sadistic psychopath who led Hindley along the terrible path that they followed, it is Myra Hindley whom the public will never forgive. She was female and as such her behaviour could not be comprehended, in any shape or form. Brady was mad, according to the Press and would plead insanity.

The body of one of the victims, eleven year old Keith Bennett, has never been found. His mother campaigned tirelessly throughout her life, to find her son's remains, even pleading with the killers to meet with her. She died in 2012. She never found her boy.

The public has been able to witness first-hand, the effects that these types of crimes have on the mothers, fathers and families of the victims. Many have spoken out publicly and given interviews over the years. Their pain and suffering has been apparent and no one could fail to be moved by Lesley Ann Downey's mother, telling of her torment. There were more than five victims in the Moors murders without a doubt.

Myra Hindley died in prison in 2002 aged sixty, of Bronchial Pneumonia, attributed to heart disease. Some wondered how that could be, since she couldn't possibly have a heart. Ian Brady, the ultimate 'control freak' remains, at the time of writing, in Ashworth Hospital, on hunger strike. Being force fed, he needs to be in control of his own death. This cannot be allowed to happen say the authorities. He has never once shown an ounce of remorse. Described by Professor David Wilson, as 'human sulphur,' he continues to exist.

'Mark'

Mark Chappell does not of course exist. He is a product of the author's imagination. Any resemblance to anyone living or dead, is entirely co-incidental.

Credits & Sources

Serial Killers: Hunting Britons and their Victims, 1960-2006: Professor David Wilson

Killing for company: Brian Masters

She must have known: Brian Masters

Somebody's husband, somebody's son: Gordon Burn

Fred & Rose: Howard Sounes

Cold blooded evil: Neil Root

BOS Magazine: Articles by Angus Dalrymple. The inspiration for the 'betting shop' scenes.

Wendy Bulman; Mike Ellis; John Gowlland; and John Nicholson for their very valued contributions.

Wikipedia: Used for additional research information.

Google Earth: Used extensively for location mapping.

AA Routefinder: Used for journey planning.

National Railway Museum: Travel and period reference.

Printed in Great Britain
by Amazon